MUTUAL HOLDINGS

Susan DiPlacido

Mutual Holdings

First Magic Carpet Books, Inc. edition November 2005

Published in 2005

Manufactured in the United States of America
Published by Magic Carpet Books, Inc.

Magic Carpet Books, Inc.
PO Box 473
New Milford, CT 06776

Library of Congress Cataloging in Publication Date

Mutual Holdings by Susan DiPlacido

$12.95

ISBN# 0976651084
Book Design: P. Ruggieri

Acknowledgments:

Many thanks to my Aunt Rose and Mary and Theresa and to my cousins Robin, Becky, and Dena for their encouragement.

Thanks to Don Capone, Jo Barris, William Reese Hamilton, Tripp Reade, Matt St. Amand, and Renee Nicholson for all their help, advice, and support.

And to Bellagio, Italy, the most romantic place in the world.

Mutual Holdings

CHAPTER ONE

Getting the work done is crucial. But getting it done right is just as important.

It takes a couple of bleats from the phone to fully break my concentration. I finish adding the column I'm on before glancing over. The display reads extension 101, my partner Tony Mancuso's number. It bleats again but I don't pick up. Instead, I cross-check the number on my machine with what's written on the form. Right now, I just don't have time for nonsense.

The phone rings again, but this time it's the buzz of the intercom. I just sigh. "You in there, Lisa?" Tony asks.

"No," is all I say.

"I have a question for you."

"Do we have to go through this every year? The answer is yes, debits must equal credits, Tony," I say and reach to click him off.

"That's not the question."

"Debits are on the left. That's all I can tell you right now."

"It's not that. I want to come in and appraise your assets."

Translation: Mancuso is horny because it's tax day and watching everyone clock all these billable hours turns him on.

I sigh and ask, "Don't you ever get tired of that line?" I've still got plenty of work looming, so I just don't have the drive for anything other than completing the work. For a couple of months during tax season, all I do is work. I eat quick meals of crappy take out and don't go to the gym or to movies or even really watch television. I just work until I'm tired and then go to sleep and get up in the morning and start again. So when the last form is finally filed, I'm ravenous.

A good meal, some rich wine, beautiful music, and my libido soars. I guess that's how I unwind.

And even though we're not a couple anymore, and even though we started seeing other people a few years ago, it usually still works out that Tony and I are both single when tax day rolls around. So we fall back into the habit of each other to chew up all that pent-up tension.

But I thought he's been dating someone for a few months now.

"I'll be right there," he says, and before I have a chance to protest, he clicks off.

Did I lock the door? I think I did lock it. I'm not getting up to unlock it. I don't have time for this nonsense yet. I just want to get finished. I grab another form off the left-hand stack and start verifying the line items against the corresponding back-up documentation. Elbow-deep in piles of paperwork, as I finish each page and toss it to the right-hand stack of completed forms, it's not much a small trill of exhilaration so much as a feeling of relief, like a noose slipping a notch looser.

There's a light rapping outside the door and I can't help but grin as he says from outside, "Open up, babe." I stay seated and start adding another column.

But then the door handle jiggles. Looking up, I see it turn. Dammit! I didn't lock the door.

"Brought you some coffee," Tony says as he lets himself in.

"I don't have time for coffee," I snap, but then instantly regret it as I get a whiff. It's strong and fresh, he must've just brewed it.

He doesn't make me admit that I do want it. Instead he sets it on the corner of my desk, just past the completed pile. "It's there if you want it," he says.

He's bringing me hot, fresh-brewed coffee, but my twelve years of familiarity with Tony has taught me that what that really means is that he's looking to get fresh with me.

"Ok. Thanks." I nod. When I reach for it, he takes the opportunity to half-sit, half-lean against the now open spot on the corner of my desk.

"Still grinding it out, huh?"

I just wave my hand across the desk in answer.

"How much longer you gonna be?"

"Tony," I sigh and try to measure my words, and tone. "You do this every year. It's April 15th, and it's 12:30 in the afternoon. We're a little..."

"It's 1:45, Lisa."

"What?" I nearly shout it. Every muscle tenses as a bolt of panic zings to my stomach. I spill some of the coffee on my lap. Hot, very hot. I stand and brush at it before it leaks through my skirt and burns me.

"What the hell are you wearing?" Tony laughs as I rise.

Looking down, I feel foolish. I've got my favorite old Rutger's t-shirt on with my beloved Armani skirt that I've been wearing since yesterday, which is now stained with coffee, and my ratty old green frog slippers on my feet.

"That's even worse that usual for you!" he says.

"What's that supposed to mean?" I ask.

He keeps laughing. "And you got haughty with me about making casual Fridays a theme day?"

"Listen," I say as I take my seat again. "I've been here all night. Working. That doesn't exactly compare with you trying to make the office into the pimps-n-hos ball, ok?"

"Oh, stop it," he says, crossing his feet and arms. "It was seventies disco theme, that's all."

"Whatever." I swivel and look out the window behind me. We're on the

21st floor, but the view is blocked by another skyscraper across the street. Still, I can tell by the way the light is reflecting off the windows at a lower angle that it is later in the day than I thought. I tell him, "I really have to get back to work here. I've got a lot to do."

"The troops are getting restless, Lisa."

"Well, then they'd better hurry. We have to get all this crap postmarked by midnight, so I want it all done by eleven at the latest."

"They are all done," he says. "Jill's finishing up the last return right now, and you have all the others right here."

"This is it?" I ask, the noose loosening even more.

Tony pushes off the desk and moves around behind my chair, placing his hands on my neck. Part of me feels self-conscious. I've been so busy I haven't had time for even the most basic cosmetic tweaks for a few weeks, including coloring my hair. I'm only 30, but a couple years ago I got my first few scraggly gray hairs peeking through the reddish brown, and they grow right out of my natural part so they're quite obvious. I haven't dyed them in weeks, but at least I've taken the time to part my hair on the other side to try and conceal them. I have a feeling that Mancuso isn't interested in inspecting my scalp right now anyhow.

He massages lightly at the top of my shoulders, telling me, "You did it again, Gladiator. Another season in the books."

"Almost in the books," I warn him as I look to the bulky stack of forms still on the left-hand side of my desk. "And I see you've been hanging out with the stockbrokers on the 17th floor again."

"What makes you think that?"

"Because we're accountants, Tony. We don't use warrior terms like 'gladiator' to describe ourselves. Brokers love that Sun Tzu shit."

"How come they get to be gladiators and we have to be bean counters?"

"Because they have inflated egos, that's why. And half of them are meth freaks. Besides. I wouldn't be a gladiator anyhow. All of them out there," I say and wave to the offices and cubicles outside my door, "are the gladiators."

"Yeah? Then what would that make you, babe?"

"I would be a centurion."

He laughs approvingly. Says, "And I guess that'd make me Caesar."

He keeps lightly rubbing at my neck. For such a big guy, he's really got an amazingly light touch. I hadn't even noticed the stiffness and cricks, but now that the gentle warmth of his palms is melting over my skin, I can feel the tightness loosening. He moves back to my shoulders, kneading softly, then works back to my neck again, his thumbs making light circles along my vertebrae.

His hands wander to my shoulders, then down my arms, rubbing up and down as he leans down and speaks close to my ear. Saying, "You put in a lot of time this year."

"Mm hm," I answer. "You know what that means."

He whispers it, softly, hot and moist breath tickling my ear. "Billable hours, babe."

I shiver. He kisses my neck.

I try to pull it together. I stiffen my back and lean forward, pulling away from him. "Enough for now," I tell him. "I still have to finish this pile."

He kisses my neck again. "I'll help you with it," he says.

I laugh.

"Oh, come on now," he says.

"You come on, Mancuso. You hate the paperwork."

"I may not like it, but that doesn't mean I won't do it."

"When was the last time you did any of heavy paperwork? I bet *Seinfeld* was still on TV!"

He laughs, because he knows it's true. But he doesn't back off. He leans down and places his mouth against my neck. Instead of kissing, he puts his lips and tongue against my neck and blows hard, gives me a big, wet, noisy raspberry. It tickles and makes me recoil and laugh harder.

"Ahh," he says as he straightens up. "It's good to hear you laugh. I haven't heard you laugh in weeks."

"Well, the thought of you doing actual paperwork always amuses me, Tony."

He moves around in front of me, devilish grin on his face. Raising his eyebrows, he says, "Know what else I haven't seen you do in weeks? Months even?"

"Never mind that," I tell him. "I just... I just want to finish up here."

"In a minute," he says. Positioning himself in front of my chair, leaning back against my desk, he folds his arms. He goes, "Where we going this year for vacation?"

I roll my eyes. "I thought you were dating that lawyer?"

"Broke it off three weeks ago. See how busy you've been? You didn't even give me any sympathy."

"Oh. Were you sad?"

"No," he grins.

"Well, then, I figured you'd have hooked up with Jill by now. You should be taking her off to Cancun or something to celebrate the end of tax season."

"Jill?" he asks, rubbing his own chin. "No, not Jill. Not my type."

I scoff.

"She's not," he protests.

It's a lie. She's exactly his type. Young, bright, with a curvy figure. But he says, "I'm not interested in dipping my wick in the company ink, Lisa."

I laugh again. Ask him, "Then what am I? A bottle of White Out that you just dunk into occasionally when you want to erase your romantic mistakes?"

He wags a finger at me and says, "You're my partner, that's different. And besides," he says, leaning closer, "since you're the workhorse partner, I just want to make sure you get the proper rewards for your efforts."

"You want to reward me? Let me draw a bigger salary, Tony."

He grins. "And we're back to the dirty talk again. For someone who's so anxious to finish her tax forms you sure are saucy."

I cross my arms. But looming paperwork never did intimidate Tony Mancuso, and he's obviously ready to play. I should finish up; it's going to take me another couple of hours at least. But the end is in sight now, and he's right, it has been weeks, actually months since I've had any fun outside of work. We pulled it off again. Another tax season with all the deadlines met.

Squatting in front of me, he places his hands on the outside of my thighs and rests his chin on my knees. Dark eyes upraised, he's giving me his puppy-dog look, working me with that mischievous charm of his. Asking, "So where are we going this year to celebrate?"

"Mm," I stretch my neck and look to the ceiling, thinking. "Where can we afford?"

He smiles and snakes his hands down my thighs. Hooking his thumbs under the hem of my skirt, he edges it up, presses his lips against my knee. "Lisa, we can afford anywhere this year. Know why?"

I smile, but I don't answer him, because that would be blatant encouragement. It's kind of our code for sexual arousal. To most people, dirty talk is all physical. To us, driven and ambitious accountants whose romantic flame got snuffed years ago, money is how we turn each other on.

"No pantyhose," he says. "I like that, Centurion." He runs his palm down the back of my calf. Warm, tingly. With his other hand, he pushes up further on my skirt, kisses at my thigh as he repositions himself on his knees, scooting between my legs. I oblige, opening my knees wider, giving him room. "You're tense, baby," he says, kissing at my thigh.

"I uh, uh," I stutter as I see the pile of papers still on my desk. He kisses higher, rubs his slightly stubbly cheek against my inner thigh. I close my eyes and say, "I worked all night."

"Mmmm," he kind of growls, nibbling at my inner thigh, his one hand stroking my calf, the other settling against my crotch. "Long night of work," he says, and I swear I can feel him grinning, waiting for me to give him the go ahead. I spread my legs wider, lean back further and scootch my hips toward the edge of the seat, pressing against his hand. His thumb searches, gently probing through the thin layer of my panties, then presses firmly against my sweet spot. I'm not throbbing, but it feels good already. He hesitates.

I glance at the door. He closed it behind him. I raise up slightly, take hold of the arms of the chair and push all the way to the edge. His thumb presses again, but doesn't stroke. I look down to catch him peering up at me. He's nearly completely beneath my desk, his huge frame folded down on his knees. He cocks a brow, dark eyes sparkling. And he waits.

I say, "All that work last night. Today. This week."

He sighs heavily.

"All of it," I whisper, "it's all billable hours."

He smiles and growls again, his thumb pressing into the cotton of my underwear, rubbing up and down. Raspy voiced, saying, "I love it when you talk dirty, Lisa!"

"All these tax forms I have to double-check, we have to bill for those, too."

"Oh my God," he says and hooks his fingers at the sides of my panties and starts to tug. I raise up for him as he pulls them over my hips and then down my legs. I have to fumble a bit. Sitting back down, raising my legs up so he can skim them down across my ankles, my slippers fall off as he pulls the undies off and discards them. He nudges my skirt back up, takes hold of my hips and presses a kiss directly against my sex, already slightly swollen. He pulls me toward him and kisses again, deeper, with some tongue, this time lingering and parting my slit. I'm wet already and starting to feel an insistent buzz.

I tell him, "Mancuso. Even the forms the interns filled out? We have to bill at my higher hourly rate for me checking them."

He mumbles something incoherent and releases my hip with one of his hands and presses his tongue against me, searching, searching, and...and...*success*, finding my pulsing clit. With his free hand he rubs at himself through his pants. But his tongue doesn't stop. He takes a long lick again, and then buries it right where I want it. "Right there," I encourage him. He goes slow at first, licking a steady rhythm, with just enough pressure to be making the throb more insistent.

A liability of knowing someone for so long is that the excitement and rush of something new can wear off. But a prime asset to being a familiar lover is that they know your body, and you're comfortable enough to tell them exactly where to go and what to do to please you.

"Up higher," I tell him, and he obliges, sparking me, driving me crazy with it. "Left," is all I have to say, and Tony's on the spot, right on the spot, working the spot, working the spot so well it won't take me long now.

People often comment on how my brain must work like a man's, because of the work I do. I don't know if there's a true gender difference in the skills. But I've also realized over the years that I happen to have a body that responds sexually similar to a man's, too.

My hands tighten around the arms of the chair, my back stiff, my face flushing. My pulse is rapping in my brain, just rapping with throbs matching the pulses of pleasure he sends with each new lick and thrust of his tongue. Pulsing, rapping, oh good. Oh, my God. "Oh, Mancuso. Oh, that's so..." That's...

That's a rapping outside my brain. Oh my God! It's on my door. I try to say, "*Wait!*" but in my addle-brained lust all that comes out is "Huh!"

And I'm so close. He's got me on the edge here and the door's opening. Tony's still licking and the door's opening. And it still feels, uh...

"Ms. Russo?" Jill asks, peeking her head inside.

"Uh! Wh..wait. Don't. Stop!" I try to holler it. But I'm too jacked up and it's just a breathy protest. And, oh, dammit! Tony thinks it was for him and he goes even harder, getting me hotter, crazier.

My one hand clenches around the arm of the chair, I pry the other away and swat at Tony's head. I'm so close I don't know if I can stop it anyhow.

Even if he stops immediately I might come. God, no! I can't, so I swat at him again, sit up straighter.

"Ms. Russo?" Jill looks to my desk now.

"Jill!" I do shout it, raising up enough to pull away from Tony's touch. I'm itching for release and still close, but the fear of her catching me backs me off enough so I won't tumble headlong over the edge -- as long as he's not working me. "Hello, Jill!" I say it too loudly, but Tony hears me and mercifully doesn't try to lunge for me.

"Ms. Russo? Are you all right?"

"Fine," I say, still talking too loudly. Every muscle in my body tense and edgy. My clit pulsing so hard and so hot and I'm shocked she can't hear it, can't see it through the thick mahogany of my desk.

"You sure?" she asks.

"Fine!" I snap. And as I do, Tony moves his hand from my hip, sliding it between my legs. I swat at him beneath the desk and he halts. Looking back up, I see the cup of coffee on the edge of my desk. Lying as a cover, I say, "I just spilled some hot coffee on myself, that's all." I mime wiping some more phantom coffee off my skirt and toss in another smack on the top of his head to let him know I'm not kidding around.

"Oh," she says and takes a step toward me. "Need some help?"

"No!" I hold up a hand, and as I do, Tony's mouth defiantly moves back on me. I haven't backed off enough yet and his mere touch rocks me hard. I try to slam my legs together, but it's no use with him there.

"I'm fine, really," I manage to grit out between clenched teeth. Tony doesn't lick this time. Instead, he cups his lips around my clit and lightly sucks.

It's like I'm sitting on a volcano. But I just can't do it. I know I'm contorted now, but if he makes me come, I'll shudder and blush harder and it'll be obvious that I'm not in pain from hot coffee. It's exquisite, the rush of feeling. And the sleazy in me is infinitely turned on by the clandestine nature of being secretly eaten out like this.

But it's mortifying, too. I've spent years working to be taken seriously as a professional. And I'm still constantly trying to overcome the sexist bias of the old-boys' network and young buck mentality on Wall Street, where they view women as disposable sex objects. And the possibility of a subordinate detecting this licentious behavior is terrifying, because it would undermine everything I've done and sacrificed to be taken seriously as a smart, hardworking businesswoman.

"What, what did you need, Jill?" I grit out and try to mentally block out the sensations between my legs. But it's no use, it's overwhelming pleasure.

"Oh!" she chirps. "I'm just finishing up the last form and I think you have the signature page for this company in here." She takes a couple steps toward my desk.

As she says it, Tony stops the sucking and presses with his tongue, the feeling incredible. "Oh no," I sigh in response to his moves, afraid he's going to make me explode.

"You don't have it in here?" she asks. As she speaks, Mancuso sets a hard rhythm with his tongue, the evil bastard.

"Yes," I say in answer to her, and he takes it as encouragement, or he's just trying to kill me on the spot, because he laps harder and faster.

I shake my head to try and clear it, keep some control over my body. "It's, um, it's on top of the file cabinet over there," I tell her and point. As she turns around, I drag in a heavy breath and exhale slowly, trying to focus away from the sensations he's causing. I can't allow him to do this to me.

"Here?" she asks me.

"To the left," I say.

Both she and Mancuso oblige. She moves to the next file cabinet and starts ruffling through the forms, and below the desk, between my legs, Tony moves just slightly left and hits the spot dead on center. I jerk, and he knows he's struck gold.

"Oh!" Jill chirps across the room, and I twitch as he nails the spot again.

This is it. I drag in another breath, but Tony really goes to work now, licking and pressing deeply. I have to come. Despite my best efforts to deny it and hold this off, the selfish, lusty need of my body is overpowering my mental will and I'm going to come.

"I found it," she says.

I have to come right now. My breath is shallow already, my heart pounding furiously.

Tony's working me, turning me inside out.

Jill heads to the door but hesitates. Asks, "You want me close this again?"

"Yes," I say, as normally as I can, praying that she'd just leave already, teetering right on the verge, trying to hold it off, feeling the blush seep to my face. Right as Tony jacks up the pace.

"Well, I only have this one more form, and then I'm all finished off," she chirps.

"I'm close too," I say, struggling to breathe. "I'm... so close."

"Hey. The party tonight, will you be coming?"

"I'm, uh...yeah. Oh yeah. I'm gonna come." Beneath the desk, between my legs, Tony laps at me relentlessly. "I'm definitely gonna come," I say, wanting her gone, vaporized, but also too far gone now to stop the inevitable climax or really care, because I need the release of the orgasm more.

"That's terrific!" she chirps. "I'll see you there."

The door shuts and I groan with it. I come immediately and hard, erupting with pleasure and shuddering violently as the latch clicks. Stuttering, "It's...it's terrific," as he keeps working away on me. I can feel myself flooding with juice, my whole body wired and my clit absolutely electrified.

Mancuso starts to back off, licking more slowly and gently now. He's pulling the delicious aftershocks out of me, still greedily lapping away, but not as insistent. As I calm and come down, my body first unwinds, then starts going limp. I ease back in the chair and Tony finally pulls off me.

He pushes the chair back and crawls out as I blink and breathe, fighting off the syrupy haze trying to leak into my head and pull me under. He's smirking as he reaches up and wipes his mouth, his chin. Leaning down close, he reaches behind me to pull a tissue off the credenza. I muster the energy to glare at him. He smirks even bigger as he finishes cleaning up with the tissue.

"That was evil," I hiss at him.

"That, my noble centurion," he says and leans close and kisses my cheek, "was beautiful. Admit it, it was damn good."

I whisper in his ear. Saying simply, "Hail, Caesar."

Tony braces one hand on the arm of my chair and leans even closer, pressing himself against me. He raises one leg, slides his knee next to my hip and takes hold of himself, again through his pants. "Little Caesar still wants some attention, baby."

It's my turn to smirk. I place my hands against his chest and push him away. "He's gonna have to want for a little while yet. I've still got paperwork to finish up. And Jill'll be back in here before long."

He groans, even begs a little bit. I can see he's turned on. I'll bet it's pretty bad, too. But it serves him right for putting me through that.

I push on him again and he backs off. Asking, "How am I supposed to get back to my office like this?" His pants are tented out.

I look across my desk to see if I can find something. My one frog slipper is sitting dead center on the desk. Of course Jill noticed it. I get a little pissed again thinking about what he did to me in front of her. I snatch the cup of now-cooled coffee and without warning I throw it onto the front of his pants.

"What the fuck!" he shouts.

I laugh. "I had a coffee accident. Now you had a coffee accident. It happens."

"What the hell was that for?"

"I thought it would help," I say. I kind of did. "I thought it would make it go down."

"It didn't," he snaps.

"I can see that."

"Now what do I do?"

"Oh, you have a change of clothes in your office. You'll be fine."

"Lisa," he fumes.

"Tony."

"How do I get to my office like this?"

"Oh." I look on my desk again and hand him a few folders. "There, just use these."

He starts to walk out.

"Mancuso, wait," I say. When he looks back at me, I drop it on him. "Since you've got those folders, you might as well approve the files. They still need checked and signed off by a senior partner."

CHAPTER TWO

Two hours later, Tony's changed and gotten through the couple of files I passed off to him. I've gotten four more checked (and my underwear back on), and Jill has dropped off the final one for my approval. So Tony calls everyone together out on the floor.

They're a ragtag-looking bunch right now. I try to keep us in corporate attire throughout the week because we do have potential clients coming through quite often to conduct proposal meetings with Tony. Fridays were always casual, and then Tony started his "theme" Fridays to make it more fun. Western, Hawaiian, and his favorite so far, '70s dance night. But even on those days, everyone looks sharp.

But not today. We started six years ago with just the two of us, Tony and me, in a small little office in Brooklyn. In one year, we moved to Manhattan, and two years after that we moved into this gorgeous office space just off of Wall Street, the financial hub of the entire world. And now, today, we've got eight certified accountants, eleven who are going to take their exams this year, and five interns that we picked up for the tax season this year. It wasn't just me who's been working non-stop since mid-February. They've all logged long, tedious hours. And they look it. I'm wearing coffee-stained Armani and frog slippers. None of them look much better. Except maybe Jill. Her hair is a little flat today and her clothes have lost their sharp line, but she doesn't look much worse for the wear overall. Poor Mark has been here until at least 11 p.m. all this week, and he's got dark circles around his eyes and his shoulders are slumped and he's wearing a strange combination of white polyester pants (presumably leftover from disco day) and one of Tony's old fraternity sweatshirts. I assume his clothes are also a casualty of coffee or lack of dry-cleaning pick-up.

Tony clears his throat and congratulates them all, as do I.

Then he goes, "As you know, we're having a party tonight." This brings a raucous round of cheers. "I've rented rooms at the Millenium Hilton where we'll be having dinner later. But before that, I've got some appetizers and drinks arranged to be at the pool, so you can let off some steam by taking a nice dip in the water. Half of you have off of work all next week, the other half of you the week after that. And this," he holds up a bunch of envelopes and waves them around. "This is our way of saying thanks for all your hard work." The cheering and applause starts again. Mark actually stands up on a chair to pump his fist and gets everyone shouting Tony's last name.

"Man-cu-so! Man-cu-so!" they chant. They love him. Even without the bonus checks, they'd love him. He's the fun one in the office here, even if he is the boss and majority partner.

Tony, he clears his throat and waves them down. "Tax time bonuses, everyone. Well, not everyone. Some of you," he stares at the five interns as he says this part, "won't be needed anymore. So there's a referral letter instead of a bonus."

He's such a jackass. We decided to keep all the interns on staff this year. They all did a great job and we've got plenty of work to keep them busy, and, best of all, we can afford to hire them. But he loves to screw with people.

I stick around just long enough to see the interns' faces first register relief, and then happiness as they collect their checks. For some people, Christmas is a time for bonuses. For us, it's April 15th.

When Tony pops the cork on the first bottle of Veuve Clicquot I go back to my office to finish up. I know they'll head to the Millenium soon and I'm starving. The weeks of pizza and Chinese and Thai deliveries have worn on me. The champagne sounds wonderful right now, too, but I want to get done and get something decent to eat poolside before the brokers from the 17th floor crash our party.

I'm affixing the official April 15th postage on the last envelope at 4:30 when everyone seems to be heading for the elevators. I give the mailings to a courier who beats it out of there as a call comes through. Our receptionist was one of the first to leave, so our maintenance guy Louis picks up and pages Tony. Quiet now, I can hear him as he picks up. Rolling my eyes as he says, "Mancuso, Mancuso & Russo. Mancuso here. How can I help you?"

He uh-huh's a couple of times and I go linger in his doorway and watch him nod and roll his eyes as the other person speaks. Finally, he says, "Listen, we'd love to help you. But today is the end of our tax season and we're closing up the office for tonight and we'll be at half-staff for a week." He nods and uh-huhs again. He says okay and then tells the guy to meet him at the Millenium. Tells him he's having a staff party there tonight. He's very clear to tell him it's a casual affair for us, that it's not a business gathering. But he'll meet him anyhow. "Eight o'clock," he says. "In Liquid Assets, right off the lobby."

When he hangs up, I taunt him. "Caesar's work is never done?"

He just shrugs. "That's our deal, isn't it? I bring in the clients."

"And we do everything else." I smile as I tease him.

Rising from his desk he says, "I checked a few of those files today."

"Yes," I nod. "I owe you one for that."

"Oh no," he says and leers. "You owe me for something else though."

Looking out of the office, I see Louis emptying a trash bucket into his large bin. "Louis, what the hell are you doing?" I ask him.

He smiles at me brightly. He says, "Just the usual, Lisa."

I get a happy tingle from that. Maybe the accountants and interns aren't fond of me, but Louis is always warm and friendly with me. "Yeah," I say. "But...why? Everyone's at the party already. You should go."

"Oh." He blushes. "I'm not done yet."

"Screw the trash," Tony says to him. "C'mon man! It'll be here tomorrow, but the food at the hotel won't last long."

"I uh, you mean, I should, I can go to the party?" Louis says.

"The fuck you waiting for, an engraved invitation?" Tony asks him. "I told you about it last week, Lou."

Louis is really cute, but very shy. I reinforce it, saying, "Seriously. Leave the stuff for tomorrow. Let's have fun tonight."

"I should really just...finish this at least," he says as he picks up another basket.

"I'll help," I say, understanding that nagging pull to have work taken care of before relaxing. I weave between a couple of desks and pick up a basket to carry it to the bin.

"Chrissakes," Tony complains, but he goes to a nearby desk and picks up a basket, then another as he marches to the bin and then empties them as I unload mine.

When we're finished, Tony says, "I'm not fucking dusting. Can we go now?"

"Yeah, yeah, thanks you guys," Louis says. "You two go ahead. I'll just empty this bin and I'll catch up." With that, he pushes the bin ahead of him out toward a service corridor.

I turn and start walking to the elevators and Tony catches up to me. Open-palmed, playful, he smacks me on the ass. He reaches over the receptionist desk and picks up an opened bottle of champagne for us as we head downstairs. The Millenium isn't far, but I'm exhausted so we hail a cab to take us the few blocks.

In the cab on the way to the hotel, Tony's uncharacteristically quiet. I'm shocked that it's still daylight out and we're already finished for the night. I remember just a couple years ago when we were still scrambling to beat the midnight deadline. Today there's a light drizzle falling down, covering the pavement. But the bitter cold of winter is gone and splinters of sunlight crack through the clouds intermittently to cast a golden sheen along the windows of the tall buildings. I'm not a native to New York, but I chose to live here, and I've never regretted it

I say, "You, um, you sure you don't have anyone else you'd rather vacation with this year?"

He takes a long pull off the bottle of champagne and looks out the window for a moment. Then, turning back to me, he passes the bottle over and simply says, "Nope."

As I take a slug off it, he asks, "Why? Have you been seeing someone?"

"Pfft," I say after I swallow. "You know I don't even have time to see television this time of year."

He nudges his elbow into my side. He taunts me by saying, "Yeah. Day-Trader Dave from the 17th floor dumped you last year in late February when you didn't give him enough time."

"He did not dump me!"

"The hell he didn't. That's why you hate the whole 17th floor."

I fume at that comment, and he just looks smug. Then he takes the bottle from my hand and takes a drink. Falls quiet again.

"Let's go to Vegas this year," I say to him.

"Really?" He perks up immediately. I know it's his favorite. Secretly, it's mine too. I have some family out there that I like to visit, but it's also the perfect place to indulge all my deprived senses.

At the hotel, Tony bounds out of the cab while I fish in my bag and take care of the fare. But he waits for me, and I catch him gazing across the street at Ground Zero. He closes his eyes for a second and I know he's saying some sort of silent prayer. I turn and do the same. It's been four years, but a quiet chill still runs through my veins at the sight, and I know it's the same for him, for everyone. Tony and I, despite all of our self-serving materialistic and ambitious flaws, we are still human.

After a quiet moment, he says, "Construction's coming along nicely."

I just nod.

Inside, he steers me through the lobby and we get checked into our separate rooms. I like it that he didn't assume I'd be sleeping with him tonight, even though I probably will. The Millenium is a very nice place; modern and tastefully decorated in the lobby with rosewood and cream colors. And right off the lobby is a nice bar, Liquid Assets, named for its proximity to the World Financial Center and Wall Street and often catering to the brokers and financial gurus. He asks me if I want to stop for a drink, but I tell him no. I'm feeling grungy and looking shabby and I'd rather get changed and dive into the pool first, especially since there will be drinks and appetizers there. But then at the elevator he presses the floor for the pool instead of our rooms. "I wanna get changed," I tell him.

"You're fine," he coaxes. "Let's grab some food first. I invited some of the guys from downstairs and they'll clean us out."

My stomach rumbles and I realize I haven't eaten all day. So I agree to it. When we enter the pool area, I stop to put down my bag and slide off my jacket in the warm, humid air. I toss them on a lounge chair at the back of the room, and then he coaxes me to move closer to where everyone is. Most everyone is in the pool, only a few of the interns are gathered around a couple of lounge chairs, still dry, but pulling appetizers off a tray that a waiter is walking around with.

A loud cheer erupts from the pool when they notice us. I know it's for him, not for me. And sure enough, Mark is the first one to come over. He climbs out of the pool, wearing swim trunks instead of the white polyester pants. He slaps Tony on the back and thanks him for the generous bonus. And the party. And everything. He pumps Tony's hand up and down and nods, says, "You're a great boss, Tony."

I look away with what I hope is a pleasant expression on my face, wish I could slouch even smaller and just disappear behind Tony's massive form. With his 6'3", broad shouldered height, it's easy for me to hide behind him if I want. But not when I'm already standing in the open. But then Tony nods in my direction, and Mark says, "You too, Ms. Russo. Really."

That's what he says: '*You, too, Ms. Russo.*' But what I hear, what I know that translates to in less polite terms is: 'You're not as good as Tony is.'

"Thanks," I say with a smile. "You can call me Lisa, Mark."

"Right, right," he answers, and then scampers back off to the pool area.

"This was really nice of you," I tell Tony as I look around at the spread. "You outdid yourself, Mancuso."

"And you outdid yourself this year, Russo. Come on." He puts his hand in the middle of my back and pushes me forward. Loudly now, he calls out, "Gladiators!"

"Oh. Madone," I sigh. But before I can move away he grabs hold of my wrist and pulls me along.

"Gladiators," he says again. "You've worked hard, you've earned your feast. But first, I want to congratulate and thank our hardworking and fearless leader."

Oh crap. Fearless my ass. This is my fear, and he's throwing me into it. Everyone loves him, but no one likes me very much. It's something he's oblivious to.

Loudly, he says, "I give you our Centurion!"

I wave gamely to a smattering of applause. Jill is the only one to give a verbal shout-out. "Yay, Ms. Russo!"

"Lisa," I correct her. "Thanks, really."

But then Mark gives a loud "Whoohoo!" and that's nice.

One of the interns just shouts, "Respect!" I can't help but laugh.

That's when Tony swoops me off my feet and lurches toward the pool. I yelp in protest. I took off the frog slippers and didn't put on expensive shoes, only sneakers, and my skirt is possibly already ruined. But it's also my already-worn-out, favorite skirt. And I'm wearing a white t-shirt.

"No!" I shout it as he pulls up short and dangles me over the edge. I clasp my arms around his neck and hold tight. I kick and try to wiggle free without letting go of him, but it's useless. Physically, it's a joke to think I could ever try to overpower him, even for a second. But I try anyhow. Maybe if I make enough of a struggle he'll give up.

I can't get away from him, but he can't hold on to me and get both my arms pried off him either. But if Mancuso has his mind set, he's going to do it. He stops trying to pry me off him and instead takes one big leap, both of us splashing into the pool.

He releases me under the water, and I kick up and away from him, surfacing just a moment before he does.

Now, of course, everyone shouts for real. It's loud; laughing, clapping, and cheering. I scowl over at him, streams of water still coursing down his face, his dark wavy hair now in thick ringlets and his white dress shirt clinging to him, making his slightly bulged physique pop and resemble a warrior-emperor even more. He's not quite as sharp and defined as he used to be, especially like when we were in college and he still did construction work over the summers. His arms were like pythons back then. He's put on a few pounds over the years. But with his huge frame, he wears it well. And he's not doughy yet. He's just not as sinewy and lean. But he still looks formidable.

Me, on the other hand? I don't need a mirror to know what I look like right now: a drowned rat. My hair matted to my head and t-shirt clinging to me. I don't dare stand up lest I give the male interns a free show. Then again, if I don't get out and get changed now, I'll be stuck looking like this when the obnoxious, juvenile, and horny brokers show up. I know if Day-Trader Dave is with them, he won't hesitate to catcall and whistle, drawing even more attention to me.

I tread water for a minute until most people go back to what they were doing before; eating and drinking and splashing around with each other. One of the interns leans over the edge and high-fives Tony. I notice Jill looks terrific when she's wet. She'd looked just slightly less-perky than usual at the office today. Now she's in a conservative black one-piece suit. But even though she's not showing off extra skin, the fabric conforms to show off her sleek form and generous curves. Her blonde hair is pulled into a neat ponytail, smooth and clean-edged in the back. I dunk under the water to get my hair off my face, come up sideways to try to conceal those pesky grays that I know are poking around up there. When the intern moves on, I frog-stroke it over to Tony. I stay under up to my neck and say, "I'm wearing a white t-shirt."

"I know."

"You're rotten."

"What're you worried about? You've got a great rack."

"I don't really feel that all our interns should know that."

"All right. You stay close behind me as we get out and I'll grab you a towel right away."

It's a good offer, but I'm now afraid it's too late. "Oh no," I say as I glance over his shoulder. There's a cadre of men in dark suits entering the atrium. Only the one guy in the center looks different from the rest. He's in a light beige suit.

"What?" Tony asks.

"Stockbrokers." But as soon as the word's out of my mouth, they've moved closer and I can tell that I was wrong.

Tony turns around and can see the difference instantly. “Those aren’t brokers. Jesus."

“No shit,” I agree.

Brokers dress well. Some of them amazing. But there’s a uniform crispness to them in the morning that turns into uniform looseness and rumpledness by mid-afternoon. Rolled up shirt-sleeves and their ties would be off. And their suits would be nice, but not like these. These suits are still stiff and pressed. There are four guys. The hair isn’t disheveled. Their shoes are gleaming. I don’t know what these guys are.

And then there’s the one in the middle in the light suit. Impeccable doesn’t even begin to describe him. He’s got a Mediterranean complexion, but his face is also slightly tanned, just to the point where it has a soft glow. His dark hair is cut tight and close and is immaculate. They stop short of the pool and from his carriage I almost expect him to snap his fingers and have the guys around him go scurrying. But he doesn’t. Instead, he just turns his head and nods slightly, and two of the men fall back. He visually sweeps the room. Lingering on nothing, his eyes scan over everything. Even though he’s still ten or twelve feet away, I can see his eyes are light. Blue, or hazel, or maybe even green. His skin is olive and hair and brows are darkest brown, but his eyes have a light, bright pop and sparkle to them. The man in a dark suit next to him flags over a waiter and says something to him. The waiter nods in our direction as he answers him.

This time, the nod is nearly imperceptible, and the two men walk over to us, the one in the dark suit just a half-step behind the one in tan. At the edge of the pool, the guy in tan looks at Tony. Says simply, “Mr. Mancuso?” The syllables are a drawn out, well-enunciated, but I can tell that masks an accent of some sort. Maybe Italian. Or Spanish.

“Yes, I am. Can I help you?”

“We talk with the phone.” The man squats now and holds out his hand, looking Tony square in the eye. "I am Gianni Loren."

Definitely Italian. The accent and the name. And the name is familiar.

"Right," Tony offers his hand. "Sorry about the...water," he apologizes as they shake.

But this guy, this Loren, he gives a shake of his head and a practiced smile. "No problem. I apologize. I intrude on your party. Thank you, for you to speak with me."

"My partner," Tony says as he looks over to me. "Lisa Russo."

The man's eyes fall on me now. I try to stay ducked low, but don't want to be rude. So I offer my hand. "My pleasure," I say.

He takes my hand, but his eyes never leave my face. "*Piachere*," he says. In English, that translates simply to 'pleased to meet you', but he doesn't let go of my hand.

Green. His eyes are a light greenish brown. Very stunning, and very absorbing. And they're looking directly into mine. He's not just well-dressed and perfectly groomed. He's also gorgeous.

"Uh, yeah," Tony interrupts, "let me just grab some towels and we'll sit down with you." Tony says this as he moves toward the steps.

Loren doesn't release my hand. Instead, he offers me his other one, I presume to help me out. "I don't want to get you wet," I protest.

"Come," he says and moves his hand closer.

In no way do I want to offend him, so I take hold and place my feet against the wall. Quickly and fluidly, he stands up, tugging me by the hands and pulling me from the water. For the first time, his eyes leave my face. They dip lower, and hover there for a moment. I'm not surprised, but I am embarrassed. I'm wearing a bra, but it's also white, and very sheer. I can feel my nipples poking out against the wet fabric that's clinging to me.

"I'm dripping on your shoes," I say and take a step back.

The man with Loren lowers his eyes discreetly.

"No problem," he tells me and looks back up into my face. "A beautiful woman, she is, uh, you are welcome to, uh, to drip. On me."

I'm not sure how to respond, but luckily Tony is quick to react and he's got a towel that he casually drapes across my shoulders while he uses another to swipe off his own face.

I motion to them to move ahead. "Please, have a seat," I urge as I pull the towel tight across my shoulders and down in front of me to cover up. Tony arranged for us to have food and drinks up here, but it's all being carried by waiters. Surrounded with floor-to-ceiling windows that show off a breathtaking view of downtown Manhattan, the indoor pool here isn't just a rarity for a New York hotel, it's beautiful. But the area surrounding it isn't very large, and there are only lounge chairs, no proper table and chairs.

When they turn and thread their way toward seats, I glance at Tony, but I don't even have to glare at him. He mouths, "Sorry," as he runs the towel through his now shaggy hair.

As they're seating themselves, I glance over and see the other two men he'd come in with waiting by the entrance, hanging back but standing straight. Bodyguards.

That's when it clicks. The name was familiar, but it's not commonplace in the states like "Trump" or "Kerkorian". This guy Loren is Italian, I'm sure. And I'm also positive he's a billionaire. Just in his early 40's, he's one of the youngest, and also one of the wealthiest. I know I saw him listed recently as being in the top fifty or maybe even twenty-five richest men in the world. Real estate, resorts, retail, European sports franchises, even a bit of manufacturing if I recall correctly. He was heir to his father's fortune, but in the decade that he's been in charge of the family's estate, he's grown it at least ten fold. Diversified and, I do believe, well known for his generous philanthropic activities as well. And he's also notorious for his much ballyhooed bachelor status, which I also recall he enjoys to its limits.

This is the guy Tony was on the phone with? And he didn't mention it? Tony woos the big money clients all the time, but we've never come close to someone of this caliber before. I didn't recognize the guy's name at first because of my typical American myopia. I bet Tony's still not aware of who he is. But this is his portion of the job, so I let him take the lead. I'll chime in when it's appropriate and try to clue him in if possible.

Tony apologizes again as he pulls out a chair. "I thought we were meeting later, or else we'd have been more...prepared."

"No," Loren says. "I apologize. I am early. I asked where to find you. I intrude now. I understand this tax day in America, the hard work for weeks. You are blowing off the steam, yes?"

"Yes," Tony nods agreeably. "But how can we help you?"

The man with Loren looks at Tony and starts to say, "This is Mr. Loren's first trip to the states, and he's not quite fluent yet..."

"Si," Loren cuts him off with just the one word and a slight nod. "I am knowing they are understand this, already." He smiles as he says it, bows his head. "But it is good for me, yes, to learn the language. To learn, I have need to practice."

Tony nods and says, "I understand you just fine. Your English is good."

"It is bad. But it is four weeks, only. So far. I have been here for three of those weeks. The other, I start to learn in Italia, before we come here."

"Well then your English is amazing," Tony says. "I couldn't learn Italian that quickly."

"Oh." Loren's smile fades. "So you do not speak Italian?"

"She does, a little," he nods to me.

Loren's smile breaks again as his eyes fall on me. "*Benissimo*," he says, drawing it out.

Before he gets too excited, I want to be clear with him. "*Solo un po*," I say, meaning, just a little. My grandmother always spoke Italian, and we were a close family so all of the kids speak it to some extent. But now, I'm quite rusty, and it takes me a second to form the sentence. But in Italian, I tell him, "I'm not fluent."

His smile doesn't waver. Instead he speaks quickly, "You understand what I'm saying right now?"

"Si." I nod.

Still in Italian, he says to me, "I need the practice in English, but I can get tired of it. Or misunderstand. My current staff is European. French, Italian, some are fluent in Japanese and Mandarin. I have plenty who speak English, but none who are accomplished enough. That's why I want your services."

"Mr. Loren," I say.

"Gianni," he corrects me. I take a breath. I glance over at Tony, watching us, quiet. And the man next to Loren, he's watching also. He's older than Loren by probably twenty years. And he's obviously fluent in English. He's not watching us, he's watching me.

"Gianni," I say as he continues his intense gaze directly on me. I fidget with the towel, pulling it tighter even though he's looking at my face and I know logically that I'm already covered. "I'm not an interpreter." I look to Tony, and then tell Loren, "We're accountants."

"This is correct," Loren answers me. "That is what I need. For the first time, I am thinking of buying a business here, in the states. The numbers are universal. But the language is not. I need someone capable who can do the investigation and report the findings to me quickly and clearly."

"But," I glance at the man next to him, "wouldn't it be easier to just have a team do the work and report back and have him interpret, if necessary?"

As I say that, the man next to him stiffens and starts to open his mouth to respond. But before he can, Loren smiles widely. "Ms. Russo..."

"Lisa," I tell him.

"Lisa," he nods. "This is Michael Spillway."

I hold out my hand and as he shakes, the guy says, in English, "I'm his attorney, not an interpreter."

He and Tony also shake. Loren addresses me again, in Italian. He says, "Lisa, what you say may be correct. But I'm in the states now, and what I'm considering is an impulse purchase, of sorts. I haven't the time to pull my people away from Europe right now. So I inquired here. When your company was mentioned, I heard only positive things. You are still growing, and quite quickly. These are all things I can appreciate and admire. So I decided to check you out for this job."

I nod. "And you like it that I can speak to you in Italian. Even if my accent and grammar is very poor."

"None of that," he says with a smile. "Your word choice is fine. And your accent is charming." He looks at Tony and nods, "And your partner, his reputation precedes him. He is young, but ambitious. Self-made."

"We have a terrific staff," I tell him.

He turns his gaze to Tony now, and I have to admit that I'm relieved. We're partners, yes. And the distribution of work is what I consider fair and equal, but we don't handle the same tasks. Tony is the negotiator and deal-maker and office manager. I'm just the bean counter. But it also makes me realize that Loren has fast, accurate business instincts to pick up who he should be addressing as the lead partner. Either that, or he's simply old-world sexist. It's not an uncommon response with the people we deal with. Though it chafes me, I haven't got any reason to complain because I so willingly, and gladly, hand over the reigns to Tony in these areas.

But for now, I'll prefer to think it's not a subtle sexist brush-off that Loren is pulling as he negotiates with Tony and that it is instead a manifestation of his keen acumen.

"Tony," Loren says, speaking in his slightly stilted English again now. "This job I have, it is large."

"With our staff and experience, we're prepared to handle anything," Tony answers confidently.

"I hear good things about you. But I hear good things about others also."

"There are plenty of fine accountants available in this city," Tony agrees. "But if you're looking for the best, brightest, and fastest, you want to work with us."

Loren smiles. That's when Tony goes for it. Sure-footed, he doesn't even glance at me for approval first. He just says, "I do need to make it clear to you though, if you were contacting us in the hopes of getting a bargain because we're a smaller firm, I'm afraid you'll be disappointed. This time of year, and with no lead time, we won't be able to offer you a substantial courtesy discount."

Loren, he smiles again. He nods slightly. Says, "When I eat steak, I do not pay for a hamburger. Yes?"

"But we're not steak," Tony answers him. "We're kobe filet."

"Ahh, *benissimo*!" Loren says and claps his hands once. "I think then, Tony, that I am satisfied. We will be doing some business together." Abruptly, Loren rises. "I use too much of your time tonight. Tomorrow, we can talk again?"

Tony rises, and before he can speak, I answer for him. I can tell by the look on his face he was about to tell them that we're closed tomorrow. But I can also tell he's not yet aware of who this guy is. Or his net worth. He pushed him fast and quickly to get him on board, but that's just Tony's manner, because he's also got great instincts. But instincts can't ever make up for lack of knowledge. So I say, "*Si, grazie*. Tomorrow."

We make the arrangements with Tony being agreeable. Loren doesn't even nod to the men waiting at the doorway as he exits. He just leads the way, with his attorney a close step behind him and to his right, and the other two fall in line.

They're barely out the door when Tony turns to me with an incredulous look on his face. "What about Vegas?" he asks.

"It can wait a day. Or longer. However long it takes. You don't know who he is, do you?"

He looks me in the eyes, but I refrain from smiling. He asks, "Is he a whale?"

"Tony," I say. "This guy is Moby Dick."

His eyes narrow. "Seriously?"

"Billions."

He exhales slowly. I loosen my grip on the towel around my neck and move it to the sides, once again exposing my chest.

"What does he want?" Tony asks, still looking in my face.

"He wants us to do a job for him. His very first venture in the States. And he wants us."

His eyes fall to my chest. I straighten my back and take a deep breath. Though it's humid in here, the wetness is keeping my nipples at attention. "I'm quite certain he'll be willing to pay a very generous fee."

Tony looks back to my face and all he says is, "Let's go upstairs."

"What about them?" I ask him, nodding to everyone still frolicking in the pool. Finally, even Louis appears, brushing by us with a wide smile. From the pool, there are definitely more cheers of "Lou!" than there were for me.

Tony, he turns toward them and yells out, "Everyone!" Naturally, they all turn to him. "We're going to get cleaned up and have a few cocktails in the bar. Dinner's on Lisa tonight in the Church and Dey. 9 o'clock. You're all welcome to come, but it's not mandatory. Enjoy yourselves." With that, he gently takes hold of my elbow, turns, and starts pulling me out. I nod to our things sprawled on a lounge chair and he scoops them up with his free hand without letting go of me, and he leads us upstairs.

Mutual Holdings

Susan DiPlacido

CHAPTER THREE

Alone in the elevator, Tony still grasping my arm, he asks, "Your room or mine?"

"Whichever one is nicer," I answer.

I watch him punch the numbers, see him hit the top floor, the suites. My room wasn't a suite. "Asshole," I say.

He laughs. Then says, "About this guy. Tell me again."

"Hotels, resorts, clothing, I think."

"You're sure about this? Billions?"

"One of the fifty richest men in the world."

"You're making me hard," he says.

"He likes us 'cause we're Italian. I get the feeling he's going to start doing business in the U.S."

"You are so fucking hot, Lisa," he says.

"I think it's a due diligence project," I whisper.

"Oh my God," he sighs.

"You know what that means, right?"

He can't take it. He releases my elbow and pulls me close around the waist. A trill of excitement rushes through my veins. I turn into him, pressing my damp body against his. We should be cool, but I can feel the warmth of his skin through our wet shirts. Stretching, I tilt my head and he bends down for me. I whisper it in his ear. "Huge billable hours." As I say it, I reach down between his legs and stroke once. He wasn't lying, he is already stiffening.

We both start laughing.

Once out of the elevator, we move quickly down the hallway. He drops our bags and jackets as he looks for the key, so I pick them up and carry them in as he gets it unlocked and holds the door open for me. I toss them aside and spin around, press him back against the door. I go right for his belt buckle and fumble with it before getting it undone. But the button and zipper go easily. Reaching inside, I dip under his boxers and take hold of him, hot and fully hard. He groans with my touch, places his hand over mine and starts guiding me as I pull him out and push the boxers out of the way, completely exposing his erection while his pants and shirt are still on and clinging to him.

"Tell me more," he begs, grinding his hips, thrusting into my hand, guiding me with his hand controlling mine.

I watch his face as I say it, but he's looking down, watching my breasts rise and fall as I breathe and speak. "He says it's a huge organization. We'll need a whole team working on it."

He shivers with that, his one hand still guiding me along him, picking up the pace, his other goes to his brow and he closes his eyes. I want to climb up on him, I want to wrap my legs around his waist and get him inside me, feel him grinding inside of me the way he's pumping into my hand.

But I love driving him wild like this too. He looks so sexy, leaned back against the door, throbbing in my hands, shameless. Aching in my crotch, I decide to hold out and really give it to him good. I drop to my knees and release his penis and pull at his hips, urging him to slouch a bit more for me. He's just too tall for me to take him in my mouth without him bending a bit. He obliges, of course.

I take a long lick first, savoring the salty-sweet tang. I swab the head with my tongue and place my lips around it and suck lightly. He groans again in answer so I take him in all the way, letting him graze against the back of my throat before backing off, inhaling, and diving down again. This time, with more pressure, more tongue. After just a few strokes and sucks, if I wanted, I wouldn't have to do anything, because he starts undulating his hips, moving and grinding, fucking my mouth at the rhythm he wants.

But I'm not one to do anything half-assed, so even while he thrusts into me, I suck and lick. He goes more quickly, all the while he groans and pants, running his hands through my hair.

Before long, he pulls me off, saying, "Oh shit." I look up at him, questioning, and he answers me with, "Lisa baby. I think I'm gonna come soon."

I can tell he's edgy already. Probably from being pent up so long from at the office earlier today. I feel a little bad about the coffee thing. He tugs on my shoulders, pulling me up and I oblige, but I take hold of him again. I don't stroke, I just hold tight, and his hand immediately covers mine again and squeezes tighter around his cock, trying to ease off and hold out probably.

I press against him, my tits aching, the tightness and wetness in my cunt exaggerating by the second. I rub against him and he snakes a hand up under my t-shirt. Over my bra, rough, he first runs his thumb across my distended nipple, making me sigh. He squeezes, gently at first, but as I increase my pressure around his cock he squeezes me harder. I start rubbing him again and his hand loosens and allows me to. While I jack him, he maneuvers his hand under my bra, roughly pushes the cup aside and kneads at my tit. "You looked so hot down there," he tells me.

It's awful but I can't resist it. Just above a whisper, I ask him, "Did you see him looking at me?"

"Ohh," he groans and then nods. "Yes."

I stroke more quickly. "Did you see him looking at my tits?"

"Yesss," he draws it out, nearly hissing the word. He also opens his eyes and looks down at me. Panting, gritting his teeth, he pinches my nipple. It feels so good I almost yelp. But I don't lose my rhythm on him, stroking faster, holding tighter. I lean back slightly and plunge my other hand on him, rubbing at the head while I keep pumping his shaft. He thrusts again, driving himself up and forward into my fist.

"Tony," I say to him, watching his engorged cock as I stroke away on him. "Baby, listen."

"Uh," is all he says, but I know he can hear me and I look up to his face. He's watching me as I watch him. "I'm, I'm gonna come," he says.

I stroke again, move my other hand down and cup his balls, feel them tighten and rise. I stroke quickly, cup him tighter, just as I know he's starting to come, I say, "We're gonna make a fortune off this guy."

He loses it completely. He groans really loud, long and drawn out, just like his ejaculation. Hot and white, a stream shoots out of him, covering my hand and splashing my t-shirt while his whole body goes tense and rigid, his hand no longer massaging my breast, just a deliciously firm, static squeeze on it. But I don't stop. I pump him again and get a spasm and another jolt of semen, so I do it again. And again, until I'm milking him dry. When he finally draws a breath, I back off, move more lightly until I'm just caressing him, and then finally holding him, feeling him starting to soften as his grip on me loosens.

It was glorious watching him get off. It's been a while since I've seen that. But now, itchy and tense and still craving him inside me, I'm wondering why I egged him on.

He slumps and chuckles, leans down and starts sucking lightly on my neck. I shiver with it, take my hands off him and hold lightly to his sides. Tony saying in my ear, "Sorry. I just couldn't hold out." He takes me by the waist and picks me up, finally. I wrap my legs around him, clinging tight, arms around his neck. He takes a few steps and stumbles slightly, but doesn't lose balance. With me still on him, he kicks off his pants and moves us to the bathroom. In there, he nudges at me and I loosen my grip, let him set me down again as he says, "Let's get in the tub, get cleaned up. I'll make it up to you there."

He's in a suite up here, so he's got a nice marble Jacuzzi tub we can slip into. I'm still hot, but the wet clothes are getting uncomfortable. And I imagine that he's getting cold now that he's gotten off. I turn the faucet and check the temp and let the tub start filling, then start taking off my clothes while he does the same. He unbuttons and peels off his shirt, exposing his broad chest with thatches of dark hair on his pecs that run into one single tantalizing line down his stomach. Sometimes, like right now, I want him so bad it makes me weak and almost queasy.

Tony never was a neatnik, and he shucks off his clothes and tosses them aside. I pull off my shirt and bra and toss them into the pile with his stuff, and carelessly kick my sneakers off. But even though it's possibly unsalvageable at this point, and despite my anxious lust, I still take the time to smooth out my skirt and then try hanging it up in the other room.

He splashes into the tub and comments, "You and that skirt. Let it go, baby."

"I can't," I tell him as I gently fold it over a chair.

"What is it with that thing?"

Over my shoulder, as I pull off my underwear, I tell him, "My cousins gave it to me." I get a stab of loneliness as I say it and move slowly back to the bathroom. I linger, completely naked, at the door.

He looks at me with a smile, and his eyes travel up and down my body. But it's obvious that his libido is low, because he continues the conversation instead of saying something suggestive. "Lucy and Marina?"

"Yeah," I nod. "And Eva. When I told them we were starting the business, they all chipped in and bought me that nice Armani suit."

"You wore that thing all the time that first year. I'm surprised it hasn't worn out before now."

"It's all I had that first year." I smile. "Remember those days?"

"I hated those days," he says, and I drop my eyes. "Ahh, Lees, I didn't mean it like that. You know I had a great time with you."

"When we had time to have fun," I smile and nod.

"Exactly. Every day was like tax season back then. And we were always shuffling and struggling to make the rent at that shitty little office."

"I know." I do remember those days. Looking up at him, I say, "But I think we're doing better now."

"I think we're doing well enough you could afford to buy a new suit and stop worrying about that skirt, Lisa."

"It's not the money," I tell him. A chill starts to hit me, so I move to the tub and carefully climb in, positioning myself between his legs and settling with my back to his chest. It's warm, even a bit steamy. Relaxing, I lay back against him and he reaches up and smoothes my hair back. Settled, I say, "I've worn that skirt every single tax day so far."

He splashes warm water up over my shoulders and runs his hands across my belly. I wonder if he can feel the rumbling emptiness in there. Unfed hunger. Un-satiated lust. Unfulfilled love.

He asks, "You miss them, don't you?"

I just nod.

He leans his chin on my shoulder, and I know he's looking down my body, inspecting me as he splashes more water across me, this time across my breasts. Then he says, "We'll make sure to look up Lucy and Marina when we're in Vegas this week."

"I'm thinking we might not make it there this year, Tony."

He's silent. Eva still lives in New Jersey, but he doesn't mention giving her a call. I know it's not a slip of his memory. I also know it's for the best.

But he does say, "They gave you that suit, huh? You guys ever get anything for Lucy?"

"Yep. When she started working in the restaurant we all chipped in and got her a set of really nice copper cookware."

"That's nice. How about Marina? What'd you get her?"

"A case of vodka."

"Oh Madone." He laughs. "You guys are so rotten to her."

"We are not! We love her."

"Lucy gets a set of cookware and you get an Armani suit. And you give Marina vodka?"

"Tony," I sigh. "You've met Marina. What would you get her?"

"Oh. I guess vodka's fitting." There's a long silence Then, I know he can't help himself, so he asks, "And Eva?"

"We got her a nine millimeter Smith & Wesson."

"Oh for Chrissakes." His hands slap the water in disgust.

I refrain from laughing. "We don't judge each other. That's why we all get along."

"Yeah, well, there's a difference between not judging someone and willingly arming them."

"She is what she is," I say, and then twist my neck around to look at him. The heat and steam and my fatigue could make me snippy, but I don't even have the will for that right now. Instead, the heat and steam and my fatigue are conspiring to make me throb. I can't stop thinking about how good it felt to be jerking him off a few minutes ago, I can't stop thinking about how he looked – so primal and wanton and unable to control himself, just pumping against me, needing relief and pleasure.

I can relate to that. He did a great job on me earlier today. But I'm still all wound up. I hardly even thought about sex for eight weeks, and I certainly didn't do anything about it. And now that the work rush is over, all that long-subverted energy is frothing out of me. "Let's not talk about Eva right now, ok?" I suggest. There are more pressing matters at hand, matters I wish he'd put his hands on and soothe. I push back against him and raise my hips to give him the hint.

He takes the hint immediately. His hand dives down between my legs, cups my pussy and gives a squeeze. I sigh and arch my back, raise my hips even more. He shifts his legs, first lowering them and then sliding them together and under me, and then pushing up and out against my knees, opening me up. He slinks down further in the water so that now I'm basically laying on top of him, with my butt against the base of his belly and my back against his chest.

I'm almost entirely out of the water this way, and I catch a small draft of cool air. But his hand between my legs goes to work. With my legs spread wide, it's easy for him to split my lips and find my already pulsing nub. Circling it with his index finger, his other hand slides across my torso, pleasantly splashing me with water and keeping my skin slick and smooth. He moves across my belly, up to my breasts. Another splash of warm water, more circling below and building the heat. Raised just enough from the waterline, my own natural slickness isn't getting washed away. Instead it's building up, making it slippery and easy for him to slide and work me down there just as his hand glides along my breasts.

Mancuso knows I love water. I grew up near the ocean shore, and I can never get enough of swimming and long baths. That's probably why he rented the rooms at the Millenium tonight, because he knew I'd dig the swimming pool. Three years ago, when there were only eight of us in the office, he booked a scuba trip to the Caribbean as our post-tax season treat.

Now, with his attentions, I'm not the least bit cool anymore. In fact, if anything, it's getting steamier and hotter in here. I slide my hand under my ass, twist a bit and reach lower, searching for him. But he's soft, probably completely spent for a while after that big orgasm he just had at the doorway.

It feels great, the way he's working me is sparking me already, but I want to feel him inside me. We fooled around like this back around the holidays, but didn't actually fuck. And good as this is, sometimes I can really go for an old-fashioned screwing.

It's like he reads my mind, or maybe it's because I squirm when I feel he's still soft. Because he keeps petting my body with his one hand, but he adjusts his other and goes to work on my sweet spot with his thumb as he eases his index finger inside me.

I groan and grind with it. It's good, alright. Not as good as his heavy, heated erection would feel, but good enough. I lean my head way back, twist my neck again and kiss his neck. As I kiss him there, he squeezes my nipple. Hard and erect, that pressure works in tandem with his thumb going at me, sliding up and down now, while his finger juts in and out. I squeeze around his finger, kiss at his neck again.

Sometimes, I want to kiss him so badly. Sometimes, like right now, I want to kiss him so badly it makes me heartsick.

There are standards and procedures in accounting. Once you understand the general principles, there are still fundamental rules that have to be followed, or you risk deviating from the standards and you won't get reliable results. Instead of keeping order and making sense of everything, it could create chaos. Profits could be shown as falsely increased, or potential dangers may not be seen.

Tony and me, we have our own set of personal standards and procedures. No kissing is one of our fundamental rules. I don't remember who came up with it, but I think it may have been me. And now, now I don't dare break it. Because what we have hums along without complications, and if we'd deviate from our standards, chaos could erupt. And that's not a price that I guess either of us is willing to pay.

We used to be in love. In college we were. There was plenty of kissing and fucking then. When we started the business, I'm not sure if we were still in love or if we just thought we'd make a great team. But there was never any acrimonious break up or anything. We just sort of...fizzled. Maybe it was the tax-time exhaustion. Because back in the early days, when it was just me and Tony, he had his nose nearly as deep in the paperwork as I did. Maybe we were just together too long. Or maybe we just took on another great love: Money.

We didn't have it, and we wanted it. So maybe that greed eclipsed our physical lust. So we started seeing other people. And then, when we'd break up with those other people, we'd fall back in with each other.

But a couple years ago, we decided neither of us would ever move on if we kept doing that. So we made a clean break, romantically, that is. We agreed we wouldn't date each other anymore. But all it takes is one long, lonely night and those old habits are just too tempting.

So that's how we came up with the mutually agreeable rules. If either of us is involved with someone else, we stop our sexual activities with each other. Even when we're both single and fooling around with each other, we never hold hands. We don't go on "dates". We don't cuddle, and we don't sleep over. We don't call each other pet names or whisper sweet nothings. Oh, he calls me "baby" all the time, but he calls everyone that, sometimes he even calls Mark that. And I'll tell him that he's hot, and he'll say I'm foxy. But he doesn't call me beautiful, and I don't tell him that he's so handsome, even though he is. We talk about the money we'll make, we'll talk about getting off. But we don't talk about love. And we don't kiss.

For two years, we haven't kissed.

About one month after we broke up and made up the rules, I knew I hated them because I was still in love with him.

Tony grabs me around the waist and he shifts again. He keeps his hand on me, one finger still inside, but he rotates his body, lifts me up even higher as he hangs his legs over the side of the tub now. He scootches down a bit and releases me, reaches up to the side of the tub and presses the Jacuzzi button.

"Here, get yourself some of this action," he says.

I'm slick everywhere, my sweat mixing with the steam and hot water he kept basting me with. His index finger rests deep inside me and he lines me up so that one of the jets whooshes between my legs.

I jerk and gasp it's so intense. It rockets my internal temperature even higher and the blast of pressure is sinful. He places his arm back around my waist to keep me bound to the rushing pleasure and moves his ass, and therefore mine, even closer to the jet. It's aligned just above my nub so the force is rushing around it, but not striking it dead on.

It's so fucking great I almost can't stand it. He takes away his finger and I ache for it, but with his hand gone, the water hits me more directly and I lurch with it.

"Are you coming yet?" he asks.

I have to gather my breath to speak, force out a grunted, "Nuh, no."

I'm not. But I'm panting and it's liquid heat coursing through my veins and the feeling is out of sight, the pressure just grazing the top of my clit, electric intense, so I'm not sure how I'm not coming yet. But it's so good that I'm actually glad I'm not.

And still, good as it is, delicious that he's watching me, shuddering pleasure, there's a fragmented shattering somewhere deep inside because I'd give it up to turn around and just kiss him on the mouth.

But those are the rules. He respects my mind, he enjoys my company, and he lusts my body. He's just not in love with me.

He says, "Get off now, Lisa, while you can. Tomorrow we'll start working again."

He slides his hand under me and comes at me from that angle. Beneath my ass, reaching between my legs, he plunges two fingers inside me. Making me feel just as needy for it and shameless and driven as he was when I was pumping him to pleasure, when I cupped his balls and made him groan. I inhale sharply and it raises me higher, just slightly, just enough for the jet to hit me dead center on my pleasure button, just as I get a visual of his face as he came. That does it for me.

Tony bites my earlobe and says, "You'll be too busy, making the big bucks tomorrow, baby."

I cry out as I come. My mouth still longing for his tongue, my body still longing for his erection, but my traitorous clitoris reacting to the physical, my hard-wired brain seizing on the memory of Tony coming as he was backed against the wall, covering my hand with his hot semen, him being made jealous and aroused by another man studying the tit that he was holding tightly. I clench around his fingers and shudder, but his arm around my waist holds me in place and the geysering water sends me rushing until I can't stand it anymore, but I can't stand to be without it either. So I undulate my hips, up and down, letting it hit me and reverberate through me, then backing off to recoup for a second, then going back on it. Just like when I milked him, each added spurt another jolt of condensed pleasure.

Until I have to stop, it's just too much. So I press down with my hips to get the pressure off me, and he slides his fingers out of me.

But ever the devil, he slides his fingers up, directly across me, pressing and rubbing where I'm oh-so-tender, sending a few last spikes of prickly jolts right to my core. Making me curl up, making me half-grunt, half-sob with how good it is.

He gives me a minute and splashes more water along my torso, keeping me warm as I cool off. When I'm calmed, he playfully slaps my tummy and says, "I hope that was worth the dinner you have to buy everyone now."

CHAPTER FOUR

Even though I'm now turned out and worn down and all I really want to do is climb into a bed and collapse for the rest of the night, the growling hunger in my belly urges me on as I get showered and into fresh clothes and Tony does the same. We have a little extra time and this is a celebratory night, so I go the distance and put on makeup and style my hair, being careful to arrange it to hide the scraggly grays cropping up.

As I'm primping, I hear Tony in the other room, clicking on a keyboard, and then shortly thereafter saying, "Lisa. This guy, Loren. You were so right about him."

"What'd you do? Google him?"

"Lisa, he owns entire sections of Europe. His family was wealthy, but after his father left everything to him, he bought compulsively and everything he touched turned to gold. I think he might have more money than God."

"You know," I tell him. "We're probably going to need help with this job he has for us."

"Yeah, that's fine." I hear him walking toward the bathroom and he pokes his head in as I'm dabbing on mascara and says, "All the more billable hours!" He waggles his eyebrows with a wicked grin.

"But, I mean, everyone's getting ready for vacation. And we're going to need a couple of people. I can't risk switching the staff over in the middle of an audit."

"Oh. Shit."

"Yeah, I know. And he wants to talk to us tomorrow. He says this is an impulse purchase. If that's true, he might want us to start immediately."

"Oh no."

"Oh yes. Do you want to risk this account?"

"Oh, Russo," he says. "We're going to have to talk to some of our crew tonight."

"*We're* going to talk to some of them, or *I'm* going to have to talk them?"

He gives me a sheepish look before ducking out of the doorway.

We're ready early, but instead of going to the bar we go directly to the restaurant and order a few drinks in their smaller lounge. I thought it would be busier, but then I realize that they have a large section of tables blocked off for our party.

It's a lovely space, with dark hardwood floors accented by the soft, creamy ceiling and it has a beautiful mural along the one wall. Tony orders a fresh bottle of white wine. When the waiter tries to hand him the cork to sniff, he reaches out and takes the bottle from his hand and slugs a huge gulp from it. I can't help but crack up as he says, "It's great." Appalled, the waiter retreats and Tony fills my glass. It is good, but although it's crisp, it's not so delightful because each sip just sets my stomach growling more. Thankfully, others start arriving before long so I sip more eagerly, loving how although it's leaving a longing in my stomach, it's already lighting up my head with a mellow, fritzy humming.

When we get dinner I'm tempted to order one of everything on the menu. They have a big array of seafood, which I love and haven't had in a long time. I don't order everything, but I do splurge on a surf and turf combo of a fillet and lobster tail, and each bite just gets progressively better. The steak is tender and juicy and the lobster is salty, buttery rich. It even makes the wine taste better.

As we're finishing our meal, Mark comes over and thanks me for the dinner.

"Have a seat," I tell him. I'm full on food and the wine had me slightly buzzed, but now I'm feeling a bit dragged down already again. I glance at Tony, but he saws off a big piece of prime rib and shoves it in his mouth and I assume I'm on my own with this unpleasant job. Tony gets to hand out bonus checks and throw parties. I get to cancel vacations and assign more work.

"Mark," I begin, "I have a big favor I want to ask you..."

But Tony cuts me off, blurting out, "Can you reschedule your vacation, Mark?"

I'm stunned, but relieved too. That was a pretty big bullet he just bit down on by asking that.

Mark, he just sits there, looking at me.

Of course.

"It's just that, well, we have an opportunity for new business," I tell him.

And Tony backs me up immediately. "This is a very big opportunity that could become quite lucrative, not just in the short term either."

Before I can start to explain it, Mark looks at me and asks, "Is this, by any chance, about the guy that was at the pool earlier?"

We both nod, and again, before I can explain, Mark says, "That was Gianni Loren, wasn't it?"

"Yes," I tell him.

"How the hell did you know that?" Tony asks him.

"He's in Forbes, Fortune, all the big lists," Mark explains. "Of course I know who he is. I just wasn't sure that was really him. So what's he interested in?"

"Well, I'm not certain what it is yet," I tell him.

"We're meeting with him tomorrow to find out and make arrangements," Tony explains.

"Yes," I jump in. "And from what little he explained to me it's about him possibly acquiring a rather large company here in the states."

And Mark, you gotta love Mark, he says, "I'm in. All the way. Whatever you need, I'm in."

I'm stunned. No one deserves this vacation more than Mark does, and no one's been looking forward to the time off more than he has. "Are, are you sure?" I ask him. "It could be a big job. More long hours. And I'm not sure how long it will last either."

He nods again, saying, "It's a once in a lifetime opportunity. I'm in. Just one thing though," and he looks to Tony as he says this part. "I get an extra two weeks vacation when it wraps up."

"Done," Tony doesn't even hesitate to answer.

"Who else are you going to have help out?" Mark asks.

"Well, I'm not sure," I tell him. "Probably Jill."

"Definitely Jill. She'll do it. And she's good. I don't think she's too burned out from the tax season either." He looks around the room until his eyes land on Jill. He leans closer and says, "You might want to ask her soon. She started drinking merlot at dinner and she seems to be hitting it harder now."

We take his advice and Tony immediately catches Jill's eye and waves her over to our table.

She thanks me for the dinner as she takes a seat and takes a generous gulp of her wine.

"Jill, I know you've worked really hard the past couple months and are really looking forward to vacation next week, but I have a favor to ask you," I say.

This time, it's Mark who interrupts me. "They're taking on Gianni Loren as a client and they want us to work on the account!"

Clearly, he's quite jazzed about the prospect.

Jill looks from me to Tony, then at Mark. She takes another gulp of her wine and asks, "This isn't some sort of belated April Fool's joke, is it?"

"I'm afraid not," Tony says.

She sighs heavily and places her glass down. But I can tell from the way her eyes are already curling to reveal a smile that the sigh wasn't one of exhaustion. In fact, she's smiling, but her eyes are glistening already, like she's on the verge of tears. "And, and you want me to help? You're serious?"

"Jill," I tell her, "we want our very best working this job. You're our best."

"Oh Ms. Russo!" She covers her mouth and tosses her hair off her shoulder. Finally saying, "Yes, of course! Thank you so much for this!"

Next thing, she bounds up and comes around the table and gives me a little hug around the shoulders. I laugh and pat her back. "Thank you, Jill. We really appreciate you helping us out."

"And Tony!" she nearly squeals as she leans down and hugs him even tighter. "I won't let you down, I promise."

"I know you won't, Jill," he says as she still clings to him. He looks over her shoulder at me, and as she pulls away, she stops to give him a kiss on the cheek.

Even in the soft lighting, I can see him blush. Not his type, my ass.

But I don't care. They are our best, and with both of them willing to help, I'm certain we can handle anything Loren tosses our way.

I take a long sip of my wine, closing my eyes to savor the flavor. When I open them again, I see them coming through the door, and this time I know I'm not mistaken. "Oh shit," I say.

"What's up, Lisa?" Tony asks.

I nod to the lounge area and say simply, "Brokers."

I try to be a sport about it. Everyone is finishing their dinners and milling about anyhow. So after I take care of the check I go up to the small bar where Tony's entertaining the brokers. They offer me a shot, and though I hate to refuse and seem priggy, I do turn it down because I'm already lit up and I don't want to get drunk and be hungover for the meeting with Loren tomorrow. Tony, of course, doesn't turn down the shot. I hang around for a while, listening to their banter. But when Day-Trader Dave comes over and starts hitting on me and won't take the hint and eventually lunges to kiss me, I back away and decide to call it a night.

On my way out, Tony catches hold of my shoulder and leans down and asks me quietly, "Whose room are you going to tonight?"

"Whose room is nicer?" I ask as my answer.

"I won't be long," he tells me.

"Yes you will. It's ok. Unwind. Have fun for a while."

"I can have more fun with you," he says.

"Oh, I'm sure. But I'll be there. No rush." I give him a wink so he knows it is alright. Then I add, "Just don't buy Dave any drinks."

Climbing on the elevator, it strikes me as I push the button for the top floor.

It's a Sisyphean task, really, trying to make someone fall in love with you. At least, when that person already loves you, it's a repetitive trap. But I can't help it, either. I've been climbing the mountain and pushing the boulder uphill for years now. And it's not so much the possibility of reaching the summit as it is the glorious fulfillment I get when I do, sometimes, arrive there that must keep me going. And sometimes, like today, tonight, it feels so right, it feels like he really is with me.

It's not like I have a choice anyhow. I can't change my heart's desire, I can't somehow eviscerate my love for Tony. I date other people and try to fall for other men, but every day, I work with him. Every day, I laugh with him. Even when we're having sex with other people, every day, I long for him.

So I do what I can. I carry that love like the boulder and keep pushing it up the hill, trying to please him, trying to impress him. Trying to get him to fall back in love with me. And sometimes, like today, I get so close.

I know he loves me. He always has, and he probably always will.

And maybe, someday, I'll reach the apex again and he'll fall back in love with me.

Somedays, like today, it feels like he's even trying to help me push that boulder up the hill, like he wants it, too.

The difference between me and Sisyphus, I don't think my boulder is a punishment.

As the light dings as I reach the uppermost level in the building here, after the day we've already had together, I can't help but feel like maybe, just maybe, I'm nearly there, poised right at the zenith.

Upstairs, it's such a relief to kick off shoes and strip off my clothes. The room is nice with a huge plasma TV and a view of the Statue of Liberty. I wash off my makeup and shake out my hair, and instead of flipping on the television I enjoy the quiet and peace of simply gazing out the window onto the harbor.

My stomach finally filled and my body relaxed from the earlier activities of the day and my head clouded by wine, I flop down on the bed and stretch out, waiting for the one final piece of the puzzle to satisfy my desires: Tony.

Mutual Holdings

Susan DiPlacido

CHAPTER FIVE

I wake to hear him cooing my name.

"Lisa."

It's so soft and gentle, and his arm is already around me, pulling me back against him.

"Lisa," he breathes again.

Foggy, I blink, but it's dark. I close my eyes again, think I was dreaming it. But just as I'm getting pulled back under, I hear my name again, barely above a whisper.

"Mmhmm," is all I say in answer, not wanting to bother with speech in case it breaks the spell. It feels too good as it is.

Tony is close behind me, not quite pressing against my backside, but I can feel his body heat and presence, and I know it's him because if this is real, I'm familiar with the size and feel of his body, the touch of his skin. I know it's him, because if it's a dream, I don't dream about anyone else.

Using a whisper touch, he traces a line down my naked spine with his index finger. Gliding slowly under the blankets, he follows the curve of my waist, up over my hip, and moves back up along my side, brushing over my ribs, beside my breast. He lingers there, still using the lightest touch, and swirls around a few times, marking the areas where the soft swell begins.

I stretch a bit next to him, sigh lightly, but I'm still not sure if I'm ready to rouse completely. I'm still not sure where I am or what's going on. He tickles his fingers down my belly, swirling repeatedly around my navel, dipping softly in and out of it. I twist my head against the pillow as a soft incoherent mumble escapes his mouth. Feeling the texture of the sheets brings it back to me. I'm at the hotel, it's the night after tax day. And it feels like Tony is finally ready to make love to me.

That rushes back, too, with a stab to my heart. He's not ready to make love. But he is ready to fuck.

That's close enough. Sometimes, it's even better anyhow. Maybe this is just a dream. Tony wanders his hand down lower across my stomach and there's nothing to interfere, because I stripped before getting in bed and feel asleep completely naked, while waiting for him.

When I wonder what time it is, how long I was waiting before I fell asleep, that's when I realize this is definitely real and not just a dream. He's tracing lines back and forth where my pubic hair starts. I shift my legs, my head still tranquilly fuzzy, so close to sleep, slightly confused and blurred. His fingers dance across my thigh, silky smooth and the insistent ache between my legs keeps me from closing my eyes and going back to sleep.

He inches closer, spooning up behind me and pressing close against my back. I settle against him, nuzzling my shoulders into his chest. It sends a quiet echo through my body, a pleasant throb to my cunt. Using his chin, he brushes the hair off my shoulder and away from my neck, then lazily runs his tongue along the area. Fingertips only, he slowly drags his hand back up and traces an elongated figure eight pattern along my arm.

Hushed, "Lisa."

"Mmmmm," is all I say. Another subdued thrum goes through me as he presses his hips closer, his erection settling between my legs.

"Lisa," he whispers again, close to my ear. "You awake?"

I simply sigh again through heavy breaths, so he nuzzles against my neck and reaches around more strongly with his arm, hugging me close.

"Baby, you awake?"

"Mmm-hmmm," I answer dreamily and place my hand over his, rubbing at his fingers, his forearm. He moves lower, massaging my tummy and aligning his groin. Licking along my shoulder again, he gently presses at the base of my abdomen, pulling my back towards him even closer and naturally letting himself slip inside me.

"Finally," I think I say. It feels so good, him filling me up, heating me up.

"This ok?" he asks me.

I just answer with a soft, "Mmmmm," of approval and a slight arch of my back.

"Good," he mumbles to me, wrapping himself as close around me as he can. He starts to rock back and forth slightly, adding that bit of friction to the wet heat. I sway with him as he sets a lulled, slow tempo - making it drowsily flow through us both. Tingles of sensual pleasure waft through me, mixing with the dulled need as he refuses to speed it up. Slow and easy, just languorously undulating.

He kisses my shoulder, sliding his hand down my belly and wiggling it between my legs. His fingers search out the hard little nub and start to massage it. He matches the cadence of his sways inside me, rubbing slowly but firm, letting the heat smolder on its own, the rocking motion doing most of the work, refusing to fan the flames. But it heats up anyhow, like a slow burn.

Every slow, deep rock back and forth ticks it up just a little more. Excited quivers start to pulse through me, the air around us gets dense and balmy as his breathing quickens. My stomach strains against his arm holding it in place, trying to contract, trying to buck and push harder, increase the speed. But he won't let me. He keeps moving slow, back and forth against me, deliciously sliding into me, gliding in and almost out before slowly pressing back in again. I start humming and mumbling. Not words, just soft noises of encouragement.

His index finger slides up and down against my pulsing clit with even pressure, almost groggily, but exactly where I need it. He holds me quiet and tight, listening to me just keep humming "Mmmmm, mmmmm," in front of him.

He answers me the same way, low and breathy, chanting my name as he rocks into me, slides against me. "Lisa," he says, burying his mouth against my neck. "You feel so good. You feel so good to me, baby."

"Mmmmm, Tony."

"Mm, mmhmm. Lisa." Still going slow, he's placidly hitting the plateaus and lingering, the skin of my back flushed against him. "That feel good to you?" he asks, already knowing it does. "Am I getting it right for you?"

"Mmmmm. Hot," I say simply and as a fever starts to run through me, with one arm I throw the covers off of us, never interrupting the easy sway. Tony obliges, blowing cool air against my neck. "Mmm, mmm, mmm," I tense in front of him, moans coming more quickly. Even though he's going so slow and easy, it feels so good to have him inside that I think I could come even if he wasn't massaging me up front. But it's so good on the outside, my clit overwhelming me again, and as he slides his fingers against me it makes me contract and come from there as I start to shiver. Inside, I grip tight around his cock, holding him in as he pushes again. He hits the same spot, slides his finger against me again, probably enjoying being squeezed so tight by the reverbs of my orgasm.

Just a few thrusts behind, it expect it to catch him too, still rocking slow, back and forth, my quivers slowing down and settling. He pushes deep on the instroke, sliding into my tight warmth and settling there for a long second. Then he pulls back and goes deep again, squeezing his arms tight around me, he presses his whole body against me as close as he can.

He doesn't shudder though, and when he speaks again I can smell the tequila lingering on his breath. Quietly, he asks, "You came, right?"

"Mmm hmm. You didn't yet. You can keep going."

"You sure?"

"Mmm hmm." I want him to keep going. It was a mellow orgasm, and I can definitely handle more. He takes his hand from between my legs and I miss it immediately. But mercifully, he stays tucked deep inside me. He strokes my stomach and then moves higher, caressing my breasts, then holding on to one. Unexpectedly, he pulls almost all the way out and then thrusts deep again, burying into me.

"Oh, so good," I sigh.

He kisses my shoulder, works his way to my neck. He sucks there a minute and thrusts deeply a couple more times, but he's not falling back into a rhythm.

"Oh, God, Lisa," he whispers in my ear, the hot breath tingling me. And then, he asks, mumbling it, "What're we doing?" He shivers lightly, and I wonder if he's coming, but I don't think he is. He kisses my neck again, moves higher and kisses my cheek, moves toward my mouth. When he's at the corner of my mouth he halts and thrusts again, groans with it this time. "I want you so bad, baby."

"I'm here," I tell him.

"Huh uh," he says and pulls out of me. Before I can protest, he moves and climbs over me, on top of me, so I shift and turn so that I'm facing him, and I wrap my legs around his waist, hoping, waiting for him to enter me again.

Instead, he eases down on me, stomach to stomach, chest to chest, his bare skin warm and smooth against mine, the hair on his body tickling me on my breasts. The weight of him on top of me is something I haven't felt in a long time and it's overpowering, overwhelming.

"Like this," is all he says, but instead of getting inside me, he moves lower, dips his head and kisses my temple, my cheek. He kisses my neck and then raises up, his eyes closed. He inhales deeply and opens his eyes, watching me. He dips to my mouth and hovers, but then raises up and pulls back with a sigh. Finally asking, "Can I?"

I nod, my chest nearly exploding with anticipation.

He dips again, still watching me, and presses his lips against mine. In answer, I kiss back.

He pulls up, still watching me. Now I can't help it. I reach up and knot my finger through the thick waves of his hair. That's when he closes his eyes and comes back and really lays one on me.

Open mouthed, his tongue peeking out, he kisses me full on the mouth. Now I can taste the tequila he'd been drinking, but it mingles with his unique, warm saltiness. It's familiar but different than I'd remembered, because even though it's been so long, I never did forget how he felt and tasted when he kissed me. It's almost like sitting down to your favorite meal after years away, and it's the same cook, but he's updated the recipe. So even though it's really great, it's not exactly what you've been longing.

But it is great. He nibbles a few times and then suddenly plunges deep, thrusting his tongue in and then taking it away. This time he's the one who starts to make the "mmmm" noises. Humming and sighing, he tongue fucks my mouth, sloppy and greedy, breathing heavily. It brings me right back up again, giving me butterflies in my stomach. Until, abruptly, he groans and shifts his body higher as he reaches down between us and takes hold of himself. Lining himself up quickly, he plunges in, hard and deep, forcing the breath out of me, rocking my whole body with it.

He props himself up on his elbows, closes his eyes, and goes to work. Pumping fast and firm, every once in a while driving really deep and lingering as I clench around him, I can tell he's taking all the pleasure he can out of it.

It's something I've always admired about Tony – his enthusiasm for things. It's why our staff loves him. It's why he can reel in the big clients for us. It's just how he is, he really gets into things. When he wants a client, he goes after him, and he really does enjoy it, too. Around the office, when he's pleased with something someone's done, he lets them know, and he gets truly excited about it. He's big and he's loud and he puts all his energy into whatever he's focused on at the time.

And he fucks the same way. Like earlier today when we first came up to the room together, he came so quickly and so hard for me because he just couldn't hold himself back. He made it up to me, so I don't mind. And whenever we used to fuck regularly, even back in college, there were times when I'd catch him controlling himself, making sure to take care of me and get me off first. But sometimes, sometimes, he just couldn't help it. It was like I drove him wild and he'd get so into it that his rushing energy would eclipse his gentleman tendencies.

And I can tell that now, right now, the same thing is happening. He broke a two-year rule to kiss me, he wanted it that bad. I've wanted it that bad, but I never had the guts to take the chance. That kiss got him wired and set him off, and now he's fanning his own flames, getting himself off with that unbridled enthusiasm.

I can't help it, it turns me on.

Tasting and smelling the lingering tequila and feeling the way he's moving, I know he's at least a little bit drunk. I don't care. When he starts mumbling, it's the garden variety nonsense at first. Heavy pants and then, "Jesus, baby, you feel so good."

"So do you," I tell him and thrust and wiggle against him, moving not so much to please him but to heighten my own swirling desire, getting what I need while he takes what he wants.

He goes shallower but much more quickly, hot and fast friction. "I, I, I..." he stutters, and I think he's edgy.

I already came once, but now he's got me hot and driven again and I don't want to be left behind, because I know if he comes he'll be completely finished for the night. And if he's drunk like I think he is, he'll pass out and won't be able to help finish me off. And this time, with his pelvis crushing against me, it's got my clit buzzing again, but even better, the rapid pumping of is cock is making me throb deep inside.

I clench tighter and hold my breath, driving myself against him. Him muttering again, "I, I love...Lisa. Oh my God, I...love..."

I inhale sharply and take hold of his shoulders, suddenly my brain swimming and my blood singing, every thrust of his hitting me inside and out, lapping against both my sweet spots, and now his words piercing my heart. It's taken so long to get back here, but I've hoped and dreamed of him falling back in love with me. I knew I wasn't alone in feeling it today. And now, now he's so close to telling me. Feeling brave, feeling reckless, gathering my strength and letting it gush out, I say it as much as I can. "Me too," I admit to him. "Me too, Tony."

"I, oh fuck," he says, his hips gyrating and pumping wildly, driving himself into me, putting me on the brink. He pounds in again, grunting, "I love..." and just a few more thrusts and he pushes me over, it starts from the inside this time, deep in my belly, contractions of sheer euphoric pleasure crashing through me, sweeping, and as he thrusts again the pressure outside triggers and wraps into it.

Tony keeps thrusting, and stutters again, "I, oh, Lisa, I love," and then suddenly blurting it all out in a rush, saying, "I love fucking you, Lisa!"

"Ooooh, fuuuck," I moan, sickening mental realization suddenly dawning, revealing my mistake, but the physical still too good and overtaking me and I shudder, coming hard even as my heart bottoms out.

"Oh, oh, yeah," he encourages. "Come for me, baby."

Writhing, I squeeze my eyes shut, turn my face away and let go of his shoulders, unwrap my legs from his waist. But with his thrusting it keeps me shuddering, my tits shaking and stomach involuntarily contracting, my muscles still tensed. Indomitable pleasure mixed with the stinging pain.

Mercifully, he stops thrusting, his last trite admission falling off his tongue with ease, shouting it, "I'm gonna come!"

He pumps again, rapidly, quickly, three hard thrusts, and then buries deep in me, stuttering, "C...Cuh, Coming," as he unloads, warm and sticky, deep inside me.

When he's done, he collapses down on top of me, but the weight is too heavy so I push against his chest as I slither to the side. Obliging, he rolls over and catches his breath. He just says, "Oh my God."

I guess I should be complimented that it was solely me getting him off, that he wasn't thinking of all the money he'd be making soon. Then again, I don't know if that's what he was thinking about it, I don't have any idea what he was really thinking, especially when he kissed me like that.

He was drunk, he wasn't thinking. He wasn't thinking anything, he was just doing, moving, taking what he needed.

That's how it's supposed to be with us.

But he broke the rules.

And once again, the boulder slipped out of my grasp and rolled back down to the bottom of the ravine, landing with a distressing *thunk*.

Laying there, exhausted, turned out, pissed off, and completely let down, I could cry. But I don't. Because it was just one kiss, just a couple of sighs, and I let it explode and unleash.

Enough. I need to lock it down, and fast.

I can't let this, I can't let myself, destroy everything we've built.

Reaching over, he slaps my thigh, then shifts and pats my tummy. "Oh, Lees," he says. "I'm a little buzzed but that was out-fucking-standing."

I turn over on my side but don't answer him.

He snuggles up closer to me and starts lazily massaging my breast and kissing my shoulder. Cuddling me.

I want to pull away, but I don't want to make a scene either. So I wait it out and it's only a couple of minutes before his movements slow and then stop completely. Listening, I wait until his breathing deepens. I lift his hand off me and slide out of the bed quietly.

Maybe he thinks it's time to start relaxing the rules and doing what he wants, but now I see the danger in it. And the brunt of the peril falls on me.

I'm not breaking the rules anymore. No more kissing. No more cuddling. And no sleeping over.

I search in the dark until I find my bag, and then I drag it into the bathroom, being careful to be quiet and not wake him. Like it matters. He's probably passed out. I slip on some clothes and then slip out into the hallway, easing the door closed behind me. I pad down the hall and climb on the elevator, punch the button to take me to the floor where my, less-expensive, not-as-nice, non-suite room is. But once I'm on that floor, even though I'm tired, I don't see the point in settling down just to get back up in a few hours. So I don't even enter. I just go home.

Susan DiPlacido

CHAPTER SIX

It's around 3 a.m. when I get home and outside my door is a rush delivery. Looking at it, I see it's from my cousin Lucy, and I nearly break into tears when I realize that in my haste to leave Tony's room last night I forgot to get my skirt that I'd hung up neatly. I consider calling him to grab it for me, but I'm not ready quite yet to deal with him. I reason that it probably won't be wearable again after that dip in the chlorinated water and resign myself to having lost it.

I open the package, and inside is a batch of her homemade raspberry, dark chocolate brownies with a brief note congratulating me on finishing tax season. I take a small one and let it melt across my mouth, savoring the bittersweet richness. I get a pang of guilt for not having talked to her in a while and next thing I know I'm stuffing brownies in my mouth more quickly than I can swallow.

Disgusted with my gluttony, once the pan is half-gone and I'm getting a sugar rush mixed with a slight sickness in my stomach, I pack the rest away in the fridge and check the clock.

It's late here, but with the time difference, I'm pretty sure she's still closing up the restaurant, so I give her a call.

"*Buona sera*," she answers, and I recognize her lilting voice immediately.

"Lucy," I say. "Thank you for the brownies!"

"Aw, you're welcome. Get it all finished for tax day?"

I sigh. "Finally. How's Danny?"

"He's great, Lisa. Thanks. Busy working, you know."

"Are they filming already?"

"No, not yet," she says. "But he's been spending some time rehearsing. Learning lines."

"Good for him."

"Yeah," she says, but I can hear the hesitance in her voice. "He's with his co-star a lot. And she's..."

"She's not you," I say. "Don't worry about it. He loves you, Lucy."

"Yeah," she sighs. Getting upbeat again, she asks, "So how's Tony?"

"Oh Madone. He's no Danny."

"Lisa. What's wrong?"

"Oh, it's fine," I tell her. "I just feel like I'm stuck sometimes. Like, I'm waiting forever for him to come around."

"He loves you, Lisa," Lucy says. "I know it."

"Yeah, the problem is I don't think he knows it."

After a silence, she changes the subject and asks, "You seen Eva lately?"

"I haven't," I tell her. "But little Rick's graduating in a couple of weeks!"

"Oh, thanks for reminding me. What are you getting him?"

"Cash," I say. "He wants to travel to Europe for the summer."

"Youth," Lucy says.

Despite the sugar flowing through me, talking to Lucy actually soothes me enough that I'm able to fall into a fairly deep sleep that night.

In the morning, the first thing I do in the bathroom is pop my birth control pill. I made one lousy mistake last night, I don't want to make another one. Then I go back to sleep for a couple of hours since our meeting isn't until later in the day and for the first time in months, I don't have anything pressing to do. Once awake, I linger around the apartment, taking my time, but I still end up getting to the office twenty minutes early.

Tony isn't there, and since no one else is either, I put on a couple pots of coffee, both decaf and regular. It occurs to me that Gianni Loren will probably want something more exotic and that I should have stopped at Starbucks or something.

With ten minutes before the meeting to spare, Tony breezes in. And sure enough, he thought of those comfort details, because he's got a courier with him and they're hauling an assortment of Starbucks coffee and Krispy Kreme doughnuts and even a tray of deli sandwiches. I get out plates and silverware and start arranging the stuff as Tony pays and dismisses the courier. By the time he's done, he catches me with a half a glazed shoved in my mouth.

I smile guiltily at him.

All morning I'd prepared myself on how to act. He may have slipped up and caused some of my confusion with that kiss, but those words he was mumbling weren't intentionally misleading. I just got carried away. And today, of all days, we can't afford the least bit of tension or discord among us. We have to be working together to nail down this account.

He checks his watch and leans back against the counter. Crossing his feet, he says, "You took off last night."

I nod and wipe my hands on a napkin. Fearless, smiling, I look him in the face and explain, "I needed to shower and get clothes from home."

"Oh," he says. Then, "Listen Lisa. I uh, last night, I was a little drunk. But I wanted to say that, well..."

I cut him off by slapping his arm and saying, "It was fun last night, Mancuso."

"Yeah, it's just," he clears his throat and folds his arms. "I um, I wanted you to know..."

The ding of the elevator interrupts him. Glad to have this ended, I raise my brows and say, "It's all good, Tony. Now come on, let's do this."

He looks at me another second, but then pushes away from the counter and heads to the elevator.

When Loren exits, Tony greets him, shaking his hand and thanking him for coming in. His lawyer is again close on his heels, and the two bodyguards behind him. I glance at the bodyguards. They look similar to the other two from last night, but they're different guys.

Loren seems bright and eager, greeting Tony warmly, shaking his hand and saying, "To-ny. Hello! Good to see you again." He looks around the place, taking his time to really examine and admire, even though there's not much to admire. Nevertheless, he makes an approving face, saying, "This is a very good office in New York, yes?"

"Thank you. It's still small, but like you said, we're growing."

"No problem," Loren says. "And I think this small comment, it is not true. I know about real estate and the price of it in this city. This is great."

He's in a suit again today, but he's not wearing a tie. His shirt is a lilac color and it's open at the neck. His suit is again impeccable, but it's not tan. Today it's a soft mist green, single breasted. He looks like spring incarnate with the way his light eyes pop out with that suit, especially with his nearly gilded skin color. He looks fantastic, but not a whit like a New Yorker.

It's refreshing.

His lawyer and his bodyguards, however, they're in respectable navy blue.

Gianni turns to check out the rest of the office and catches sight of me. "Ahh!" he says and holds out his hands as he walks toward me. He takes both my hands and quickly leans in and kisses my one cheek, then the other. Still holding my hands, he pulls back and says, "Good afternoon, Lisa. You look..." he hesitates for a second, and a slight furrow crosses his brows, but he brightens again and says, "Wonderful!"

He ducks closer and asks, "This is good word, yes?"

"*Buon giorno*, Gianni," I say. "*Si, e benissimo*."

"No!" he says forcefully and drops my hands, holding up a single finger. "Today," he says as he glances over at his lawyer, "we speak English. All day, all the time. Today is a day of learning...English."

"Okay," I nod, smiling. I can't help it. His energy is positive and contagious. If he were an American, or poor, people would probably think he was a nutcase. But being Italian, and so freaking rich, I'm sure most people find his manner quite charming. I know I do.

Spinning around, he says to Tony, "You see this greeting I give her? This is how we say hello where I am from. I am knowing that it is different in America and in New York. But you, Tony, you will allow me this greeting soon? When we are more friends? I am, uh, I tell you now, I like the women very much, so you do not have to worry. When I give you the kiss, it is just a kiss. Okay?"

"Actually," Tony laughs, "I'm a bit hurt that you didn't lay it on me this time."

"Ahh!" Gianni exclaims and immediately obliges, swooping over to him and placing his hands firmly on Tony's arms and leaning in and kissing his one cheek, and then the other, as Tony responds in kind.

It couldn't be less gay looking, except for maybe the most severely homophobic, and yet it couldn't be more ridiculous looking in a New York, Wall Street office.

But they both laugh, and I can tell it's genuine and that it's not just me who likes Gianni's flashy and eccentric style. "Can I offer you some coffee?" Tony asks him. "Something else?"

"Have you wine?" Gianni asks.

"Uh," Tony rubs his chin. "Yes. Kind of. We have some champagne left, I think."

Gianni laughs, saying, "I make a joke, about the wine. Accountants, they do not have the wine in office. Even in Europe, they have no wine. But you do. You do better and have the champagne. I like this company even more now," he nods approvingly.

"Gianni," the lawyer behind him says.

"Yes, yes, Michael," Gianni says. "I know. Too early for the wine. Oh-kay." He claps his hands together and rubs them. "Let us get to the business, huh?"

With that, Tony guides him toward his office. The bodyguards stay at the elevator, but Loren walks beside Tony, and I fall in step with his lawyer and follow them.

Once in Tony's office, he points them to chairs, but before sitting, Loren moves across the room to more closely study the painting on the wall. It may be a masterpiece, but I think it's an ugly thing in a tackily ornate frame. It's not real, just a reproduction of a Rubens.

Loren says, "I know this. I study the, uh, *come si dice*, artwork, painting, very much. This is Rubens, si? A Baroque, yes?"

"Yes." Tony smirks and looks down at his desk to avoid my hostile glare, which would probably make him smirk even bigger. But at least he knows I'm glaring and he doesn't say what I don't want him to say. Instead, he just says, "I'm impressed you know that."

"You also love the baroque art?" Gianni asks him.

"Uh, well." Tony scratches his temple. "I'd like to have time to learn some more."

"I understand. So, this picture, you have it why?"

Silent, I shake my head, mentally begging him not to say it. Just please don't say it.

"It reminds me of someone," Tony answers him.

He said it.

Now I just pray that Gianni won't make the connection. The painting is *The Education of Maria de Medici*, and it shows Maria kneeling before the gods learning music and literature But the focal point of the painting is off to the right, where the three graces are blessing Maria with beauty. The graces are suffused with a golden light, and they're nude.

After a few heavy seconds, Gianni squints his eyes and turns from the painting to me and grins.

I blush.

Tony says one of the nude graces, the woman on the left, looks like me. I think she looks nothing like me. But, apparently, Gianni made the connection, too.

Normally, I'd be flattered to be compared to a great master's painting. And on most levels, I am, because the woman in the painting is lovely. However, in this office, and especially now when I'm trying to appear formal and give off the impression that my mind is essential for this client, it completely undermines my professionalism to have a man looking at a painting of a nude woman and having him compare it to me. Especially when the woman in question isn't simply nude. She's standing in contrapposto with one knee slightly bent, a rather seductive pose. And instead of looking at Maria, as the other two graces are, she stands directly facing the viewer, with her eyes seemingly gazing back at them.

As Gianni looks at me, I can see that randy sparkle in his eyes, the same as when he first watched me at the pool last night. He tilts his head and asks, "Lisa. You are also a fan of this painting?"

I try to get him focused back on my mind by saying, "I'm an accountant, Gianni. To me, baroque is very bad, because it's means you're out of Monet."

As soon as I say it, I regret it, because I'm afraid the pun is over his level of comprehension of English right now. But I can actually see his quick intelligence register on his face as he remains blank for a second, and then his brow twitches into the slightest furrow before it breaks, and I can see he's decoded it. He smiles and nods. "*Benissimo*," he says. "Michael, do you understand this? It is a joke."

"Yes, I get it, Gianni," his lawyer answers, nodding politely, but I swear I can pick up a hint of annoyance in his manner. Looking at me, he says, "Very clever."

"It's an old joke around here," I tell them both and motion for them to sit.

Instead, Gianni checks his watch and says, "I have enough here. We should go now."

Looking panicked, Tony goes, "Wait. Don't you want to at least discuss the project before you go? If you give us some idea about it we can get back to you with estimates if you prefer, or..."

"No," Gianni answers. "We all go. Now. We talk later. First, I think I show to you the project. Maybe that can help you most, yes?"

"Oh," Tony says, probably relieved his stupid painting didn't kibosh the whole deal. "Sure, that'd be great."

As Gianni and Michael turn to leave, Tony and I exchange quizzical glances, but fall in line behind them anyhow.

Outside the building, double-parked, there's a limo waiting, and I get completely curious about where we're going. As Gianni opens the door for me to get in, I'm startled by a sudden flash of light in my face. As I blink and focus on the retreating photographer, Gianni says, "*Mi dispiace*. Paparazzi."

Holding out a hand to escort me inside the car, what he says is, "They sometimes wish to photograph me."

What I understand, in my lower-middle class brain, is: This man and this job is a world away from what I'm accustomed to.

Michael stands by, but Gianni nods to him, saying, "You go with Lisa. I take Tony with me. He will like." Wordless, Michael climbs in next to me. After Michael is in, the bodyguards also climb in, one in the back, and one moves to the front.

Turning around in my seat, I look out the back of the limo to see what they're going to be getting in. I can't hear Tony, but I see him light up when Gianni shows him the gleaming red sports car and directs him to get in. I'm not sure what it is, but I've never seen one before, and it looks expensive.

I look at Michael and say, "He sure is an energetic guy, huh?"

Michael sniffs but doesn't look at me. He checks his watch and says, "Ms.

Russo, I'm American by birth, but I've lived in Italy for over 30 years working for the Loren family. So I'm no longer attuned to the current American slang vernacular. Perhaps *energetic* is what your culture is calling it these days."

"Oh," I say.

Michael falls silent after that, and the bodyguard doesn't speak either, so I just watch the buildings crawl by, getting more curious as Gianni cuts ahead of us in traffic and gets on the Brooklyn Bridge. Before long, I realize we're all the way in Queens. I can't imagine what Gianni's interested in out here.

We pull into a large deserted lot and follow the red car as Gianni speeds along. When we stop, the bodyguard exits and holds the door. Michael climbs out first and I follow. I squint in the sunshine but shiver from the still brisk spring breeze.

Tony and Gianni standing in front of me, Gianni says, "What do you think?"

"I'm sorry," I tell him as I look at Shea Stadium looming directly in front of us. "I don't think I understand. You want to talk about this deal over a ballgame?"

Gianni laughs and motions to Shea. Then says, "No, Lisa."

I look at Tony, but he's just beaming, looking like he's ready to die and go to heaven right now.

I knew Gianni Loren was loaded with money, I'd even used the word billions when talking about his net worth. But the reality of that must not have really clicked with me. But now it does. He looks at me and winks.

Gianni, he says, "I wish to buy the Mets!"

CHAPTER SEVEN

Gianni takes the lead, and with a couple of gentlemen from the stadium, he gives us a tour of the ballpark. We start on the field. The Mets are away, so it's quiet inside with the stands empty and no balls popping into gloves or cracking off of bats. But we're gathered around home plate, and as I squint up into the clear spring sky, it feels surreal.

Along the tour, Gianni explains that he'd like us to begin immediately, and this time, I'm not quite sure that it's the lure of a big paycheck so much as the awesome surroundings, but Tony doesn't hesitate or hedge. But he's not so awe-struck that he loses his edge as he starts the official negotiation. I'd love to listen in on this deal being made, not just for curiosity, but also because I try to learn by watching Mancuso work. But immediately, Gianni's lawyer Spillway presses his hand against my back and shifts me aside gently and leads me down a long corridor, one side of which is enclosed in glass so that we can look down upon the lush, verdant field.

He actually starts explaining what the job will entail. A small part of me registers indignation, because I'm quite aware of what the job will entail. But I smile and nod and listen closely for any surprise cues anyhow. But as he's explaining how the stadium is leased by the Mets from the City of New York, which is something any self-respecting New York baseball fan already knows, I realize that he's not clueing me in so much as playing divide-and-conquer with Tony and me.

Slick as he is about it, and though I do admire his protecting of Gianni, I don't stumble when he finally tips his hand. He wraps up his speech and asks, "So you think you can handle this, Ms. Russo?"

"Yes. It's different, and it'll be a big job, but we can handle it. And I'm a Mets fan, so it'll be very enjoyable for me."

"So," he says. "Given the depth of the investigation, can you give me a rudimentary quote on your services?"

I glance over his shoulder, down the hall where Mancuso and Loren are still speaking. I tell Spillway, "I believe my partner is discussing that with Mr. Loren right now. Would you care to join them?"

As we approach, Tony and Gianni shake hands, and I know it's a done deal already. Spillway, he pats Gianni on the back to immediately insinuate himself back into the conversation. But Gianni simply says, "We are complete here." And then he breezily leads us back outside.

Behaving, and still a bit guarded and not wishing to encourage him, I refrain from even looking at Tony to try to discern what they came up with. But I can tell from his relaxed stride that he's pleased.

Outside, in the glowing sunshine, as we approach the vehicles, I ask Gianni, "So, what is this car?"

But Tony answers instead of Gianni, saying, "It's a Ferrari Enzo, Lisa."

"Oh," I say. Gianni nods.

Mancuso says, "It's based on Forumla 1 cars. It's a 6.0 V12 that can go from zero to sixty in under four seconds, with a top speed of over two hundred miles an hour."

"Very good," Gianni nods. "I think you like, huh Tony?"

"Like it?" Tony says. "I love it."

I like it too. It's a pretty combination of sleek performance lines and sexy curves.

"Lisa," Gianni says to me. "You like to ride? With me? We return to office?"

I can see Mancuso's face tighten as he tries to conceal his disappointment. I know he's dying to get in it again, and since I know it means more to him than it does to me, I should decline. But considering that he already did check it out, and considering that I'll probably never get another chance, I would like to see what the fuss is about from the inside. "Yes?" Gianni asks as the doors don't open out, but rise up, revealing the cockpit. The sun glints briefly in his green eyes, making them appear momentarily translucent.

"Yes," I say, and he offers me a hand to help me step in.

Tucked inside, he looks over and raises a brow as he turns it over and the machine roars to life, sending subtle vibrations through my entire body. "Hold on," Gianni tells me. "You are ready? This will be quite a ride."

I have a feeling he's right.

He says, "All day, we speak in English. But now, we sing in Italian! Oh-kay?"

"Okay," I nod.

Suddenly, drowning out the roaring engine, the stereo bursts forth, and the opening notes to Verdi's *Rigoletto* resound through the air. Simultaneously, Gianni puts us in motion and loudly sings along to the famous first line, "*La donna e mobile!*"

Smiling, looking out the window as New York rushes by, he only has to prod me once. His voice isn't operatic by any means, and that's just the thing to encourage me.

Exhilarated by the hum of the engine and amused by his animated bellowing of the lyrics, I join in and sing it loudly in Italian, where it sounds forceful and lovely. But in English, the words mean: *Woman is fickle, like a feather in the wind.*

Mutual Holdings

CHAPTER EIGHT

When we pull up outside the office, we have to wait a few minutes for Gianni's entourage and Mancuso to catch up. I felt weightless and giddy on the ride as we zoomed along, singing with abandon. But now, with the music silenced and the engine cut off, I feel more like I'm falling back to earth rather than just stepping out of the vehicle as my foot again touches New York concrete. Soon, Tony will be pulling up, and he'll be excited about the job, eager to tell me the deal he worked out, and it'll get him all worked up. And after yesterday and how I responded, and responded, and responded to him, he'll be completely flummoxed if I turn him down.

I can't be rude to him, especially when none of this is his fault. And I am curious to hear where we stand with this deal. But the specter of last night's disappointment still clings to me thickly. It was like the car ride had stripped it away, as we cut through the wind and parted the air, it had been torn away with the breeze. But now that we're still, it catches back up to me, hovering around. And now, today, I have to walk back down the mountain and prepare to start pushing the boulder up the hill again.

Chasing my love isn't a punishment, and it's not a curse. But sometimes, like today, it's exhausting because I realize that no matter how hard I push or how high up the mountain I get, Tony isn't in love with me anymore. So even when I get to the brink, that boulder is going to slip from my grasp and roll back down the hill.

Some days, like today, it breaks my heart.

Outside, on the street, before I can invite Gianni inside to wait for everyone else, his cell phone rings. He excuses himself and checks the display before answering. He breaks a smile and answers in Italian, saying, "*Pronto, cara mia*!"

I take a few steps away to give him privacy, but I can hear him as the tone of his voice changes. He loses the carefree lilt as he says, "No, no, Angelina! *Mi dispiace, mi amore.*" A short silence, and then he turns slightly away from me, but I can still hear him, speaking in Italian, apologizing and pleading with the woman on the other end. He's telling her he didn't mean to upset her, he's telling her he'll be there soon.

I smile as I look away discreetly, trying to afford him as much privacy as possible in the middle of a weekday afternoon on a corner on Wall Street.

As he disconnects, Mancuso and the rest of Gianni's posse arrives. Tony invites them back inside, but Gianni declines, saying he's got other business to attend to.

"I am very late," he tells Spillway. "For a meeting with Angelina. She's very angry."

"Oh hell," Spillway says and turns to me. He asks, "Where's the best fine jewelry shop?"

"Um, I'm not sure. Graff, maybe, on Madison Avenue?" I give him basic directions.

Turning back to Gianni, he says, "You go to the airport. I'll call to get the plane ready and I'll pick up a...?"

"Necklace," Gianni says with authority.

Tony's looking at the Ferrari lovingly as Gianni climbs back behind the wheel and starts easing it out into traffic. That's when disaster strikes.

As he's pulling out, a bike messenger suddenly weaves across traffic, directly in front of him. I see it coming and shout to the messenger, "Oh my God! Look out!"

Gianni halts and avoids hitting the guy, but the taxi behind him doesn't stop as quickly and it ends up jerking into his right rear tail, the sound an instant, diffused cracking.

That's when Tony shouts. Loudly, "Oh my God! Not the *car*!"

Up comes the door of the Ferrari as Gianni climbs out to check it out. Always hovering close, Spillway sprints from the limo right behind the bodyguards as one of them rushes to Gianni's side and the other stands right at the heels of the taxi driver. As the poor cab driver looks at the car, his face goes pale. Looking down at the crumpled rear end, with yellow paint now marring the previously perfect candy-apple red finish, the only thing the cab driver can say is, "Oh my God."

"Relax, relax," Gianni urges him. "You are not injured?"

"No," the cab driver says, while Gianni's bodyguard breathes down his neck.

"Then it is fine," Gianni says.

Spillway jumps in with that, insisting, "It is not fine! Look at it! Look at you, Gianni. You could be hurt."

"I am not hurt," Gianni says.

"Are you sure you're not hurt?" Tony asks the cabbie.

"I'm not hurt," he says.

"Are you sure you're okay?" I ask Gianni.

"I am not hurt," he insists.

"The car is hurt!" Tony says.

"It is fine," Gianni says.

And at that moment, appearing just as quickly as the bike messenger had, a photographer swoops in closely and pops a flash, capturing Gianni's consoling expressing.

"Get that film!" Spillway hollers. Cat-quick, the one bodyguard lunges at the photographer, but he evades and takes off running at top speed down the street.

Before the bodyguard can give chase, Gianni takes hold of his arm, saying, "It is fine. Let him go."

"It's not fine!" Spillway shouts. "And this car is not fine!" He hands his card to the cab driver. "You're responsible for this, cupcake! This may be a no-fault state but if he's hurt it'll blow the roof off your coverage and you're liable."

"My dispatcher is gonna kill me! It, it wasn't my fault!"

"Oh, it was your fault," Spillway insists, baring his teeth in true lawerly-shark fashion.

"It wasn't his fault," Tony interjects. "It was that asshole's fault!" He points in the direction of the now long-gone biker.

"It is not bad," Gianni says. "The car, it is fine. You think it is fine, Lisa?"

I look down at it. It's definitely not fine. I don't know how much the car costs or what repairs will run, but I do know that the cab driver definitely won't be fine if he has to pay for the damages. I just shrug and say, "It's...not bad. It's maybe a little...crunched."

"Crunched?" Gianni asks, and I just nod at him.

"Crunched!" Tony's nearly shouting. I can see he's distressed as he looks at it. "It's fucking smashed!"

"Oh my God," the cab driver says.

Inside, I'm dying for him.

The bodyguards move and lean in closer to inspect the damage. They don't speak, but they both shake their heads.

"I don't see that it's that bad," I say, trying to defuse the situation a bit. "It's a little crunched is all."

"You don't see it?" Tony nearly shouts. "Jesus, Lisa! Stevie Wonder could see it's smashed!"

"You can't drive that, Gianni," Spillway says, pulling him aside and talking in a hushed tone so the cab driver can't hear him. "The taillight is knocked out and you don't even have a license in this country! I'm trying to intimidate this guy so he won't report it. We're screwed if he does. It was completely your fault."

"It is fine," Gianni insists. "The car is fine."

"Oh, it's not fine," Tony says as he paces, inspecting the damage from multiple angles. "It's smashed alright."

"I have to go," Gianni says. "I must meet Angelina now. She is angry."

With that, Spillway rolls his eyes but stands firm and says, "You can't drive this. It needs to be fixed."

I may be the only one who notices the cab driver quietly slink back into his taxi.

Drive! Be free! I want to shout to him, but I think it's better if I don't call attention to him and allow him a quiet escape.

"I...I...I have no one to fix it," Gianni says.

"I have someone," Tony says. "If you want to leave it here, I'll get it fixed for you."

"Tony," Gianni says. "You can do this?"

"Sure. It'll take a week or so. Just leave it with us. We'll get this fixed up while we crunch some numbers for you. It'll be fine."

"Crunch the numbers? Like the car is crunched?" Gianni asks.

"No, not like the car," I laugh and explain. "It's just an expression accountants use when they're working."

"Oh," Gianni says. "No problem. Oh-kay. Is good. Michael, we take this car now," he says as he nods to the limo. "We'll stop together for necklace for Angelina." Pointing to the now damaged Ferrari, he says, "Tony, you take this car, and then for me, you fix this and smash the numbers!" His full attention falls on me again. Staring at me, he puts his hand over his heart and bows slightly. He says, "Lisa, I must tell you this. You are a pretty woman."

"Thank you," I blush, looking down, feeling as though his eyes are piercing through me.

He goes, "It is good you are smart and pretty, because you have a very bad singing voice."

I laugh.

"It is terrible!" he insists. "But still, I look forward to seeing you again."

As Gianni piles into the limo and speeds off, I can see the heavy rise and fall of Mancuso's chest as he slowly takes a 360 around the car. Traffic streaming around him and horns honking don't speed him up in the least. As he slides in behind the wheel to re-park the car, I think he might be hyperventilating. When his door eases down, the passenger one pops up and he shouts out to me, "Come on, Lees! Let's park this bitch!"

I know I shouldn't. After last night, I should try to emotionally distance myself again.

Still in park, Tony revs the engine.

Camus argued that Sisyphus wasn't so tragic. That in his consciousness, as he pondered his fate while getting that breathing room to go back down the mountain and chase the rock, that is where his victory was. Because it is his fate, it is also his purpose. So although he is condemned to travel back down and start pushing that boulder again, his awareness of the situation doesn't destroy him, because it's the struggle itself toward the heights that fills a person's heart.

I climb in the car.

CHAPTER NINE

As he weaves through the streets of Manhattan, I'm not surprised that Tony's handling the car with care. But I am curious as to where he's going. Before I can question him, he says, "I'm thinking, I don't know any good mechanics in the city."

"Oh Jesus." As he steers us toward the Holland Tunnel. I know where he's taking us, and I know why. Sure, sure, he can trust his pals at home to fix this up. But he also can't resist the urge to take it home and show it off to everyone. What does surprise me is how he keeps the stereo off and concentrates on the road, keeping the speed down even as we get on less congested streets that he knows better. "What are you doing?" I finally ask him.

"What?"

"You're driving like an old lady."

"I am not," he says, but I can see his knuckles clenching around the wheel.

"This car is meant to be raced, you know," I say.

"This car," he says and glances over at me, "isn't mine."

"Oh come on," I scoff. "This car is a dream come true for you."

"Not quite, Lisa," he says as he flips on his turn signal over fifty feet ahead of the next turn he wants. I laugh at him. I've never seen him like this before. I would've expected him to get behind the wheel and make for the nearest highway so he could start opening it up.

"This car is almost a dream come true of mine," he says. "Someday, maybe, I'll have something like this."

"Well. It'd be a waste if you'd just baby it like this."

"I wouldn't." He glances at me with a wide grin, saying, "I'd enjoy the hell out of it."

"Then what are you doing now?"

He half shrugs and looks straight out the windshield. "If something's not mine, I figure I should be careful with it." He glances at me again. "Especially something precious, Lisa."

"Oh. So a Ferrari is precious?"

"This isn't just a Ferrari," he corrects me. "It's an Enzo. The best of the best."

"Enzo," I repeat, liking the way it falls off my tongue. Now, confused again, I ask, "So where are you going?"

He smiles and says, "I said I'd be careful with it. I didn't say we shouldn't enjoy it at all." He waits a beat and then tries to be smooth about changing the subject. He goes, "So. You want to hear about the deal I worked out with Gianni?"

Looking out my window, smirking inwardly, I say to him, "I'm not giving you head while you drive this thing."

"What?" He sounds shocked, but it's feigned. "Why would you say that? I'm trying to talk business with you here, Ms. Russo."

"Oh come on, Mancuso," I laugh. "You're like Pavlov's dog with the dirty business talk. You're driving this hot car and you want to talk about how much money we're about to make."

"No," he says and leers over at me. "I want to talk about how much money we're going to make while we work at Shea Stadium for the next few weeks."

"While we smash the numbers for Gianni Loren," I say, making Tony laugh.

"He's a trip, isn't he?" He adjusts his hand on the wheel again, his other arm rested lazily next to my thigh. But it's the hand clenched around the steering wheel I get engrossed in. His shirt sleeve is rolled half-way up his forearm, and as he moves his hand, the tendons in his hand ripple and shift. One strong vein on the underside of his wrist meanders up through the meaty, muscled flank of his forearm.

"So," I say. "What are we billing for this job?"

He sighs, but it's not a harried sigh, it's one of contentment, I can tell by the placid look on his face. But then his brows furrow together for an instant, and still gazing out at the road he says, "You know what? I don't think I want to talk about it right now."

"Why?"

He glances over at me. "Because if we start with the dirty talk while I'm driving this car I might have an unassisted orgasm."

"I don't have a problem with that," I say. "Less work for me."

"Yeah, but this car's already been crashed once today. I'm not taking any chances on explaining that to Gianni Loren."

"Pfft," I say. "He'd just say, 'No problem, Tony.' It's Spillway you'd have to worry about."

He smiles. "You in a rush to get back to the city?"

"If you're going to keep driving at this breakneck speed, I certainly hope not."

Next thing I know he gets on the highway and starts moving back east. I'm surprised. I figured he'd be heading directly for his old neighborhood in Newark to show off his little prize for the day. He keeps the vehicle at a reasonable speed as he guides it steadily along the dark pavement, and I can't figure out where he's going.

"Where are you taking this to get fixed?" I ask him.

"Ahh, I'll take it to my friend Rob back home."

"Then how come we're going this way?"

"You'll see," is all he says.

"You know who could fix this up right for you, don't you?"

"Madone," he sighs. "I'm not taking this to your cousin."

"Eva and Vinny have the best exotic custom shop in the state and you know it."

"Yeah, well."

"Well, then?"

"Look," he says. "I don't want to owe a favor to Vincent Vendetti, ok?"

I don't think he'd owe Vinny a favor, but I also see his point about not wanting to get mixed up with them. I give him credit for it. Most people? They don't want to consort with Eva or Vinny either – until they need something from them. They have no trouble sneering at them behind their backs, but they also have no trouble when they could be useful to them. Tony's not like that.

Soon we're in Hoboken, and he makes his way along Hudson Street until he finds an area with a view alongside a quiet pier that he seems to like.

Slowly, he pulls in and puts the car in park with us facing the river, looking beyond to the skyline of New York. The doors flip up and he climbs out first, so I follow. The early evening sun glints off the river, leaving golden sparkles in the small waves. Beyond us, the sun plays the same tricks on the intimidating buildings, flashing off the unseen windows and making them sparkle with gilded promise.

Below us, at our feet is a healthy collection of cigarette butts and a few random soda cans along with some other unidentifiable litter. Tony kicks one of the cans aside as he makes his way to the front of the car. Joining him, I pat his back and ask, only half-joking, "Inspecting your empire, Caesar?"

He grins, but it fades quickly and he says, "Not quite."

"Not quite *yet*," I correct him.

With the sun already lowering at our backs, his face is in half-shadow, but his strong features look handsome as ever.

Crossing his arms, still looking out across the river, he says flatly, "Today, with Loren? I billed you, Mark, and Jill out at two thousand bucks an hour."

I suck in a breath, my knees actually going weak. I don't think it's the greed so much as that it's just a staggering amount.

"This is it, Lisa," he says, still looking at the city sprawling before him instead of me. "All my life, I wanted to do something big like this. I wanted to make my parents proud. It wasn't easy for them, they had to work really hard to put me in college. And now, it's like...it's like it's nearly here. This car I'm driving right now, this job for the Mets. It's like we've been working so hard and reaching so long and now it's finally right within our grasp."

I slide my hand down and place it around his waist, looking up at him instead of the city beckoning beyond. Asking, "Then what's wrong?"

"Because it's not ours yet," he says. "I'm close. I'm so close to the life I wanted. It's like I'm test driving it though, and I still can't afford to buy it."

"You will," I assure him. "Soon. Can't you feel it? You're living the life you wanted."

"I feel like I'm renting Gianni Loren's life, that's how I feel."

When we were just young kids back in college and we first hooked up, it was based more on attraction than an emotional connection at first. But we grew together, and I guess in a sense we grew up together, too. We just always clicked so easily. Over the summers, he'd have to go back home to Newark and take construction jobs to help make money for his tuition, and I'd have to go back downstate to my home in Atlantic City to work to save and make mine. But we'd find time to meet. If he'd have a couple days off he'd come down and visit me, or sometimes we'd meet in the middle at Point Pleasant or Asbury Park. I think it was around our third year in school that we were sitting on the hood of my car. It wasn't even my car, I shared it with my mom, and it was a beater; a nondescript twelve-year-old Skylark that we picked up used. I can't remember now where we were, but were gazing out at the ocean and he was talking about how we'd break out someday.

As we sat on the hood of that crappy car, he was promising me we wouldn't be forever trapped in a dingy little town on the Jersey shore, working like dogs just to survive, waiting for our lives to begin or get better as we just got older and time slipped away. Even though our parents drove us crazy, he promised me we'd never forget how hard they'd worked to give us a better life. He promised me we'd make them proud. He promised me that we'd actually do it. He promised me I wouldn't have a job for the rest of my life, that instead I'd have a career. He promised me we wouldn't have to deal with shitty, sour bosses taking their frustrations out on us. He promised me the city.

Tony Mancuso, he promised me that we'd do all this together.

And then, when he was done talking, as the sun set behind us, he promised me he'd love me forever as he kissed my mouth and sighed in my ear and made love to me as the sun set at our backs and the waves lapped at the shore in front of us.

Now, as I tighten my arm around his waist, he drapes his over my shoulder. I wonder if our synergy is still strong enough that he's thinking back on that, too.

He says, "He's interested in you, you know. Loren, I mean."

"Oh," I say and though I'm not chilled, I snuggle more closely against his side. "Don't be silly."

"Lisa. I've seen him look at you. He's interested."

"He's got a girlfriend, Tony."

"He's got a lot of girlfriends, Lisa. He's an unrepentant playboy."

"Mmm," I nod. "Googled him again this morning, huh?"

"I'm serious here."

I laugh. I look up at his face, but it's now fallen mostly into shadow and I can't tell if he's jealous or not. But from what I can see, he's placid. It disappoints me. But I say, "I'm just a guinea girl from Jersey. What the hell would he want with me?"

"You know Lisa, you always were a pretty girl." As he says that, I self-consciously reach up with my free hand and touch the hair gathered at the crown of my head where I'd arranged it to conceal the escalating grey. But I'm also reminded of Gianni's deep stare when he called me pretty earlier. "But now," Tony says, "you're more than that. You're a sexy, whip-smart New York accountant."

"Excuse me," I say. "But I'm a partner at a hot-shot New York accounting firm."

That does it, he cracks a grin with that remark and looks down at my face. It quickly fades. "Remember how we used to talk about how we'd do this someday, Lisa? Are you living the life you wanted?"

This is it. With his reticent tone and the way he just mentioned the past, I know those old memories are close at hand. And he's asking me if I'm happy. I could take the leap right now and tell him that he's lived up to nearly all his promises. But I could tell him it's the one promise that doesn't seem to have stuck that means the most to me – that he'd love me forever. I made the same promises to him back then, and I don't know if he realizes that I've kept my word. All the other dates and even Day-Trader Dave weren't anything. I was just drifting and experimenting, because he was doing the same.

Right now, I could tell him that I love him. I could tell him that's the life I want.

This amazing deal with Gianni, it's called due diligence. It's what one company does when they're interested in another one. They fact-find and investigate to determine the risk level, often involving a takeover or merger.

Me, I've been doing due diligence on Tony for over 12 years now. I know he's completely solid. But the risk lies in me telling him that I'm still in love with him, and him not being able to reciprocate. Where would that leave me? It wouldn't be an amicable merger.

I'd then have to decide if I really could endure the punishment of Sisyphus

– knowing for certain that there's no hope of ever keeping the rock at the top of the mountain. What if Camus was wrong and the purpose and sheer will of trying isn't enough and it truly is torture?

Sometimes, at important moments, it's just not smart to take the leap. It's better to keep your head down and just keep pushing up the hill.

He's waiting for an answer, so I say, "Billing at two thousand dollars an hour? That's quite a good life."

It takes a moment, and in that second I wonder if I've miscalculated. But then Tony breaks into a wide smile. Even in the rapidly deepening shadows, as he looks up and back out across the river, I can see the telltale lines at the corner of his eyes form as he laughs lightly and shakes my shoulders. He says, "It's a good number, isn't it?"

"Mmm," I sigh. "You know, even with three of us working on it, it'll probably take three weeks, at least. That's...oh shit, Tony, it's gonna be around a quarter million dollars. At least."

"Took you a while to figure that out, didn't it?" He tightens his arm around my shoulders.

"A quarter million dollars."

He groans at that. Sometimes, like right now, he's just so easy. He's also so bold, so shameless that even out here in the open he doesn't even look around. He just reaches down with his free hand and rubs roughly at the fly of his pants.

It turns me on. "Want to get back in the car?"

"No," he says. "Too small in there. C'mere." He maneuvers me so I'm directly in front of him, my back to his chest. He goes, "Say it again."

So I say, "A quarter of a million dollars."

With one efficient swipe, he brushes the hair off my neck and leans down and half-sucks, half-bites on me. His arms clamp around my waist, pulling me back against him, letting me feel the rigid length of his hard-on pressed against the soft flesh of my ass through our clothes.

It feels great, and I sigh with it. But my eyes dart around, checking for interlopers. The sun is low at our backs now and the light is getting soft and dusky. As I look across the river at the tops of the tallest buildings falling into shadow, I can't help but wonder if there's anyone over there who can see us. It's far to the naked eye, but in a city like New York, there are thousands of binoculars and telescopes put to illicit use every minute of the day.

It's like Tony reads my thoughts, because he comes up for air, licking at my earlobe, sending shivery spikes of pleasure through me as he whispers with sultry breath right in my ear, saying, "Look over there, look at your city. Let them see you."

It's mid-April, but the day was unseasonably warm and dry. With the sun rapidly sinking, the air is taking on a spring crispness, but the chill of winter has been burned off.

Tony snakes a hand up around my throat, holding and caressing, then moving lower as his fingers fumble with a button on my blouse. When he gets it released, he dips lower and nimbly undoes another, and then a third. A breeze licks through the wide opening, wafting against my breasts, hardening my nipples. Tony undoes another button.

I scan the area again as he pulls the hem of my shirt out of my skirt and it falls open, completely exposing my stomach, leaving my breasts only covered by the thin, silky fabric of my bra. Self-conscious, I check for interlopers but don't find any. With a libidinous growl, he lowers his lips to my neck again, sucking as one of his strong, big hands cups my breast. My knees going weak, I look up to the sky to center myself, but it doesn't help, it only dizzies me more. Directly above, the sky is already the softest shade of diffuse blue, with a couple of early stars already competing for attention, nestled above pink-streaked clouds fanning out above the city skyline.

Abruptly, giving me no time to protest, Tony uses both his hands, rapidly pulling the straps of my bra down across my shoulders and then plunging lower, pulling the fabric of the cups aside and down, exposing my tits for the entire city to see. The wind surges with a shock of cool air bristling against my naked skin. He hands go to them again, but not to cover me. Instead he cups them underneath, avoiding the nipples entirely, just massaging the weight of them.

He stops sucking at my neck and rises just slightly, his chin over my shoulder, and I know he's looking down at me, inspecting my flushed, protruding nipples. The warmth of his hands work in contrast with the cool wind and it's sheer exhilaration. I want him to cover me, I wish he'd move and give some attention to the rest of my breasts, massage my nipples the way they crave. But he doesn't. He dips lower, releases one of my tits and slides that hand down to my knee, then back up again, under my skirt and across my thigh. Reaching between my legs, holding me there. I can't help it, I squirm with it the pressure and warmth.

It's so risky out here like this I almost can't stand it. Longing for him, longing to face him, I try to slither around in his arms, but he's got me tight. Him sighing,"I'm so hot for you, baby."

"Get in the car," I tell him. "I'll go down on you there."

"Huh uh," he answers, squeezing between my legs, intensifying the pressure as he cups and rubs the underside of my breast, pointing my distended nipple to the beckoning city. "I have to fuck you, Lisa," he breathes. "Right now."

I nod in acquiescence.

"On the car," he growls. "I have to fuck you on this Ferrari."

I nod again, breathing hard, thrills coursing through my veins, teetering between being scared of being caught and being completely turned on at the danger of it.

Next thing I know, he releases me and I want to moan because I miss his touch already, the cool air hitting my skin where he'd warmed it, seemingly rushing up my skirt and leaving a draft where he was. But he's moving fast and rough, hiking my skirt up for me, pushing it roughly over my hips, above my ass as he turns around to face the car.

I pull away from him to turn around, efficiently pulling down my panties as he helps me step out of them. One arm around my back, he tries easing me back against the hood of the car, draping me across it, but it's way too streamlined. The curve dips down quickly and too low and he's too tall to be able to get any leverage that way.

"Turn around," he commands as he rises and guides me at the hips. I lean forward, bracing my hands on the hood and offering my ass before him. Rushing, hungry for him, my eye catches a last glinting reflection from the now sinking sun as it shines off the face of my watch.

"Wait," I say to him, and behind me I hear him groan. Over my shoulder, I ask, "Mancuso. How much is this car worth?"

"Oh fuck," he says, fumbling with his belt buckle. "Nearly seven hundred thousand dollars."

Rising, I unclasp my watch and try handing it to him.

"The fuck?" he asks.

"We can't scratch it," I say. "Put this in your pocket."

His face is flushed and I know he's dying for it, but he smiles and takes it from me, shoves it in his pants as he smirks and starts unhooking his. "I thought you were just trying to get me hot with that."

"Did it work?"

"Oh yeah," he nods, shoving his watch in the same pocket as mine.

I turn around and lean down again. I brace my hands, waiting for him. Behind me, I can feel him close and I hear the zipper on his fly going down. "Watch the buckle, too," I warn him. With one fluid motion he takes hold of the buckle and yanks, whipping the belt off and tossing it carelessly on the ground.

As he lines himself up, I turn around and face the setting sun, only the top quarter of it now visible on the horizon. The head of his cock is pressed between my lips already, his one hand on my hips. I know he's about to enter, and I'm fully wet and ready so I close my eyes and say, "Show me, Tony. Show me how you drive a hard bargain. Just like with Gianni."

He enters with a hard shove, rocking me forward on my hands, filling me to the hilt, forcing my breath out of me. He doesn't answer me, he just grunts. Immediately, he drives into me. Deep, hard strokes, holding my hips but thrusting so hard I'm having a hard time keeping steady, my hands sliding against the polished, smooth veneer of the lacquer.

Letting go of me with one hand, he reaches around in front of me, searching out that hard, pulsing nub and going to work on it. It weakens me too much. I lock my knees to stay raised up for him but with another demanding thrust he forces me off my hands. My arms buckle and I sink down, supporting myself on my forearms, arching my back. My tits graze the slippery finish of the exotically expensive red paint, finally some longed for contact against my nipples.

I love this angle, the head of his cock grazing my cushy G-spot when he jacks into me while directly outside he fingers the same hot area. Edgy already, I rock back against him and clench around him.

Tension building, panting, I'm on the cusp when he takes his hand away. I muffle a scream of frustration.

Wanton and desperate, I'm still aware someone could be watching but I don't care. Instead of just being complicit I shift my weight to one arm and thrust the other between my legs to finish myself off. Just as I touch myself, my blood singing, he takes hold of my wrist and pulls my hand away.

"Not yet," he growls. Leaning over me, pressing me down and flattening my chest against the hood, he grips my wrist near my face as he supports himself on his forearms. I'm staring at his hand and arm, the same coiled strength

I was watching as he was steering the car along the road, the vein now throbbing and pulsing with life.

His mouth near mine, breathy, demanding, he's panting but he says, "I'm gonna fuck you on his car."

"Uh-huh," is all I can say.

"I'm fucking you on his Ferrari. On *his* Ferrari," he says, almost angrily. But I still can't tell if he's jealous because of the car, of if he's jealous because of me. Either way, I don't care. "I'm gonna make you come," he promises, and by the way he keeps driving in, I know he can do it even without the still-longed-for stimulation on my clit.

"Oooh, do it," I moan to him. "Please, do it. Let me come, Tony. Now."

"I'm gonna *make* you come, Lisa," he says again and thrusts hard. "I'm gonna make you come on his car. All over his Ferrari."

"Oh, oh God," I plead, dying for it. Egging him on, saying, "Seven hundred thousand dollars, Tony. It's an Enzo."

"You're gonna come on his Ferrari, but you're gonna come for me. Around me."

"With you inside me," I say as he thrusts deep.

"We're gonna come together, baby. Same time, okay?"

"Uh huh," I agree. "On the Enzo."

"With me," he grunts. "You'll come with me," he's panting, hard. He's pounding into me, hard. "You'll come for me. I'll make you."

"Make me," I tempt him.

"Make me," I dare him.

"Make me come, Tony," I beg him.

"Soon, baby," he promises.

Open mouthed, I just pant. Wishing, longing for one thing to make it complete. His mouth right near mine, if he'd kiss me, if he'd thrust his tongue inside, I'd probably come from that. But he doesn't. I'm dying for it, so I do the only thing I can. I raise up slightly, the most I can with him covering and smothering on top of me, still pounding into me. As the last sliver of sun slips below the tree-line in front of us, I do it. Hungrily, greedy, open mouthed, I clamp my lips along his wrist and suck.

The taste rushes across my tongue, filling my mouth with his salt and sweat, lapping and licking along that protruding vein, feeding my desire with the feel of his flesh. His fist was clenched and he opens it for me, thrusting his thumb inside my mouth. I suck on it. Lord help me, do I suck on it as he fills me and thrills me deep inside with every shocking thrust. Sloppy wet kisses, soaking his hand nearly as wet as I am inside, around him.

"Sweet Jesus, Lisa," he groans as I clench around him, rock back against him and press a kiss into the middle of his palm, inhaling the tang of his musk. "We're gonna come," he says. "We're gonna come. Now!"

And then, good on his promise, he reaches down with his free hand and all he has to do is press his index finger directly on my clit, and I explode.

I cry out with it, and he was clearly ready too, because he buries deep. He shouts, and I swear, it's stuttered but loud. "Fah, feh...Ferrariii!" he says as he comes.

"Enzo," I sigh.

Laying there, he relaxes on top of me and I can feel the exaggerated thrum of his heart beating wildly with his chest pressed against my back. He leans his head on his hand, and face to face, looking me in the eye, he's so close he could easily kiss me. As badly as I needed to have that orgasm when I did, it's even more than that that I wish he'd kiss me. If I could wind the clock back and choose one or the other, I'd spend eternity in that restless, high-strung, pleadingly frustrated state if I could just have the pleasure and relief of a kiss from him right now.

But I don't have that. He doesn't do it. For a moment, I swear he's thinking about it. But then he blinks and peels himself up and off of me. Away from me.

It's not inky dark yet, but the soft, diffused light is rapidly fading as darkness encroaches. Sexually satisfied and emotionally unfulfilled, I pick myself up on shaky arms and carefully flip around and raise myself up, quickly pulling my skirt back down. After he zips his pants, he bends over, resting his hands on his knees and taking a deep breath. He watches as I arrange my bra straps and tuck my tits back inside. I'm glad for the dimness as I button my shirt because I know my face isn't just flushed, it's flaming.

"Holy hell," he says as he picks up his belt. He loops it around, but before he bothers to clasp it, he reaches in his pocket and pulls out my panties. "Here," he says as he offers them to me. "Thought I'd keep them from getting dirty."

"Thanks," I say and begin the ungraceful process of stepping into them. I have to hope they're substantial enough to sop up the wetness from both his ejaculation and my juices combined as it leaks out of me. When I'm done, he hands me my watch, and it's in those moments that I remind myself not to get pissed at him. He gave me what I said I wanted, he gave me what the deal was. We have an agreement, and I got pissed last night when he stepped over the line and broke the rules by kissing me, and now I'm rapidly unraveling because he's backed off and didn't step over the line and break the rules.

I've given him no clue, no indication of my feelings either way. So I have to suck this up and deal.

He makes it more difficult for me. Watching me, quietly asking, "You okay?"

I just nod.

"That was a little...rough, I guess. Did, did I hurt you?"

I'm thinking, *No, you don't hurt me, Mancuso. You fucking destroy me.* But I'm saying, "It was great. I'm just spent, that's all."

Outside, the temperature is falling and I use that as an excuse when I shiver.

Back in the cockpit of the car, he starts it and revs the engine, contentedly sighing, "Ferrari," and then looking over at me.

I can't help it. It breaks my ugly disappointment as he has that expectant look on his face. So I answer him, sighing it, "Enzo."

It brings me up even higher as he struggles to figure out how to turn on the headlights. I mean, it takes him nearly three minutes, and by the time he's got them on, I have the giggles.

On the road, ever the tactless, he asks, "You leaking all over that seat over there?"

"Jesus," I snipe, but press my thighs together and shift my weight. "I hope not."

"I hope you are," he says.

I just stare out the window, still unable to determine what he's getting at with those comments. Still too gunshy to ask.

I was right though. Instead of going directly to a garage, he first takes us to his parents' house where he honks the horn outside in the driveway. After a couple minutes, the porch light comes on and his father tosses open the front door. I can tell he's pissed. But his anger disappears immediately. His jaw drops before he's even got the screen door opened and he sees his son leaning casually against the exotic race car.

"Huh?" Tony prods him. "Huh? Dad, whaddaya think, huh?" Tony's voice instantly falling back into that natural Jersey twang at the sight of his father.

While they coo over the car, his mom comes out and gives me a warm hug. Interrupting the festivities of the men by asking her son, "Anthony? Anthony! When you gonna marry Lisa, huh?"

She always asks. But I wonder if she can smell the sex-scent clinging to me as she asks tonight, putting an extra edge on her voice this time.

They try to push us inside to get something to eat, and I am starving. I know Tony must be ravenous too. But he brushes them off, saying he's got to get hold of the guys at the shop to see if they can help him as he points out the damage to his parents. His mom says, "Oh, it's not too bad."

His dad shakes his dead and yells, "Not too bad! It's smashed!"

"It's not perfect," she says. "But I don't see that it's smashed."

"Chrissakes woman! Ray Charles could see that it's fucking smashed to shit!"

"Daniel!" she cries. "The neighbors. Watch your mouth."

"Fuck the neighbors," he says, making her shriek again.

"Shhh!" she warns him.

"I have to listen to that goddamn mutt of theirs at two in the morning every night!"

"But that's not obscene!" she yells at him, holding out her hands, pleading.

"What?" he asks. "I'm not saying anything here. I'm just saying, this damage isn't what I'd call 'not so bad'. It's fucking smashed up!"

"I don't think it's that bad," I say. "The damage, I mean."

Tony stares at me but says quietly, "It's smashed."

"Fucking right it's smashed!" his father shouts.

"Lisa, Lisa honey," his mom says to me. "Does my boy speak to you like that? Saying the f-word like that?"

"No," I shake my head and lie. "He's a gentleman, Mrs. M. You raised him right."

"I'm a gentleman," his father insists. "What'd I say? It's a car, not a person. And it's a car that's fucking smashed."

A half-hour later, after we've eaten a couple sandwiches and Tony's gotten hold of his old friend Rob, the mechanic, we're at Rob's shop as he looks over the car with an appreciative whistle. "It's gorgeous, T."

"It's not mine," Tony tells him.

"Yeah, yeah." Rob nods. "Shame it's all fucking smashed up back there."

I sigh.

Tony asks, "So can you fix it?"

"Yeah, oh yeah," Rob nods. "I can do it. Take me a while though."

"How long?"

He shrugs. "Week. At least. Maybe two."

"Listen Rob," Tony says. "I'll pay top dollar for this, but I want it done right, so if you can't handle it, just tell me."

"I can handle it, T. No problem."

"Yeah. Well. One other thing. This isn't mine," Tony says. "That week or two that you've got it? You can't be taking it around for joyrides all up and down the Jersey shore."

"Tony," Rob says. "Seriously. I'm offended here."

"I fucking mean it!" Tony shouts. "You can't drive it around. And don't go driving it and then trying to fuck with the odometer to cover it up, dude."

"I am a fucking professional," Rob says, indignant. "I wouldn't do that."

"It's my ass if you fuck this up," Tony warns him. "And if it's my ass, I'm taking it out on you. Understood? Do not drive this car, Rob."

"Tony. Trust me. I won't."

"Promise me," Tony insists.

"Tony."

"Promise me, Rob."

He sighs. "I promise."

"Promise me what?"

"I promise I won't drive the car unnecessarily."

"Alright."

Outside, Rob loans us another car to drive back to the city. As we climb in, after Tony's behind the wheel, I say to him, "You know he's going to drive that car all over, right?"

"We'll be lucky if he doesn't drive to Mexico and back for Chrissakes."

CHAPTER TEN

In the middle of the first day of working at Shea stadium and poring over the books with Jill and Mark, I realized that this was the biggest, and coolest, job I'd ever had. I couldn't believe I was getting paid to do this. The swag was unbelievable. Just walking around the place there were hats and pens and mugs and anything you could imagine adorned with the Mets logo. I snagged some decent booty and packed it up and shipped it to my cousin Marina in Las Vegas. She's not a Mets fan, but her boyfriend is and I knew they'd get a kick out of the stuff.

The second week, when the Mets returned from a road trip and the players started filtering onto the field as Jill and Mark and I, and even Tony, sat tucked in an office in the upper tier with our elbows deep in papers and our laptop files bulging, it seemed like a dream. Mark was inspecting payroll, and Tony was looking over his shoulder with nebbish glee. Jill was checking merchandising figures and I was accumulating all the different contracts and lease data. I looked out onto the dazzlingly perfect bluegrass and saw the crew painting fresh foul lines. Then, my eyes fell to the golden dirt on the infield. Mike Piazza stepped into the cage and started taking batting practice. I looked up at Tony with his arms crossed, his eyes focused on Piazza as he took a long, strong swing and launched the ball over the outfield fence. Tony's mouth fell open in amazement, watching the trajectory of the ball as it glided away. That's when I knew this wasn't the coolest job yet, but I also realized that we'd probably never have anything better.

I can't help it. I know Mancuso will disapprove, but this is a once in a lifetime shot. So the next day, I call up my cousin Eva and invite her to meet me at work to watch the batting practice show.

I meet her outside a special entrance and lead her up through the catacomb-like hallways. I thought I was safe because Mark and Tony left about an hour ago to take care of a couple of things at the office, and I know Tony's going to pick up the car tonight. So I only expected Jill to be in the office. But Tony's standing at the window, watching as they set up for batting practice. He turns as we enter, but he only glances at her and then fixes his stare on me. He's not glaring, but I know he's not happy.

Things cooled between Tony and me right after that trip back home. He dropped me off at my place in the city, and we started work the next day at the stadium. That was a Friday, and we never got together over the weekend or so far this week. He's been occupied with keeping an eye at the main office while it's at half-mast while still squeezing in a couple hours out here in Queens. Me, I've just been busy here. I'm pretty sure that bringing Eva here will turn the cool to a definite chill.

Even though Tony grew up at the other end of the state from my family, he's all too aware of who Eva's family is, and who her "family" is. I don't think Tony blames her for being the daughter of one of the most feared mob bosses in the tri-state area. But after her father's murder it was apparent to everyone, not just family and "family" members, that she was a little more than just a daughter when she got engaged to his second-in-command, Vincent Vendetti.

I can't say I approve of all of Eva's decisions and actions, though most of what I think I know is sheer speculation. She's very careful to not even acknowledge the shady aspects of her business and life, let alone speak openly about it. And I do know that Vincent isn't just a strategy on her part. She's known him and circled in his orbit longer than I've known Tony. Or, maybe, it's better to say that Vincent circles her orbit. He's always worshipped her, and I know she loves him deeply. People talk about a love they'd die for. I think Vincent would do that for her. But I also know that after her father's murder, bodies turned up all over Manhattan, Brooklyn, and up and down the Jersey shore, proving that he had zero problem killing for her.

Tony finds the whole thing stereotypical and sickening. But to me, she's just my cousin. I grew up with Eva, and she was always good to me.

Eva knows Tony dislikes her, but I guess that's something she's used to from most people. Most people, in this city, they'll go out of their way to make a good impression on a wiseguy. There's the obligatory disgust, but usually also a twinge of admiration or mystery that these guys inspire. But with Eva? She doesn't get that same leeway. Something about her being a female somehow makes it more grotesque, or unforgivable. When she sees Tony, she squints her deep blue, kohl-rimmed eyes and simply says, "Mancuso."

"Vendetti," he calls her and nods.

"Not yet," she says. Holding up her left hand, she wags her finger quickly, the obscenely large diamond glinting so brightly it nearly obscures the fact that there's no wedding ring, as she says, "I'm still a Russo for now."

He may not like her very much, but Tony's not a prick, and he extends his hand and gives her a quick but firm shake. Playfully, he digs her, asking, "How long you gonna string Vincent along?"

But Eva doesn't miss a beat. "How long you gonna string my cousin along without even giving her a ring?"

"Uh," he says. "I don't think your cousin is waiting."

"Well, neither is Vincent."

"Yeah right," Tony scoffs. "He was born waiting for you."

She smirks. "It won't kill him to wait."

"Oh really?" Tony asks. He stares her in the eyes as he boldly says, "I thought death was a very real and very common occupational hazard for you two."

I can tell it truly zings Eva, because her nostrils flare. Just as I'm ready to tell Mancuso to back off, her voice drops an octave and is quieter as she says, "Perhaps. But at least Vin and I acknowledge that we don't just simply work together."

Now it's Tony's turn to bristle.

I have to admit, I'd like to see him squirm a little bit, because maybe it'd give me some clue about his true feelings. But more than that, I don't want the discomfort between these two to rise to acrimonious levels, because I do love them both. Also, though it's just Eva's nature to be aggressively protective of me, I can speak up for myself, and just because I haven't lately doesn't mean she should have to.

So I break their barbs by saying, "Tony and I do work together, Eva. But I'm not wilting like a hothouse flower waiting for more."

"Well," she says, "you deserve more."

"If I deserve more of anything, it's money," I say with a wink at Tony. "After this gig, I'm thinking my salary is going to take a nice hike."

"Watch it with that filthy language in front of your cousin," Tony warns me. "She may be tough, but she's still a lady."

"Hey, I don't fucking mind," Eva says. "You're accountants. I figure you talk cash all day long. Her love life, I'll stick my nose into that. But her paycheck, that's on her."

"Thank you," Tony says. "Now, if you'll excuse me, I have to get going. I have to see a guy about a car."

"Oh yeah," Eva says and reaches inside her purse. Pulling out a set of keys, she hands them to Tony. "That Enzo, right? Here you go."

"What, what is this?" he asks, looking down at the keys.

"Figured I'd save you a trip across the river," Eva says coolly, but the spark in her eye is evident. "So I brought it to you. It's right outside."

"You, you drove it here?"

"Sure," she drawls as she drops herself into a chair. Kicking up her feet on a desk, she goes, "Who do you think your pal Rob had to get the parts from?" She's enjoying this now, I can tell. Putting her hands behind her head, leaning back, she goes, "Wasn't easy, either. Those are rare, let me tell you. But it's worth it, she looks gorgeous again, came really nice. Vin says it's one of the finest machines he's ever driven."

Tony holds up the keys. Blushing, asking, "Vincent drove this car?"

She nods. "Sure. How could he resist? Come on, don't worry, we didn't abuse it, Mancuso. I mean, I opened her up a little bit on the highway a few times. So did he. But that's what it's made for, right?"

"It's, it's all fixed?" is all Tony can ask.

"It's perfect," Eva says.

I can see how badly Tony's struggling here, so I jump in again. "Eva, thank you," I tell her. "Tell Vincent thanks, too."

"My pleasure sweetie. I was shocked you didn't come to me in the first place. Could've at least saved you Rob's fee." Looking directly at Tony, she goes, "But I guess maybe you didn't want to drive it that far."

"Yeah," is all he says. Then, collecting himself, finally, he says, "Thank you. This was important."

Eva dips her head slightly, lowering her eyes.

"I'm uh, I'm gonna go check it out," Tony says. "I mean, I'm sure you did a great job, and all, I just..."

"Go to it," Eva says, but she eyeballs him the entire time as he gathers his things and leaves the room.

"You are so bad," I scold her once he's gone.

Like a lazy cat, she stretches in the chair and says, "I know. But I'm so fucking good at being bad." Straightening, glancing out the window, she asks me, "So what's up with you two these days?"

I take a deep breath. "Same old thing. We work together. Sometimes we play together."

"Lisa, honey," she says, "you're still in love with him, aren't you?"

"Yes," I admit.

"Does he know it?"

"I don't know. I don't think so."

"What the fuck are you waiting for?" she asks me.

"Eva, you don't understand. If I push him, I could lose him."

"If you don't push him, you'll never get anywhere."

"I don't know what I'd do without him in my life," I admit. "Besides, look at you, still trailing Vincent along."

"Yeah, well, I only trail him along because I don't know what I'd do without him in my life."

"That's ridiculous," I say. "He loves you. You should know that."

"I do," she says and she looks at me and smiles.

It's because of my cousins that I've never been insecure about my looks. I'm not vain, but I see how beautiful they all are, and I know my looks are similar. Eva is the most striking of all of us though. Her features are similar to mine, but instead of having deep reddish brown hair and dark eyes like I do, she's got nearly black hair and inordinately deep blue eyes. I also know she's got more money than me, Tony, and probably our whole office combined. That wasn't always the case, though. When we were young, none of our families were blessed with much extra income, and Eva's father struggled to make ends meet before he rose the ranks. But even now that she's flush, she refuses to move away from her childhood home in Atlantic City, and her stylistic choices reflect her lifestyle. Thick black eyeliner that nearly eclipses her naturally lush lashes. Tight jeans and a low-cut shirt with a black leather jacket. Though it's soft and tailored, it still gets the point across. She looks as tough as she is. But still, when she smiles, she can't conceal her graceful beauty.

"I know he loves me," she says. "And I love him. It's just that, believe it or not, I don't love his lifestyle." Her smile fades and she gazes out the window.

"You're right," I say and suck in a breath, knowing I'm walking on dangerous ground. "I don't believe you. You love that life."

"Yeah, well," she tilts her head and briefly licks her lips. "It's a love-hate thing, you know? Like...like smoking. People who smoke love it, because it feels good. And even though they know it's bad for them, they figure it's worth it. But once someone they love gets lung cancer, then the danger of it really sinks in. The trouble is, it's already got its teeth in you by then. So even though it's hurting you, you don't want to stop because it's so pleasurable. So you start to resent it even while you still love it. I love my life...for me. And I hate my life...for him." Coldly, she says, "That life has taken enough from me already."

I know she's talking about her father. And I know she's scared senseless of the same thing happening to Vincent. Much as I'd like to, there's nothing I can do to help her. So I nudge her shoulder with mine and try to lighten the mood. I go, "But from what I hear, you're so damn good at that life."

She smiles again. "I am. I am so fucking good at being bad, Lisa. I was born for this life." Abruptly, she points out the window and says, "Look! Piazza's gonna be taking some swings!"

"Isn't this cool?" I ask her.

"Know what would be cooler? If you'd just straighten things up with Mancuso and really enjoyed all you've got."

"I just don't think it'd be smart to rock the boat right now."

She cocks a brow and says, "I don't see what you're worried about. You need to pull the trigger here and either suck it up or move on."

"Nice choice of words, Eva."

"Oh, fuck you, you bitch," she laughs. "Pardon the pun, again, but you need to take your shot, Lisa. You know he has to love you."

"How do you know that?"

She looks at me like I'm stupid. "Because I know you. How could he not love you? You know, for being so book smart, sometimes you're really stupid."

"That's mean," I say, genuinely hurt.

"Oh, c'mon, Lees. If you seriously believe it's not the right thing to do to tell him that you love him, then you're being dumb."

"It's not dumb," I say. "It's calculated. You know, we've worked really hard to build what we've got, and we're finally getting somewhere. I'd be jeopardizing that, too, you know."

"No you wouldn't," she says. "He needs you for this business."

"Mm, not really," I say. "I just do bookwork. He does all the handling of the clients and handling of the staff. I couldn't do any of that."

"Yes, you could," she says.

I refrain from telling her how just how little the staff likes me.

Eva says, "I know why you think that. It's kind of like how I need Vincent for my...job. No matter what, in this life, with my gender, I can't ever be protected or in charge, in name."

I swallow thickly, because I know she's right. Those rules are so old and so solid that it's impenetrable, even for her. It scares me for her.

But she just shrugs and says, "Of course, that's not why I love Vin. It's just a happy coincidence. But you, Lisa? It's not the same. You can do all those things without Tony. And I think deep down you know you can. You just don't want to. But you shouldn't have to suppress your love either. We may be smart, modern, metropolitan women, but deep down we're also old fashioned, passionate, Italian-Jersey girls, too. I think Tony can handle that from you."

I just shake my head. Finally asking, "What is it with you anyhow? Why are you pushing me to him? You don't even like him."

"That's not true," she says. "He doesn't like me very much."

"I wouldn't say that."

"Oh come on," she scoffs. "He can't stand me. I actually respect him for not faking it and kissing my ass. He's got balls. Besides," she says. "It's okay. I'm used to it. Not many people do like me."

"Plenty of people like you, Eva," I lie.

"No they don't. Plenty of people are afraid of me so they act like they respect me. There's a big difference. Anyhow, it doesn't matter what Mancuso thinks of me. You love me. And if he loves you, that's more than enough to satisfy me."

"He doesn't dislike you," I say. "He's just...I think he's afraid of you the way you're afraid of Vincent, that's all."

"If he's afraid of you getting hurt, that's a pretty good indication he loves you, Lisa."

"No," I say. "There's a big difference between not wanting to see someone caught in the crossfire and wanting to spend the rest of your life with them."

"Is there?" she asks. "I'm not so sure about that."

I've never felt sorry for Eva before. I know she's had it rough at times, but she always seemed to hold her own. Now I realize that she's not joking when she makes that statement, and I realize just how few people she trusts and loves in this world.

She may be a killer, or something close. But she's my family. And despite anything - just like my father loved his brother, Eva's father, no matter what he did - I love her. I put my arms around her neck and give her a hug. I say, "I'm really happy you came down here. I've missed you."

She hugs me back tightly. Then she goes, "You know what we need to do? We need to get those two hookers Lucy and Marina back in town for a couple drinks sometime."

I laugh and let go of her and tell her about Lucy's brownies. Then I nudge, saying, "I'm sure they'd be glad to be bridesmaids in your wedding. That's one way to get them back on this coast."

She nods, just says, "Soon." And then she points out the window, her jaw dropping. "You see that! Holy crap did Piazza tag that one!"

"Eva. You um, you and Vincent. Did you really drive that car all around?"

"Pfft. You kidding me? We drove it to Graceland and back in one day! That sucker can FLY!"

CHAPTER ELEVEN

During the third week of us working on the Mets acquisition research, Loren comes back to town and requests a dinner meeting with Tony and me. He went out of town after that first day, and Tony's only had a couple of brief phone conversations with him since then.

Luckily, things have been so busy with this project that my dealings with Tony haven't been the least bit strained. I put on that business-as-usual face the first day after the Ferrari fuck-fest and we've continued it since then. And since then, he's been friendly with me but hasn't made any advances. I've since resigned myself to the fact that on tax day he was just exceptionally horny, and I was available. Maybe he remembers the kiss, maybe he doesn't. And the Ferrari? How could anyone resist something like that? I thought maybe he was getting possessive of me when he thought Loren was interested. But now I realize that he wasn't jealous for me; he was simply jealous because of the car.

But it doesn't really matter anyhow. For all the detail work we accountants do to verify and fact-check, the bottom line is still the most important aspect of anything. And the bottom line between us is the same as ever: He's not in love with me. So I bury myself in work and try to forget my feelings, or at least sublimate them, until I can move on or actually change them. Or change his.

The evening Gianni returns, Tony and I meet him at Ono for dinner. I've been living in Manhattan for over five years, and been making respectable money with Tony for the past couple, but this is still the kind of swank place that I've never been to. It's nestled inside the Hotel Gansevoort in the heart of the meatpacking district, and I know it's been getting great reviews for the "cui-zen". Outside, with its cool blue-green and purple lighting, the hotel looks more likely to be in Miami than in New York, and it's just as stunning inside the lobby with its bold reds. At Ono, the O-bar splits down to the main dining room, with the ultra-hip Garden of Ono bar on the outside.

Now early May, the days have lost their bitter edge and already the sun has been warming the city by day. But it's evening now, and I don't relish the thought of freezing outside if we go to the Garden. Tony and I arrive first, and standing there waiting, he looks over at me and says, "You look...nice."

"Yeah? Thanks. You look good, too."

"That's not a suit," he says with a nod, meaning my dress.

It's new. I splurged on it when I heard about the dinner. It's not racy, it's just a simple, knee-length black dress with a cut that I thought flattered my figure. "It's not appropriate?" I ask. I won't lie, I had occurred to me that maybe I shouldn't deviate from a suit. But this seemed nicer, yet still professional looking. I wanted to look more worldly for Gianni. I wanted to look stylish at Ono. Maybe I wanted to impress Tony.

"No," he says. "It's fine. I've just never seen you wear something other than a suit before."

"You've never seen me have dinner at Ono before," I say.

"Sure," he says but looks away.

But now I'm twice as concerned about being cold if we go out to the garden. The dress is conservative, but sleeveless, and I'm accustomed to the warmth of a jacket around my shoulders.

Luckily, once Gianni arrives, we go to the main dining room that's dominated by a long sushi bar and we get seated under the Japanese clip-art chandeliers. I'm now used to Gianni's entourage, and Michael and the bodyguards look as they usually do when they enter. But Gianni is dressed for evening in a luxurious black suit with a gold tie. He looks a bit more tanned, but the most striking thing about him is his voice as he speaks. He greets Tony warmly first.

Gianni asking, "Are you fixing my Enzo?"

Tony laughs. "I have it here tonight. She's all fixed up and ready to go."

I can see the wistful look on Tony's face as he hands over the keys. He can't help himself from saying, "Take care of her."

Gianni nods once, but then he turns to me. "Lisa, it's great to see you. Have you been enjoying your time in Queens?"

It's only been three weeks, but already the cadence of his speech is more rapid, and he's not over-enunciating as much. His accent is still there, but now it's more lilting instead of stilted.

"Yes," I nod. "*Grazie*."

"Excellent," he says, pulling out my chair. "You look lovely."

"Thank you," I say, and I am a bit flattered. I've been busy with the Mets research job, but not strung out like during tax time. I've had Sundays off and most evenings free. So in that spare time, I've managed to work the gym back into my regular routine and even squeezed in a trip to the salon to get my hair trimmed and have the gray taken out. I splurged on this new dress. "And you sound different," I tell him. "You've been speaking a lot of English, haven't you?"

"Yes, yes," he nods. "Can you believe it? I have been speaking only English. Two nights ago, I have my first dream in English."

"I hope it was a good one," Tony says as he takes a seat.

But Gianni looks at me instead of Tony as he answers. Staring directly in my eyes, he says, "It was a wonderful dream."

I blink and look away, certain that I'm reading more into his gaze than I should.

Once seated, everyone else at the table orders the famous robatayaki, but I can't resist the appeal of lobster.

Though I accept a glass of wine, I make sure to only press my lips to the glass but don't drink any, wanting to stay sharp and focused for any questions or discussions.

However, Gianni keeps the talk light and away from business, at least, away from it in the direct sense. Instead of asking about the job, he asks vaguely probing questions about our firm. Tony gives a brief history of our startup, and then Gianni asks him, "I have met two of the partners. Who is the mysterious second Mancuso of Mancuso, Mancuso and Russo?"

Tony just smirks, so I say, "Tony is both Mancusos in the firm name."

Gianni looks at him and smiles. Says, "You name yourself twice? Are you twice the partner?"

"Only on paper," Tony answers. "Because of circumstance. I had more money than she did for the initial investment."

Gianni smiles. "I know something about that." Swirling the wine in his glass, he laughs and says, "It is funny, yes? That you name yourself twice?"

"I think so," Tony smirks. "I'm not so sure Lisa does."

"Ah, she should be flattered. You saw more than her investment money. Is that it?"

"Exactly," Tony says. "She was the best. I was just trying to catch a tiger by the tail." As Gianni smiles, Tony congenially turns the tables and asks him, "How long have you and Mr. Spillway here worked together?"

"Longer than I can remember," Spillway answers, but it's in a good-natured tone.

"Longer than I care to!" Gianni says, but he's smiling as he says it.

"He was just a lad when I started with the Loren corporation," Spillway says.

"Oh," Tony says. "So you're a company man."

Spillway nods, takes a long drink of his wine. "His father whisked me away from the states and never let me go."

"And we're a better company for it," Gianni says and toasts him casually.

Once Gianni digs into his food, he starts to question us. I have my mouth stuffed with a buttery clump of lobster as he says, "So tell me please now, Tony. Do you think this baseball team can be a worthwhile investment for me?"

I glance at Tony, because I've made sure to keep him fully informed so that he could speak intelligently in case Gianni cornered him when I wasn't around. I assumed he'd want to do the talking and take the lead in a situation like this. It happens, more often than I'd like to admit, that even though I'm primarily working the account, Tony needs to handle all the communication simply because he's a man. And though Gianni's very polite to me, he is quite literally from the "old world" and I'm not sure I should be too aggressive. But Tony swallows a mouthful and says, "I can update you if you like, but it's probably best to talk to Lisa."

There's an uncomfortable moment when Michael's eyes fall on me, but Gianni doesn't avert his gaze from Tony. Instead, he asks him, "So you are not so comfortable discussing the details with me?"

"I'm perfectly comfortable," Tony says. "But I also like to give you what you pay for. You paid for the very best work, and that came from Lisa. She did the majority of the work."

"Ahh," Gianni's face lights up now and he looks at me. "Lisa, you are my main number smasher?"

"Yes," I tell him, but I lower my eyes. As I begin talking and explaining my findings, I keep them lowered, only glancing up and holding his eyes for brief periods – just enough to let him know that I'm focused on him, but not long enough to break my concentration on my dialogue, because his eyes are twinkling under the lights and his smile is contagious. And even though I love Tony, Gianni is, admittedly, strikingly handsome enough that it's pleasurable to look at him.

But as I get deeper, Spillway starts to interject with questions, and I have to admit they're pointed and astute, leading me toward more explanations.

Gianni nods, clearly absorbing, but simply listening instead of speaking.

By the time I wind down, our dinner has been finished but we're still sipping wine and I finally allow myself a few long drinks from my glass. Spillway seems satisfied, Gianni leans back in his chair, quietly flicking his middle finger lightly against his wineglass. Other than his one finger repeatedly flicking, his body is still, and his gaze is fixed on his glass, but I've a feeling he's actually looking through it. His smile is gone, and I can tell he's deep in concentration. Then his finger falls silent.

Knowing I did my homework correctly, I still feel uncomfortable with his change of demeanor and I glance briefly at Tony for reassurance. He's also looking at Gianni in these tense moments, but he catches my eye briefly and winks, then averts his eyes back on our client.

Abruptly, Gianni speaks. He doesn't look at me, he's still looking directly ahead. In Italian, he asks, "Can I afford to purchase this baseball team?"

At first, I think he's speaking aloud to himself, mulling the decision over mentally but asking in a rhetorical way, which is why it would come out in his native tongue.

But then he looks directly at me. He repeats the question, still in Italian, but this time saying, "Can I afford to buy this, Lisa?"

I inhale deeply, respectfully answering in Italian, apologizing first, and then simply saying, "I don't know."

Spillway jumps in now, in a firm voice, but obviously following his boss's lead by keeping it in Italian, saying, "She has no way to determine that, Gianni. Don't be ridiculous."

Again, I glance at Tony, who's now got his eyes fixed on me. I'm sure he can tell by my expression that I'm lost, but that we're not in trouble. Yet. I don't think.

Gianni now, saying, "Then she must find out. I have assigned this project to her firm."

"Gianni," I say. "All due respect. I can't possibly make a determination about your financial standing without a thorough examination of your holdings."

Across the table, one word, the same in both English and Italian comes from Spillway's mouth. "No!"

"*Sì*!" Gianni barks back, glaring at him.

"Have you gone crazy?" Spillway nearly shouts, but keeps it in Italian. Leaning across the table, he says, "What a waste of money. What a waste of her time. You have a fully competent staff who can..."

"*Abasta*!" Gianni growls, leaning forward in his seat.

Easily translated, *abasta* simply means *enough*. That's the only word Gianni used, but the halt and shift is perceptible. In cultured business speak, that one word and the tone of Gianni's voice aggressively declared, "I'm the boss. You aren't. Back down. Now."

He stares at Spillway for a long second before looking back to me. His expression softens, but remains serious. "This is what I want," he says to me, still speaking in Italian, keeping Tony in the dark, clearly infuriating Spillway. "I will need you to conduct whatever investigation you deem necessary. Immediately. Can you do this for me?"

"I, I," I stutter, stalling. I feel lost. If this were Tony he was talking to, Tony would know exactly how to proceed. But I haven't a clue. I'm not a deal-maker, I'm an accountant. Reeling at the thought, I say what does come to mind. "It, that job, it could take months. At least. I know of your holdings, and I know they're vast, but I can't even estimate right now without having more information."

A playful glint comes back to his eye and he cocks his head. He says, "Que? You mean to tell me that Google doesn't have everything about me, including my shoe size available for you to know?"

"They have your shoe size, Gianni," I tell him. "It's a size ten. But not everything else. Don't you have others who can..."

Across the table, Spillway dares interrupt by saying, "Yes, he has plenty of..."

"No," Gianni says firmly, answering both him and me. "I am asking this of your firm. Can you do the job?"

"Can I? Yes, I can do it," I tell him. "But as I said, it would take months..."

"You would have to be in Europe," he says. I can feel my own jaw go slack. "I apologize," he says. "But that is where my businesses and offices are. And I need you to start immediately. I am returning to Italy in two days. You would come with me."

I'm dying. My head is swimming. We had wine at dinner but I intentionally sipped on the same glass so that I wouldn't be affected. But now I feel drunk. In response, I pick up the glass and drain it, hoping maybe it'll clear my head.

I glance at Tony again, wanting to bring him into this and let him take over. But for all his breezy verve, Gianni's been quite precise in his dealings. And I know it's not an accident that he's switched back to Italian. Perhaps when Tony handed me the reins on the Mets discussion, Gianni took that as a cue that I'm the leading lady for everything. Maybe he's more comfortable discussing something of this magnitude in Italian, as he'd warned me of in our first meeting. Or maybe he's freezing him out intentionally. But either way, I don't dare disrespect him by straying from the course.

"I apologize, Gianni," I say. "But I can't even formulate an estimate of something like this on the spot."

"*Capiso*," he says. Meaning: *Understood*. He leans back in his chair again, takes another glance at that wineglass that intrigued him. Quietly, he says, still in Italian, but making it ring sweetly in my ears, "I'm prepared to offer a two million dollar upfront retainer. Plus expenses and additional billings as we exceed."

Oh my God, I think.

"Oh my GOD!" Spillway says, in loud, clear English.

My head swirls as my breath goes shallow.

I glance at Tony, who is literally leaning forward on the edge of his seat. He doesn't speak Italian, but the word "million" is similar. In Italian, it's simply "milione."

Dazed, reeling, as I'm struggling for an answer, movement behind Gianni catches my eye.

A gold dress, shimmering as it rapidly approaches. Refocusing, I see the woman striding, cutting with laser precision through the restaurant. Gianni's bodyguards hustle behind her. "*Stronzo*!" she barks as she halts at the table and throws down her purse.

Stronzo, that's Italian also. Loosely translated, it means asshole. She was definitely addressing Gianni.

Without even turning, Gianni says, "Angelina."

"Dear lord," Spillway sighs.

The woman, she's fabulously, unbelievably beautiful. Her gold dress shimmers and clings to her curves, her hair is a luxurious mass of tamed dark waves and curls, framing her burgundy-colored lips and gleaming dark eyes. Also in Italian, she asks, "Who is this?" as she glares at me.

I'm shocked. I suddenly feel silly for previously thinking I looked pretty in the tasteful and simple black dress I'd gotten for tonight. It's not just the dress though. Even if I was dressed in her clothes and standing in her spike heeled shoes, I'd be nothing more than a pale knockoff compared to her exquisite beauty. And she's seemingly threatened by me? I'm not just shocked, I'm flattered.

Gianni turns to her and bestows one of his smiles on her. "*Cara mia*," he drawls slowly as he gazes at her and rises. Motioning to Tony and me, still speaking in Italian, he says, smoothly, "We are conducting business still. My accountants."

She sniffs and pierces her eyes through him. "Enough with the business tonight. I want a drink."

"Please," he says to her. "Have a seat."

"I don't want food," she hisses. "I want a drink."

"Angelina, just one minute..."

"Now," she says.

Gianni nods to the bodyguards standing behind her, letting them know they can again fall back, and they quickly obey and retreat.

"Amore," he says. "We were just finishing..."

"Andiamo!"

She's saying, "Let's go." But in agitated, spoiled girlfriend-speak, she's also jerking his chain just as effectively as Gianni jerked Michael Spillway's when he simply told him "enough."

Gianni reaches inside the breast pocket of his suit jacket. He pulls out a long, black velvet box. Opening it first, he then holds it up for Angelina to inspect.

Reaching down, she first touches his cheek as her face softens into a suggestion of a smile. Then, she pulls the item from the box, holding it up briefly to reveal a dazzling diamond bracelet.

All is quiet and calm as she drapes it over her wrist, and Gianni gently clips it on for her. Once done, he admires it briefly, and then kisses the back of her hand.

He takes a deep breath and turns back to us at the table. Spillway is sitting with his hand on his forehead, and Tony is still staring at this feminine, demanding creature standing at Gianni's side. To me, Gianni says, "Lisa, would you mind accompanying us outside to the garden for a few moments?"

"Not at all," I say, rising. "Tony," I say sharply enough to get his attention and then I nod for him to rise.

Gianni places his hand at the small of Angelina's back to guide her along. But as Michael also rises, Gianni halts to say to him, "We are finished for the evening with business. Take care of this bill and I will contact you tomorrow." With that, he nods at me again with a smile as Angelina sighs with boredom, and Tony and I follow them outside to the garden bar.

The Garden of Ono is even trendier and more exclusive than the restaurant, but of course, as we follow Gianni, we aren't just allowed entrance; we're greeted warmly and escorted directly to one of the gauzy cabanas. The days have been warming with ample sunshine, but night still carries a slight chill. But we're kept toasty warm by the multitude of fiery heat lamps and lanterns surrounding us, giving off a serene red glow. After he orders a bottle of wine, and while Angelina is deciding on a cocktail, Gianni asks me, "Lisa. We have a deal?"

I say the only thing I can say. "Can I speak to my partner about this?"

"*Si.*" He glances at Tony. But then warns me, "I need an answer this evening."

I gently tug on Tony's arm to lead him out of the cabana. Following me, he places a hand on my hip and leans close asking me, "What the hell is going on?"

I lead us to the pond lined with reeds, aiming toward the sleek bar. I refrained from alcohol at dinner, but now I long for a drink. But behind me, Tony halts and goes, "You were so hot telling him all about the Mets, Lisa."

"Tony," I say.

"I mean it, baby." He places his other hand on my waist. Right in my ear, he says, "Sometimes, like right now, I just want to bang the knowledge right out of you!"

"Tony," I turn around and look at him. "He wants to hire us to audit his entire corporation."

His hands still on my hips, looking down at me, he studies my face for a couple seconds before smiling and just saying, "Get the hell out of here."

"I'm not kidding. That's why Spillway was so pissed. He wants me to go to Italy and conduct a full audit."

"Well, but," Tony stutters. "That, that'd take weeks."

"Months," I correct him.

"You're serious about this? Why? Why would he want that?"

"I don't know," I shake my head. Glancing to the cabana behind us, I get self-conscious of Tony's hands on me like this. We're at an unbelievably important junction, and now I know that I've gained Gianni's intellectual respect, and I don't want that being undermined by him seeing me being held like this. Gently, I push Tony's hands off me and take a step back, using my conservative business voice. I tell him, "When I was finished explaining everything, Gianni asked me if he could afford to buy the team. I thought it was rhetorical, but then he got very serious about it." Just on the far side of the pond, I glance around Tony and spy into Gianni's cabana where he stands closely with Angelina. He leans close to her, and even from here I can tell that he's gazing at her with longing, while she stands looking petulant and bored. Looking back up to Tony's face, I say, "He wants to know tonight if we'll do it."

"Oh my God," Tony sighs, but his eyes spark with that devilish glimmer. "Can, can you imagine how much this'll cost?"

I take a deep breath and tell him. "He offered us a two million dollar upfront retainer."

"That's obscene!" he nearly yells.

"I know," I laugh. "It's true though. I'd have to leave in two days and go back to Italy with him. Two million upfront plus expenses and additional billings."

"Are you trying to make me come in my pants?"

I can't help but laugh. I'm glad it's hitting him as hard as it did me.

This time, he turns and looks over his shoulder, probably checking to make sure that this is real and that this guy wasn't just an extended hallucination or that this is now a mirage. I tell him, "He's waiting for an answer. He wants one tonight."

Eyes back on me now, Tony asks, "Can you do it?"

I just give him my "Duh, of course" look as an answer.

"I mean," he goes, "Italy. Do, do you want to do it?"

"I don't know," I say. "That's a long time to be away. And I'd need help. I'd have to take Mark, at least."

"You know I can't go, right?" he asks me.

"I know," I say. I do know it. It's a big job, but we can't close down our entire office here in New York for the sake of it. Tony would have to stay here and operate the day-to-day business as usual. From the time we've met, I've never been away from him for longer than two weeks at once. I love the thought of the job, it sounds amazing. And I love the thought of going to Italy and spending time there. Of course, I love the offer of the money. But I hate the idea of being away from him.

Tony says, "Two million bucks, Lisa."

He does the unexpected. He does the unthinkable.

He leans in and kisses me.

It's soft at first, just his lips brushing against mine. Almost like a reflex, I close my eyes, take a deep breath of the same air he's breathing, and let go and kiss him back.

More insistent, his arm wraps around my waist, pulling me close into his world as he presses firmly. His tongue peeks out, licking, teasing, coaxing me open.

"Tony," I sigh and wrap my hands around his neck, my whole body weak.

I forget myself; I lose myself. I just respond.

It's better than a fine wine, it's better than the savory lobster, it's better than two million dollars. I feel like I'm spinning. He pulls away for a second and takes a breath and I steal a look up at him. His eyes closed, a light sigh, and he moves back in. Wet, warm, tonguing me and licking and sucking and kissing, seemingly all at once. It dizzies me but he holds me tight and keeps me steady.

Dazed, I pull back to glance at him again, but this time, his eyes are open too. He's not watching me, though. His mouth still nuzzles against mine, but he's looking off to the side, staring intently. Almost hostile.

Following his line of sight, I remember where I am, out in public at the garden bar, and Tony's looking directly into the cabana across the pond where Gianni stands next to his girlfriend. Even from here, I can see Gianni's eyes locked with Tony's.

I inhale sharply, stunned. Before I can react, Tony kisses me again, hard and deep, working my mouth like he hasn't in years. But this time, I don't give in. Gianni's eyes flicker, and now they lock with mine. I do the unexpected, the unthinkable. I push Tony away. Insistently, I push on his chest and then reach and pry his arm off my waist, taking a step back. All the warmth I'd felt surges to the heat of anger.

Tony grins wickedly at me and licks his lips. I turn away, but quickly, catching me by the wrist and holding tight, Tony says, "C'mon Lisa, don't be pissed."

"I'm pissed!" I tell him, wheeling on him when I'm satisfied that we're now cloaked from Gianni's view. "What the fuck was that?" I demand.

"What?" he asks.

"You know you're not supposed to do that. We aren't supposed to do that anymore."

"Two million bucks," he says. "I got carried away with the moment."

I can feel my face flaming, my heart beating wildly. "You got carried away so you put on a little show for our biggest client? Is that it? You're pissed that he talked to me about this instead of you?"

"What?" he asks, seemingly truly shocked. "No!"

I don't know if I'm actually infuriated at him for what he did, or if I'm just infuriated at myself for mistaking what he did as something else.

"You had to put me in my place, is that it? Do you know how hard I work to be taken seriously in this old-boy's network? And you can't stand it that someone important respected me so you had to make me just a fuck-toy in front of them?"

"Oh my God, Lisa! No! That's not it!"

"Then what? What is it with you Tony?"

"I, I...I just got so excited. I forgot."

"You forgot? If it was all about me, why were you looking at him?"

Now Tony's face flames. Even in the already backlit red glow, I can see his complexion deepen as his carriage stiffens. But he doesn't answer me.

I do it. It may not be smart, but I give the boulder the biggest push I possibly can. I say, "I love you, Tony."

"Uh," is all he says as he holds out his hands. Then, "You know I love you, too, Lisa."

"No, Tony." I shake my head, knowing he's not getting it. So I make it crystal clear. "I'm in love with you. I'm still in love with you."

This time, he is speechless. Not a stutter, not a mumble, not a sigh. Nothing. Just silence as he stares at me.

He's not saying anything, and I know exactly what that means. It means he's not in love with me.

"Oh, this is just great," I say. I wish I could vaporize myself to escape this whole thing. If I could somehow suck those words back up and eat them down, I would.

Worse, as Tony stands dumbly in front of me, Gianni, with his arm around his gorgeous girlfriend, rapidly cuts through the crowd and makes his way to us.

"Lisa," Tony whispers, almost apologetically. He reaches for me again, tries putting his hands around my waist, probably to console me.

I can't stand it. Infuriated, I can't have him touching me right now. Two-handed, with all my might, I shove against his chest. Fortunately, it's strong enough and it pushes him off me.

Unfortunately, we were standing very close to the pond, and instead of easily stabilizing, his foot catches on the edge. He stumbles, and next thing I know, his massive frame tumbles back through the reeds and he splashes into the water.

This time, he shouts it: "LISA!"

Oooh. He's only saying my name. But the translation is simple. He's calling me a bitch.

Just as he's rising to his feet, completely drenched, wayward reed and fronds sticking to him, Gianni arrives at my side. He glances at Tony, but otherwise ignores the situation. Instead, he looks at me with a smile and says, "We are leaving now. Have you a decision for me, Lisa?"

I look at Tony. He looks confused, he looks trapped. He looks cold and wet with his dark suit clinging to him, water ridiculously streaming down his face. He looks like a lot of things, but he doesn't look like a man in love.

Escape. Yes.

I say, "Gianni. I'm going to Italy with you."

CHAPTER TWELVE

The next day, I'm back at Shea packing up all of our company files and cleaning up the office we worked in. At noon, I send Mark back to our Wall Street office with several boxes of files and ask him to start making our travel plans to Italy. Coming back from the ladies' room, I hear Jill speaking in a hushed voice inside the office. I don't mean to pry, but it's not just the volume of her voice but also the timbre that gets my attention. Instead of her curt, businesslike tone, there's a sultry lilt to her words as she says, "I've missed you. I'll finally be back in the office later tonight."

I hover outside the door, half of me not wanting to intrude, and the other half rudely curious. She says, "I want to have you on right on my desk."

I'm scandalized.

She laughs. Says, "I hope she doesn't make me go on this trip. I want to stay here with you, baby. I'd miss you too much."

My heart sinks. I take a few steps back and then retreat to the ladies' room.

Last night, after Gianni walked away, I didn't even bother looking at Tony again. I just turned and left, briskly carrying myself out of the scene of my utmost embarrassment. He called after me, but I knew I'd do something stupid like break down or cry if I was confronted with him trying to smooth things over, nor was I in any mood for the way he would've yelled at me, even though I so richly deserved it. I saw it on his face, I didn't need to hear him telling me how he feels, or doesn't feel, about me.

But now, hearing Jill on the phone with him, it hits like a sledgehammer all over again.

No wonder he'd cooled off with me the past couple of weeks. No wonder he looked so shocked and trapped when I blurted out my heart to him. Just like I'd always suspected, he's found the younger, prettier version of me and finally wiggled his way into Jill's pants. No dipping in the company ink, my ass. He's probably been dipping into her kinky ink for a couple of weeks now.

It makes me feel twice as good about leaving for Italy. It's fantastic money, it's a great opportunity, and it's wonderful experience. But it's also an escape from my humiliation and emotions. Maybe the reason I can't get over Tony is because I'm always around him. It's awful hard to ignore that boulder and not push it when it's right in front of my face as an obstruction every day. So now it's time to finally walk away from it.

One of the things we have to do as accountants is reconcile accounts. We have to match the book balance to all the corresponding back-up data. Sometimes, even with multiple passes and industrious research, it's just not possible to make the two balance. In that event, you have to make an adjusting entry, or write off the excess funds. I guess it's time that I finally reconcile my emotions about Tony with the truth. I'm in love with him, but he's not in love with me. I'll never be able to make him love me. So it's time to write it off and move on.

I wait a respectable amount of time and then approach the office with a sure-footed stride. Jill is flipping through files and sorting them. I say, "Jill, I'm going to need help with the Loren account in Italy."

"Yes Ms. Russo." She keeps her eyes lowered.

"You and Mark are the senior accountants in the firm, but I hope you don't feel slighted if I only take Mark. I think it's extremely important that we don't strip the New York office completely bare."

"Yes, Ms. Russo." I can see the smile forming at the corners of her mouth.

If I were jealous and vindictive, I'd make Jill go with me. I am jealous. But I'm not vindictive. If I'm truly going to move on, I have to accept how things are instead of being manipulative and trying to sabotage her.

It hurts. It's harder than anything else I've ever done in my life.

I have to turn and look out the window as I blink back a few tears. Outside the window, the ballfield is empty. I'd grown accustomed to watching the guys take their batting practice swings, but now they've left for another road trip and the stadium is deafeningly quiet.

Turning back, looking around the office strewn with papers, boxes, and assorted files, I guess I am a little bit vindictive. Because I say, "You know what? Can you please stay and finish up here, Jill?"

"Yes, Ms. Russo."

"Good," I say. "I have to go get ready for this trip." Unencumbered and free, I exhale heavily and then turn and quickly leave the building.

Mutual Holdings

CHAPTER THIRTEEN

Flying into Milan is both exhilarating and disappointing.

Exhilarating because it's my first trip out of the continental states, and it's somewhere I've always wanted to go. My father is Milanese, and he often spoke fondly about his motherland. My grandmother would tell us stories about her childhood in the old country, about her meeting my grandfather, about the beautiful city and lovely countryside of the surrounding area. So I feel as though I'm completing some sort of family circuit by coming here, finding my way back to my roots while taking a fantastical leap forward in my professional career.

It's disappointing because I'd expected a relief to overcome me as the plane first took off. Like I expected that once I'd made the conscious decision to stop chasing Tony's elusive love, it would be as freeing as Sisyphus walking away from his famed, torturous boulder. But even now, as we make our descent into the bustling airport, the phantom presence of the weight burdens me, even as I try to exorcise it as I watch the runway come into focus.

I tried to sleep during the flight, but with little success. Beside me, Mark kept softly repeating common Italian phrases that were being funneled through his earphones as he tried to pick up a rudimentary understanding of the language. But as we exit the terminal with our excessive luggage (*la nostra valigie*, as Mark proudly announces to me), the bright morning sun energizes me. Outside, there's a limo driver holding a sign affixed with our names on it waiting for us.

Gianni flew separately from us in his private jet. He'd offered us a ride, but Mark and I weren't quite ready when he unexpectedly zoomed out a day early at Angelina's request. He's not with the limo driver, and I'm chagrined to note I feel another small letdown at not seeing him. I get a lump in my throat as we load our bags and visions dance in my head of being stuck in a shabby, archaic office in this foreign country with mounds of paper and computer work to wade through as I dutifully lead Mark around every couple of evenings to sightsee to break the grueling monotony.

The depressing visions dissipate as the car begins to wind its way into the heart of the ancient city. When walking around New York, I'm at times struck by the beauty of the "older" buildings. But compared to the architectural treasures scattered around Milan, New York's old gems seem to be infant upstarts. Already I'm in culture shock, and I can tell Mark is, too.

The last of my worries evaporates when the limo pulls up to a regal, five-star hotel in the heart of the financial district in Milan. Gianni told me he'd arrange our accommodations, but I had no idea what to expect, and it certainly wasn't this.

I thought I'd seen opulence before, but it's nothing compared to this as we enter the marble lobby adorned with crystal chandeliers, mirrors and wood paneling. The level of detail is breathtaking with every single area bursting with something unique for the eye to take in. I'm just standing there, open-mouthed staring when I hear a voice behind me.

"Is this baroque enough for your tastes, Lisa?"

"Gianni," I say with a smile, turning to greet him.

"Well?" he asks, brows raised,

"This is incredible," I tell him. "Is this...yours?"

"*Si.*"

Remembering myself, I take the opportunity to introduce him to Mark. He greets him with a firm handshake that I expect will turn to an embrace by the end of the week, which he now bestows upon me, gently kissing each of my cheeks.

Looking around, I see that he's alone, and I can't help but ask, "Where's Mr. Spillway and...everyone else?"

"Michael is at the offices a few blocks from here. He gives me a longer leash when we are at home and there is less danger of me making impulse purchases. And the others are not so necessary here in Italy. They linger less obtrusively." As he says that, I glance around and do indeed see one of the New York bodyguards posted near the doorway. Gianni says, "I'm afraid I haven't much time, but I wanted to greet you today. *Andiamo.* I'll show you to your rooms."

"Oh, I know you're busy," I tell him. "We'll be fine. Just tell us where to meet you to get started."

His eyes twinkle as he shakes his head. "Always on the job, Lisa. None of that today, you have just arrived. Today you will unpack and relax and get to know Milan." Glancing at his watch, he says, "I'll meet you here this evening for dinner, yes? Let us say, eight o'clock?"

The only thing that tops the lobby is our rooms. Old-world elegance combined with modern amenities, somehow the Louis XIV furniture and high ceilings are a perfect match with plasma televisions and the marble bathroom.

Giddy in the surreal surroundings, I can't resist the impulse. I take out my phone and dial. It's only noon here, and with the time difference I know I'll be waking her up at five in the morning, but I just can't help it. It only takes three rings for her to answer, and she does sound concerned. Gleeful, I set her mind at ease as I say, "It's me, Mom."

"Lisa?" she asks. "Are you alright?"

"Sorry to wake you, Mom. But you're never going to guess where I am right now!"

"Are you drunk?" she asks me. "Oh my! Are you on vacation in Las Vegas with Anthony? Are you getting married?"

"Mom! No. I'm in Italy!"

"With Anthony?" she asks.

I sigh.

CHAPTER FOURTEEN

Gianni treats us to a lovely dinner at the hotel restaurant where I actually loosen up and enjoy a glass of wine with the meal. Once he orders another bottle, though, Mark excuses himself for the night, claiming fatigue. We'd spent the afternoon touring the city and I can tell by the set of his eyes that he is exhausted. I should be. I am, in fact. But I still can't believe I'm in Milan and I don't want to let a second of it slip away, afraid that I'll wake up back in New York and that this was just a prolonged dream. I'm also equally dreading falling asleep and actually dreaming, because I know that it will be dreams of New York and Tony haunting me, obnoxiously pushing his way into this serene landscape thousands of miles away from him.

Also, I tell myself as I allow Gianni to refill my glass, I don't want to be rude and abandon my host.

Unfortunately, my host invites my dreaded dream into the dinner conversation. He hadn't broached the subject of the obscene display he'd witnessed at Ono when Tony was macking all over me, and I was hoping he'd discern my dismay and avoid the subject. But he doesn't. Boldly asking, "You and Tony. You are partners in more than just business?"

I try to deflect by saying, "We're in Italy, Gianni. You're welcome to speak Italian if you'd like."

He laughs. "My English. It is still offensive to your ears?"

"No. You sound great. But now I can use the practice in Italian."

"Oh-kay." In Italian now, saying bluntly, "You evade my question."

I blush. "I apologize. You shouldn't have seen that...that display at Ono. And thank you for not mentioning it in front of Mark."

His eyes flare briefly, but then he looks away from me. Saying quietly, "He calls you Ms. Russo so I assumed discretion was the best option. But you and Tony, I must say, I was surprised. And I was not surprised. Tony, he is a lucky man."

"He's only my business partner."

"Ahh," he says. "Then he is not so lucky."

I laugh. "You're kind."

Leaning closer, staring at me again, he says, "I see. You wish he was more."

I blush even harder, take a big swallow of wine. "Why would you say that?"

"Lisa," he says and looks at me. "There are many things in this world that I know nothing about. But there are a few things that I do know. I know how to make money. And I know women. You are in love with him, yes?"

"Should we be discussing this? I mean, wouldn't you prefer to be discussing business?"

"No," he says simply. "When I am having dinner with a beautiful woman, the last thing I want to discuss is business."

I shift uncomfortably in my seat. "It's just that for the money you're paying me, I didn't think you'd care to be giving me advice on love."

"Lisa," he says and catches my eyes. Gazing into them, he says, "You are a lovely Italian woman in your blood, but it's so apparent that you are American by birth. All business, all the time. Trust me when I tell you this. I hired you to do business. Did you know that you were the fourth firm to do the Mets research for me?"

"What? Why?"

He shrugs. "I was looking for the best. It took me four tries to find it. You completed the work much more quickly and much more thoroughly than any of the firms before you."

"Are you saying that was a prolonged job interview?"

He looks away, and this time he evades my question by answering, "I'm telling you that I am well aware of your business worth. I am also telling you that I like you. I am not American, and therefore not every minute is about the work for me. We have a different way over here. We enjoy life. I am telling you that it is not necessary for me to pay two million dollars to simply have dinner with a beautiful woman."

"So where is Angelina tonight?" I ask him.

"Ah! You understand then, this separation of work and enjoyment?"

"Yes, I do. I'm afraid I'm just not very good about practicing it. But you didn't answer my question. Where is Angelina?" He still hesitates, and I know I'm stepping over the line, but since he was questioning me, I boldly tease him. Asking, "Didn't you have any jewelry for her?"

Catlike, a slow smile spreads across his face. "So you've noticed her affinity for diamonds?"

I rub my ear, hesitating. Still shy of treading too heavily, I say, "I've noticed your affinity for giving her diamonds."

"Well," he says. "I did two days ago. I gave her an engagement ring."

"Gianni! That's wonderful. I had no idea, congratulations!"

He takes a deep breath. "She accepted the ring. But she has not yet accepted my proposal."

"Oh. I'm sorry. What's wrong?"

"I also asked her to sign a pre-nuptial agreement," he says sheepishly.

"Well. There's nothing wrong with that."

"To her, there is very much wrong with that. She is very angry."

"I guess, maybe, she thinks it's not very romantic."

"And I'm afraid it would be tragically romantic, and foolish, to marry someone who cares only for my money," he says.

"I understand," I tell him, because I do. "She'll come around."

"She is out of town. She is away on a photo shoot. She is a model."

"Mmm." I'm not shocked. She has the exotic, stunning looks of a model. "How long have you been dating?"

"Over five years," he tells me. "You look surprised."

"Oh, no. It's just that, well...I thought you dated a lot of women."

"Oh," he says with a knowing grin. "So Google also has information on my love life?"

"Of course."

Gianni takes a long drink of his wine. His deep green eyes don't sparkle with his candid wit as he looks back to me. He looks as serious as when I watched him contemplating his wineglass at Ono before hiring me. He admits, "It is true. I do love women. I enjoy their company. But if I had my way, I would have only one woman now."

"Angelina?"

"Yes. Angelina. I like you Lisa, so I don't mind admitting to you that she is the love of my life."

"Then what's the problem?"

"Ahh," he sighs. "I am not so certain that I am the love of hers."

Looking at his handsome features, enjoying his pleasant demeanor, I shake my head and say, "I find that very hard to believe."

"Why? Because I am so rich?"

I laugh. "No. Um, well. That doesn't hurt, of course. But no. You're a great guy, Gianni. I can't imagine someone not falling for you."

As he fills my glass with more wine, he says, "Much like I find it hard to believe that Tony is not in love with you. If that is, indeed, what you desire. You never answered my question. You are in love with him?"

He's been blunt with me, so I open up to him. Simply saying, "Yes. I'm in love with him."

He looks at me softly. Kindly.

"Ahh, well," I shrug. Raising my glass, I clink it lightly against his. "Poor us," I toast.

"It's a waste, isn't it?" he asks after he sips. "The two of us here together. And instead of making the most of it, we long for others."

"I wouldn't say I was longing for him."

"I would," he says and nods knowingly, teasing me ever so slightly. "I know about these things, remember?"

I can't help but laugh. I guess I was. It is sad. And silly. "It is a shame," I agree. "Love would be easier if we could strike up mergers the same as we do in business."

"You mean... What do you mean?"

"I mean, if we could look someone over and investigate them and then just mutually agree that we're going to fall for each other."

"That, Lisa," he clinks his glass against mine and says, "is certainly an idea I could get behind."

CHAPTER FIFTEEN

Our first week of working in Milan is incredible. Gianni sets us up in a magnificent office near the hotel. It's one of his primary facilities, so everything we need to begin is at our fingertips. I still find the whole deal very odd, especially since he told me at dinner about the other firms he was courting in New York. But for what he's paying us, I'm more than happy to indulge his eccentricities and do as he asks.

Mark and I are working on Saturday afternoon, trying to make a significant dent in the initial data collection before we relax into more traditional hours. It's quiet in the office, because it's the weekend. Gianni's people work hard, but they don't submit to the sixty to seventy hour work weeks I'm accustomed to in New York, which is a refreshing change. Mark calls me over and asks, "Ms. Russo? What is this?" Poor Mark's brain is stuffed with numbers, so he's having a hard time picking up the language.

I translate the phrase for him, saying, "*Che cosa e questo*?"

He repeats me, twice, but then says, "Thanks. But, no. I mean, what *is* this?"

He's working on the hotels bundled under the Loren conglomeration while I'm doing the legwork on Gianni's soccer team. He's inspecting an invoice for what appears to be a consulting firm. "I'm not sure," I tell him.

He looks at me questioningly and I translate what I just said for him, saying, "*Non lo so*."

As he parrots my words, I look at the paper. I don't know what it is, but it seems vaguely familiar. "Flag that entry and we'll do confirmations later. I don't want to get bogged down on detail stuff yet." I want to compile a large overview so that when Gianni starts questioning me, I'll be able to give him intelligent, bold-swipe answers.

But when I return to my desk, the nagging feeling won't subside so I shuffle through several files, wasting over twenty minutes before I find the document I'd thought I'd seen. I flagged it for later review, but now, combined with Mark's, I get more curious. I do a detailed search through the electronic records I have and get a few more hits, but no more detail.

I make my way through the nearly empty offices and take the elevator down several floors to the main hard-copy records floors. It's vast; it eclipses anything I've ever seen before, and this is still only about a third of Gianni's businesses contained in this building. But it's also exceptionally clean and well organized. Strangely, when I start searching for the hard-copy documentation, I can't find it. After over an hour searching, I remind myself to stop wasting Gianni's money on this level of detail for now. I go back upstairs and make a note to resume it on Monday when I can get some help.

When I get on the elevator, it stops on the main floor and I'm surprised to see Michael Spillway waiting to board. I nod to him.

"Hard at work?" he asks me, speaking in English.

"Always," I say.

"What were you doing?"

"Oh. I had to go to the records room. I was trying to trace a particular transaction and couldn't find the documentation though."

His eyes narrow as I say that. He sniffs.

I haven't run into him much here in Milan yet, but I know from his outburst at dinner that he's none too pleased about our presence here, or the money Gianni's spending on us. I have an innate wish to make people like me, to please them. I know it's a fault, but I can't help it. It's only gotten worse since I started the business with Tony. Because for as much as Tony likes me, almost no one else in the office does. And many of the clients we deal with seem to have a genuine disdain for me. Again, it's the sexist boy's-club thing. But instead of ignoring it, I try to work twice as hard to impress them. Sometimes, there's nothing I can do to crack through and prove myself. But more often, I do end up gaining their respect.

I guess it's that desire to prove myself and please Spillway that compels me to try and convince him that even if he's against the whole idea of us, we will do a good job. I say, "It's something called Midaco Enterprises. Does that sound familiar?"

Suddenly, he reaches out and punches the stop button the elevator. He says, "So this is what you're doing? Gianni shells out two million dollars to your firm to create a broad profile and you're pissing away his money tracing nitpick transactions in the basement records room?"

"No," I say. "I was just..."

"I know exactly what you were doing. You're running out your time and hours by wading through paperwork so that you can sock it to him for more billable hours once the retainer is run dry."

"I am not," I say, totally offended.

"Gimme a break, sweetheart." Pointing at me, he says, "I was a freelance attorney for several years before I started working for Mr. Loren, Sr., and I know how this game is played. This is the biggest payday you could ever imagine. But I'm not going to let you take advantage of Gianni like this. From now on you better keep this on the straight and narrow and get the dollar signs out of your head. I don't want to see you running down details again while you're on this job."

Embarrassed because I could see how he'd get to this assumption, but furious because it's completely against my business ethics, I'm nearly nonplussed. I love to make money, but I like making it fair and square, not by ripping people off. And rich as he may be, with how generous Gianni's been with us, I would never consider sacking him. "Gianni gave me carte blanche to run this audit as I see fit," I tell him.

"Gianni's a trusting fool sometimes," he says and straightens his tie. Pushing the elevator button again so that it begins rising, he says, "That's why I'm here to look out for him. He might like a pretty face, Ms. Russo. But if you think you're the first woman he's showered with extravagance, you're sorely mistaken."

"Excuse me," I say and reach out and push the stop button again, bringing us to a halt. "Gianni Loren hired me to do a job for him. He's not showering me with extravagance because I'm a pretty face."

He snorts. Really. He snorts with derision. He goes, "You may be a capable accountant, Ms. Russo. And I hope you think you're giving Gianni his money's worth. I suppose you think you're clever by landing this account. But I'm his lawyer. And if I catch you making one false move or exploiting his generosity, I can assure you that I have a vast arsenal consisting of much more than just balance sheet reconcilements to effectively destroy you, and your whole firm, forever." Then he smiles at me, malevolent and smug. "Don't mess with a lawyer. I will bury you. Are we clear?"

What I want to say is, *I'm clear that you're a dick.* But I don't. But I don't back down either. I just say, "I'm here to help Gianni, that's all. And, frankly, I'm a little shocked at this bullish attitude."

"Bullish?" he says sarcastically. "Screw around on this account or tangle with me again and you'll get the bull by the horns, young lady."

Reaching out, I release the stop button. I don't know what else to say, so I just nod.

CHAPTER SIXTEEN

Mark and I knock off for the day shortly after that debacle. It's early in the afternoon and I'm trying to relax in my room, but I'm infinitely bothered by the episode. Normally, I'd pick up the phone and bitch to Tony about it. But since I'm still trying to distance him from my mind, I know it'd be a huge backslide to call him, especially because I know he'd side with me and give me sympathy, which would only make me appreciate him more.

I think that's one of the big problems I have in getting over Tony, is that I never stop appreciating him. And I think just the opposite has happened with him. In accounting, there's a system called depreciation. Whenever you acquire an asset, you put in on your books at full value. But over the years, you slowly write down the value of that asset as it ages, or depreciates. What often happens is that ten years later, you still have the asset hanging around, and you still use it on a daily basis. But it no longer holds any book value for you, because it's been fully depreciated. I think that over time, Tony got used to me being around, but my book value depreciated until I was at zero. I guess that's how people just gradually fall out of love.

I try to call Eva, but with the time difference, it's probably too early in the morning and she's not answering. I briefly consider calling Lucy out in Vegas, because when she was upset and lonely a few months ago, she had no problem waking me up in a panic at four in the morning and asking if she could move back to New York and live with me. I didn't just say yes, I was excited at the prospect. But she smoothed things out with her boyfriend and decided to stay in Vegas. But it's late there, and she's probably just finishing at the restaurant and trying to fall asleep, and I'm not really in a panic, I'm just a little homesick. So I don't bother her. I actually do call my other cousin, Marina. But her voicemail picks up.

I call my mom. I tell her I'm having a good time, I'm just a little homesick.

When she says, "Oh, you just miss Anthony," I know it's time to hang up.

But she's right, of course. I tell myself it's anxiety over this overwhelming job that urges me to call the office in New York. It's Saturday and I don't expect anyone to be there, but I know I'll get to hear to Tony's voice on his pickup message if I call his direct extension, and I can leave him a message about sending some of the files to our office to be looked over.

Sure enough, Tony's canned message simply says, "Mancuso, Mancuso & Russo, CPA." As his deep voice tells me to leave a message, I'm momentarily stuck, wistful at something as stupid as hearing him say our names together. But after a brief hesitation, I pull myself together and say, "Tony. Once I get Gianni's approval on Monday, I'm going to send some files back to the New York office. I'll need you to..."

"Lisa?" he says, interrupting as he clicks off the machine. "It's me, I'm here."

Startled, I go silent. I wasn't prepared to speak to him.

"Hello?" he asks. "Are you still there? Did I lose you?"

"I'm here. It's Saturday. What are you doing there?"

"Lisa, you won't believe what's going on back here. Word spread about the Loren account and we've gotten a lot of calls."

"So you're really busy, huh?"

"I'm in here making calls trying to pick off some experienced accountants from other firms."

"You're so rotten," I say, but I can't help but smile.

"All's fair in love and multi-million dollar business, babe."

I go silent.

He recovers the fumble, quickly asking, "Speaking of million dollar babies, how's Loren?"

"That's why I'm calling," I say.

"Oh? Are you, uh, working closely with him?"

"I want to send some stuff back to the office in New York to be looked over. Just basic stuff, interns can do it. Just have someone senior glance at it, too."

"Sure," he says. "I'll put Jill on it."

The jealousy that stabs deep in the pit of my stomach is vile. Not only is he fucking her, now he's looking at *her* as his top-dog accountant. A terse "Fine" is the only response I can muster.

"Are you alright, Lisa?" he asks.

"Fine."

"You sure? You don't sound like yourself. You're handing off work, and you sound tense."

"Look, Mancuso. This job is immense, okay? And I don't think I need to be wading through every stupid detail."

"Okay," he says, dragging it out, making it clear that he's pacifying me. A pause, and then, in a low voice, he goes, "You uh, you don't want to overrun the retainer and start racking up more billable hours, huh?"

"Fuck you." It just tumbled out of my mouth before I could censor myself.

On his end, silence.

I take a deep breath, saying, "I'm sorry. I didn't mean that. I'm just tired and this job is more than I thought and I need to concentrate on it."

"Lisa," he says softly. "That night at Ono, before you left..."

"I don't want to talk about it," I snap, now actually shaking. I didn't think things could get worse between us, but this is escalating rapidly into disaster territory. Nothing he could say will mollify me, because the only thing he could say to make me feel better right now is the one thing that's not true – that he loves me. And Tony may be greedy and ambitious and proud and horny and even sometimes insensitive. But he's not a liar. And he'd never toy with me. "I was drunk anyhow," I lie.

"You were?" he asks the question, but it sounds more like a sarcastic, accusatory indictment, as though he knows I'm lying.

"I'm just under a lot of pressure here," I say. "I could've used a little time off this year."

He says, "We should've taken that vacation."

I'm not sure what he means by that, and I'm not sure how to respond. Even though I'm on the phone with him, and even though things are degenerating, I miss him fiercely. I wish we'd taken it, too. But we didn't. So I say, "Yeah. I miss my family."

"You homesick, Lisa?"

No, dummy, I'm lovesick!

I say, "I have to get going."

CHAPTER SEVENTEEN

I lay back on my bed, making a maudlin little nest of my own misery amidst the expensive sheets, prepared to wallow in solitude for the rest of the evening, feeling like the weight of the boulder has finally rolled back and squashed me under its path on the downturn.

There's a slight knock on my door. "Ms. Russo?" Mark calls and knocks again.

I heave myself up, wondering what kind of a crazed lunatic he is, still plunging ahead and working after the exhausting week we've already had. Opening the door, I see he's not dressed in business attire. Instead, he's wearing a billowy silk shirt adorned with bright colors in a paisley pattern. Very Milan. He goes, "Do you want to have dinner together?"

"Really?"

"Sure. You're my interpreter. How could I order without you?"

"Oh."

"Plus," he says teasing me now, "I'd like you to keep me company."

"I like your shirt," I tell him.

"Versace." He smiles. "I went for a stroll through the fashion district last night."

"I see you didn't need an interpreter for that."

"No," he says. "Spending money on overpriced couture is pretty universal."

We decide to walk instead of taking a taxi, enjoying the mildness of the charming Milan evening. In the middle of dinner, watching Mark bend over his plate to protect his shirt, I suddenly feel really guilty.

"Mark, I'm really sorry you didn't get a vacation yet this year."

"Are you kidding? I'm in Milan, and the company's paying for it."

"Uh, you um, you aren't going to try and put that shirt on your expense account, are you?"

He blushes and lowers his eyes. "Uh, no. No no, I uh..."

"Mark. I'm fucking with you."

"You are?" he asks and seems genuinely surprised.

"Expense it," I tell him. "Thanks for asking me to dinner. I was...surprised."

"*Perche*?" he asks, meaning, *why*?

"Very good," I tell him. Feeling vulnerable, knowing I'm fishing because I'm still trying to figure out the missing link with Tony, I decide to tread lightly but go for it. I take a long drink of my wine and say, "Because I thought you didn't like me very much."

"That's not true," he says quickly.

"Mark. Come on. No one in the office really likes me much."

"That's not true at all," he says. "I like you."

"Not like you like Tony, though."

He looks me in the face. "I respect you, Ms. Russo. Everyone does. That's all it is. Everyone's just a little intimidated by you. Because you're the boss."

"But so is Tony. He's the majority partner."

"Yeah, but you're the one who does all the work. Even Tony knows that."

"No," is all I can say. "That's...No."

"Yes," he insists. "We just try to impress you, that's all."

"Now you're fucking with me, aren't you?"

"No. It's a really big deal for me that you asked me to come here and help you."

Relieved, satisfied, I lean back and say, "Thank you, Mark."

"*Grazie*," he corrects me.

"Well, I still think we got screwed on our vacations. We have a lot of work to do here, but I hope you try to have some fun. In fact, I'm going to expense this dinner." I hail the waiter and order us an expensive bottle of wine.

"Ms. Russo," Mark says with a genuine smile on his face. "I'm shocked."

"We deserve a vacation. Just don't tell Tony."

He laughs. "How do I say, I *promise*, in Italian?"

"*Prometto*."

"*Prometto*," he repeats. He looks down as he says, "I promise I won't tell Tony anything else you don't want him to know either." He looks back up at me now. Adding, "Like about how Gianni Loren looks at you."

"He doesn't look at me in any way."

Mark nods knowingly. Says, "Yes he does. I've seen it. I don't think Tony would like it very much."

"He wouldn't care a bit."

"Really? I always thought..." his voice trails off as the waiter brings our bottle of wine. Mark watches him intently as he opens it and serves up the cork. I recall Tony foregoing the whole sniffing and tasting thing and instead grabbing the bottle and slugging off it. It makes me want to laugh. It makes me want to cry. When the waiter leaves, Mark fills my glass, and as I take a sip, he goes, "I always thought Tony was in love with you."

I nearly spit the wine all over the table, but I choke it back.

Mark says, "I overstepped, I'm so sorry."

"No, it's fine," I assure him. I try to choke back the words just as I'd choked back the wine, but I don't. Instead, they come tumbling out in a messy rush. "I'm in love with Tony," I admit to him. "And he doesn't love me. I made a mess of things and that's part of why I came here to Italy to do this job, to get away from him because he's back in the office screwing Jill."

"Oh my God," Mark gasps. "Ms. Russo! This is so unprofessional!"

"Oh hell, Mark," I say. "I'm sorry, I'm so sorry."

"I love it!" he nearly shouts.

"You love it that I'm heartbroken and forlorn?"

"No. No. That's bad. That's all very bad. I just meant that I love that you spilled your guts like that."

I just stare at him.

"Ahh, we'll fix the other stuff," he assures me. "I'm telling you, you should hook up with Loren, he's got the hots for you, woman. And I don't think Tony's screwing Jill, either."

"Pfft. Jill's gorgeous. I bet you'd love to nail her, too."

"Jill's not my type, Ms. Russo."

I scoff. Asking, "Yeah? Then who is?"

Mark licks his lips, and with a slight nod of his head, directs me to the table next to us, where our waiter is currently running a crumber across that table. He's tall, with sandy colored hair and broad shoulders.

"Oooh," I say, grinning as it dawns on me.

"Um. If you're serious about us having some fun while we're here, can I ask you to translate something for me to tell him?"

"Sure. I'd be happy to."

This guy, Mark, the quiet one that I've worked with for five years now, he goes, "How do I say: I'd like to fuck you out of your shoes until the sun comes up?"

CHAPTER EIGHTEEN

On Monday, Gianni gives me permission to e-mail files to our home office for inspection. I see him only a few times during the week, but Mark and I keep plunging through files and accounts. Mark, he now calls me Lisa. We work Saturday, but knock off early in the afternoon. Mark has a date with a waiter – not the same waiter as the one he hooked up with last week, but a whole new one, and though he invites me along, I want to give him some privacy.

I lay back and doze fitfully until the phone in the room wakes me. When I answer, I hear Gianni's voice, always speaking in Italian to me now, asking me, "What are you doing lounging in a hotel room on this beautiful day?"

"Well, it's a beautiful hotel room," I tell him.

"I think we can do better."

"Gianni. This is so nice of you. But you don't have to entertain me. Shouldn't you be spending the weekend with Angelina?"

"She is angry with me," he says.

"Gianni, what'd you do?"

He sighs. Then says, "She is still refusing the pre-nuptial. She said she'd consider it if I'd do something for her. She wanted me to buy her something and I refused."

"Well. That doesn't sound like you," I say. "You're very generous with me and everyone else that I've seen. What did she want?"

"Greece."

I laugh. He doesn't. That's when I realize that he's serious. That's when I wonder again what I'm doing here, supposedly figuring out his net worth.

I stop my giggles, but can't stop the ludicrous vision of him pulling out a credit card and charging a country. "I'm sorry for laughing. And I'm sorry you're having a bad day."

"Meet me downstairs. Pack an overnight bag, including swimwear and an evening dress. We're going to have a mutually agreeable good weekend, Lisa."

Right now, he's the boss. Who am I to disagree?

Downstairs, as I exit the lobby to climb into the back of his waiting limo, I see the photographers hanging around so it's not startling as they start popping pictures. I'm still not used to the whole scene, and there are several of them, not just one. It makes me feel like I'm with a rock star on a red carpet. "Are they always around?" I ask him as I slide in.

"They don't pester and come inside the buildings, but it's not unusual for a few of them to be outside."

"What are they doing?"

He smiles and gives me an odd look. Saying, "They like to gossip about who I am dating."

I just nod. But then it hits me. They took my picture as he opened the door for me. Surely, they can tell the difference between a date and his accountant. Right? I ask him about it, but he just shrugs. Saying, "Most likely not."

"But," I say. "Angelina. Won't she be angry if she sees them?"

He shrugs again.

"Oh, right," I say. "She already knows I'm just your accountant."

He doesn't answer that. Right. She probably doesn't even recall seeing me, let alone recall who I am.

I ask, "Where are we going?"

"Bellagio," he says, rolling the name off his tongue with Italian grace.

"In Vegas?"

It's his turn to laugh at me. "You are such an Americana! No, the original Bellagio. The city that your casino was built in honor of."

"On Lake Como?"

"*Si*," he answers. "The most romantic place in the world. *La perla de lago*."

By that, he means, "the pearl of the lake". I've heard of Bellagio, from my family and other travelers. Lake Como forms a distinctive Y, and Bellagio is nestled right at the center, very similar to a woman's physique.

Gianni says, "I have been thinking all week about what we discussed at dinner, Lisa." Looking directly at me, boldly, he says, "This is something I wish to discuss with you in more detail."

Inside, I tremble, both with anticipation and fear. Fear that maybe Spillway's denouncement of me as nothing more than an expensive potential fuck-toy of Gianni's is true. Anticipation that maybe Spillway's denouncement of me as nothing more than an expensive potential fuck-toy of Gianni's is true.

"Angelina," he sighs the name. "She has spent the week torturing me again. This isn't unusual," he confides. "Other men, ridiculous demands, these are the things that make me crazy."

"But it also makes you crazy for her."

"Perhaps," he nods and stares at me, his eyes flashing. "Or maybe I just tolerate it. I enjoyed our dinner, Lisa. I think we should pursue your idea, together."

"Come again?"

"What you said, about how things would be easier if we could find mates that we picked, instead of letting ourselves fall indiscriminately."

"Yeah, but, Gianni," I say. "You've already picked Angelina."

"And you have already picked Tony," he says. "It is not working out for either of us. From what I have learned of you, I like you very much already."

I shift in my seat. "Are you serious about this? Did you actually pay two million dollars to get me over here in Italy to seduce me for kicks?"

"I am insulted!" He nearly shouts it. "Offended! I told you, Lisa, I have hired you to do a job."

"Well, then maybe we should leave it at that," I say. "I'm not sure it's such a good idea to go any further. It could get...complex. Maybe I should go back to the hotel."

"Nonsense," he says to me. "We are here, and we will enjoy the day and evening, in any way that you're comfortable. I only ask that you consider this proposal as carefully as you would examine any of your standard business transactions."

"Gianni," I say, trying to tread lightly. "It's a nice idea. And I'm flattered. Extremely flattered. But technically, on a legal basis, aren't you concerned?"

"I have papers we can sign," he says, offhanded. I must look stunned, and he says, "Come now, Lisa. I have papers for everything to protect myself."

"So," I say, trying to wrap my brain around this. "This is common practice for you."

He doesn't deny it outright. Instead, he dips his head and says, "If you have heard rumors of my...escapades, they are probably not too exaggerated." I start to protest, but he assures me again, saying, "I did not plan this with you. I hired you strictly as an accountant, and you will be expected to fulfill your obligations to the level I am expecting. But I am not going to lie and tell you that I am not also attracted and wanting to investigate this attraction. Especially now that Angelina has again left me."

I stare at him, wordless, trying to determine how to proceed.

"Unless," he says and looks me directly in the eye. "You do not find me attractive at all?"

I have to look away as I answer him quietly, "You're very attractive to me, Gianni."

"You see?" he says, with his nonchalant enthusiasm back. "I think you're lovely, too!"

"Oh Gianni. It's just, it's not that simple."

"Isn't it?" he asks.

We head north, rolling through the seemingly manicured pastures, places that would make the original Elysian Fields blush. Each place we pass gets more beautiful than the next, until I'm nearly certain I'm in the midst of heaven on earth as we come to the dazzlingly deep blue lake with imposing mountains of the Alps rising in the background.

"My villa," he says, pointing to an obscenely large mansion ripped from the pages of antiquity. Set upon a hill bejeweled with rich flowers that leads down to the lakeshore, the villa is a gorgeous, stone enclave that sprawls across the landscape.

I can't speak. I've never seen anything like this. I've never imagined anything like what I'm seeing. Not just his villa, but the entire scene. He was right, it is a beautiful day with the sun shining down, seemingly cavorting with the gentle waves. It's warmer over here than it is in the states, or so I assume. It feels like mid-summer already. I stand there, dumbstruck. Even though a man who I assume is a butler comes out to greet us, Gianni takes my luggage and urges me to follow him inside.

He says, "The first time I met you, you were swimming. I assume you enjoy it."

"I love it," I tell him.

"I'll show you your room. We'll get changed and then meet on the beach." Turning back to the butler, he informs him that we'll be dining out this evening, and that the staff can leave early.

Inside, the villa is just as astounding as the outside. Marble halls and plush velvet furniture in creamy greens and pastel oranges fill the great rooms and a spiral staircase leads us upstairs.

I can't suppress the thought of how blown-away Tony would be by all this, and it nearly brings tears to my eyes as I imagine him exploring the place and all of its treasures. Upstairs, my bed and bath would make Donald Trump blush with the luxury of its appointments. A king size bed with canopied frame with the softest sheets I've ever felt. All of the furniture must be at least 300 years old, but it's in magnificent shape.

"Quickly," Gianni prods me as he drops my small bag on the bed and then pulls the door shut behind him.

There's a set of floor-to-ceiling doors, and upon opening them, I find a spectacular balcony overlooking the lake below. It's so magnificent I have to applaud.

The drive up here took well over an hour, and by the time I finish changing, it's early evening. I regret my choice of swimwear, wishing I looked more like Jill in her sleek black one-piece. Instead I'm wearing a white two-piece tankini. The white looks good with my dark skin tone and reddish hair color, but even though the fabric covers my slightly soft middle, it doesn't completely hide the fact that I'd missed two months at the gym. I pull a plush towel off the rack and wrap it around myself and navigate back through the villa, getting lost three times in the maze-like hallways and bumping into not one, but two people in the kitchen, hurriedly cleaning up. I ask them for directions and find an exit out the back that leads to a cobblestone patio and pathway down to the beach.

Gianni is outside, already swimming in the lake. I drop my towel and prepare to plunge in quickly in the hope he won't see me before I can get hidden under the water. But no luck. The water is brisk and as I hesitate, he comes up for a breath and sees me lingering on the edge.

It's now magic hour, that luscious time of day between sunset and dusk. The twilight time that lingers, where a divine light glows with soft edges and misty rapture. The Italian Alps frame the background as he strides out of the azure lake, water skimming off his muscled skin, dripping from the strands of his short, dark hair.

Susan DiPlacido

It's the first I've seen him out of a business suit, and for as well as he wears those fabrics, it's nothing compared to the sight of him tan and shirtless, his body lean but rugged.

I know I'm in trouble right away.

He drops to his knees in front of me. In his Milanese dialect he says, "*Bella regazza. Sempre sarò infelice se con me Lei non avete pranzo.*"

This guy, Gianni, that I've been working for, that's what he says to me.

I sigh.

In English, that roughly translates to: "Pretty lady. I'll be unhappy forever if you won't have dinner with me."

And in my American, 30-year-old, single-girl jaded dialect, it translates like this: "I've paid you two million dollars to work on a silly project. The first time I saw you, I noticed you had great tits. Wanna fuck?"

I didn't come to Italy to get laid by a billionaire. I came to get away from a wannabe billionaire who likes to fuck me and nothing else. This city, Bellagio, it's sometimes called "the most beautiful city in the world". Even in a place as ancient as Italy, modern promotional taglines are now the norm. It has other names too. It's sometimes called "the pearl of the lake."

Even though I've only been here an hour and only seen a small slice of it, I can see how it comes by its name. It's a place that makes you realize that humans don't fuck up everything. The landscape alone is breathtaking, with the mountains rising beyond the deep lake; it's an enchanting marriage of Mediterranean sensuality and Alpine splendor. But the gorgeous villas and basilicas done in the creamy peach and butterscotch tones are nestled into the hillside, with cobblestone paths leading to abundantly flowering gardens. It's more than I expected.

And now, just as I thought I'd seen heaven on earth, out of the lake comes this Michelangelo-looking creature. This, this – Gianni. Looking as he does and looking at me as he does, he could be an angel.

But as he looks at me, he reaches out, wet fingers circling my wrist, skimming and tickling the underside of my palm, sending an unmistakable spark up my spine. And the glint in his eyes tells me he's closer to a devil.

I spend so much time railing against being seen as a feminine, sexual creature in the workplace. Sometimes, I get really offended when men can't see my brains and only focus on my body. But then sometimes, like with Tony, I love the duality of my nature. Sometimes, like right now, I'm not offended, I'm purely flattered to be looked at as a woman.

I guess that makes me shallow. Or fickle. Or capricious. Or maybe just lovesick and horny.

What the hell. I'll go to dinner with him.

After a brief dip in the refreshingly crisp water, we retreat inside to get changed for dinner. I don't usually take an extraordinarily long time to shower and dress anyhow, but I still, for some reason, find myself hurrying so as to not keep him waiting. But as I descend the spiral staircase, I see him seated on a plush divan in the foyer. He rises to greet me. Looking me up and down, he gives a small nod of approval but then tilts his head slightly. Asking, "Lisa. Isn't this the same dress I saw you wear to our dinner in New York?"

Self-conscious, it occurs to me for the first time that he's used to Angelina and her probably endless wardrobe consisting of an array of sexy clothes. It's then that I realize that I haven't seen him in the same suit twice. He's wearing one now, and it's a deep blue, along with a silky seafoam shirt, again highlighting his eyes.

"Sorry," I tell him. "It's the only one I have." His brows go up, and I quickly correct that sentence, saying, "It's the only one I brought with me." It's a lie. It is the only one I have.

"It is lovely," he tells me with a generous smile. "You look lovely. I'm just surprised. You have been in the fashion center of the world for nearly two weeks. I figured you'd be showing off new purchases."

"I haven't been shopping. I've been busy working."

"Ahh," he says, his smile widening. "Then we must tell your boss you will be needing some time to enjoy the city."

"Yeah," I say. "You send him a memo."

"I would like to ask something," he says now. "Have you given any thought to what I was proposing between us?"

"Yes," I tell him. "I have."

"And so? Is this a dinner date? Or is this a business dinner?"

I glance up at his face, with its subtly tanned skin and twinkling eyes. It's inconceivable that he's interested in me. It's so inappropriate to pursue this. And it's been so long since I've felt a spark of appreciation like this from anyone, including Tony. Tony. Tony who's back in New York, probably banging Jill on his desk right now for his lunch break.

I can see the papers on the divan next to where he was sitting, and I know his question is about more than just curiosity.

This guy, Gianni Loren, he's got more at stake than just his heart when he gets entangled with a woman. He's got an entire empire.

Frankly, I'm not the least bit insulted. I respect his caution.

"I'll sign the papers," I tell him.

He looks delighted as he humbly brings me the folder. Flipping through, I give them a cursory glance, skimming them quickly. I can't say that it all looks standard, because nothing about this is standard for me. But for him, I know it is.

I feel a pang of guilt, because I don't feel more guilty. The way I feel about Tony, I expect that I should feel as though this is wrong, this is a betrayal of those feelings. But I don't feel that. I came here to escape him and cut those burdensome ties. As I raise the pen, I think maybe it's similar to me picking up scissors.

I sign.

I have to admit, there's something appealing about it to the businesswoman in me. Quick and efficient, and lacking any doubt. In reality, I just signed away all rights to sue him for sexual harassment in regards to this evening. But implied in that signing is something else. It's a written acknowledgment that we find each other attractive.

It's so reassuring that it's nearly intoxicating.

CHAPTER NINETEEN

Even after all he's said and as open and forward as he's been about this date, and even after signing those papers, which makes this all seem like a buildup to an inevitable screwing tonight, it startles me when he puts his hand on the small of my back. Such a bold and familiar move. I step away and put space between us. But he takes my hand as we walk and though it stiffens me, again that sinful spark keeps me from pulling back.

At the restaurant, instead of sitting across from me, he takes a seat next to mine, presumably so he can enjoy the view of the placid lake at night. Leaning back, he rests his arm on the back of my chair and twists his fingers through the locks of hair that hang down my back, across my shoulder. It's appalling to me at first, his sudden and casual affection with me, but as I sip on wine that warms my belly while the evening *breva* kicks up, cooling the air, I reluctantly relax into it.

It's presumptuous of him, almost cocky, as though he's taking it as a given that I'm now his for the evening. But I like his confidence, and besides, his good looks and sultry demeanor are admittedly winning me over and making me curious.

Sitting on the terrace framed by cypress and olive trees, I stick a forkful of *ravioli di pesce* in my mouth, my toes curling with the buttery richness as Gianni says, "I must admit to you, Lisa. The first time I saw you, I was taken. Your face, it bewitches me." He's been pouring this impromptu poetry to me since we've been here, lacing it with compliments, presumably to weaken my defenses.

This guy, Gianni, my boss, is he serious with all this?

Of course not. I decide to cut to the chase.

"Gianni," I mumble with my full mouth. Chewing, swallowing down a gulp of wine, I say, "*Piachere*. You sound like a Bocelli song, stop it already."

"You are angelic," he says. "You look like a Bocelli song come alive."

I wipe my mouth with the napkin and lean back from the plate of food. "Listen," I tell him. "You're very nice. But this isn't necessary, you don't have to sweet talk me. With a few shots of grappa, I'll sleep with you anyhow. I think we established that earlier when I signed those papers. I'd prefer it if we kept it honest like that."

He frowns and says, "Lisa. Is this what you think tonight is about? Having sex? I don't want to have sex with you. I want to have a romance with you." But then he motions with his hand and calls over the waiter. He orders grappa for us.

"I knew it," I say, smirking.

He leans forward and looks me in the eyes, saying, "*Certo, ti voglio." Of course I want you.*

"Then stop trying to make it more," I tell him. "It's not nice."

He looks shocked. Stricken. "Lisa. This was not my intent, to anger you by telling you how beautiful you are."

"I'm not angry," I say, feeling guilty for offending him. "It's just, it's leading when it's not true."

"Ahh," he nods. "*Capisco*. It is not that I'm making more, *angelica*. It is you trying to make less. I should have expected. This is how it is between you and Tony, yes? Come now," he flops his napkin on the table and stands. Looking down at me, he says, "We go now, and have the sex, then?"

"But..." I stall, slinking in my seat, glancing around to see if anyone heard him. "The grappa hasn't come yet."

"So we can finish the meal?" he asks.

"Yes, we can finish our dinner, Gianni."

"You are sure?"

The waiter arrives with our grappa but hesitates as Gianni still hasn't taken his seat.

"Yes, I'm sure," I say and motion for him to sit.

This guy, Gianni, my boss who's trying to sleep with me, I guess he is serious.

He pulls his chair closer so that his knee brushes against mine as he sits. He raises his glass and says a traditional toast and we both take a deep swig of the grappa. I close my eyes, letting the warmth fill my mouth as the pungent scent hovers. Upon swallowing, a liquid heat courses down to my belly. He nudges my shoulder, leans close and whispers in my ear, "You are not without hope, yet, Lisa."

Tingles ripple across my skin as my face flushes. Whether it's the effects of the booze or his sultry breath, I'm not sure. "Without hope for what?" I ask him.

"If you can enjoy your food the way you do, if you can enjoy the drink, then all is not lost. You are not in that much of a hurry."

"What are you talking about?"

He laughs and places his arm on the back of my chair, directs me to look out on the night waters of the dark lake. "Why did you agree to come here tonight?"

"I, I…" I stutter like a fool. "I don't know."

He puts his arm around my shoulders, his thumb lightly stroking my naked arm. It's still disconcerting, all this physical closeness. But I figure it's a difference in our cultures. Nearly everyone around here is snuggled close, though I assume they're longtime lovers.

He says, "You came here, Lisa, looking to escape bad romance. You came here to find out if you can still find good romance. But when I try to offer it, you protect yourself and try to make it less. You try to keep it business as usual, same as in America."

"I'm not sure I know any other way to do it," I tell him.

"But it is not all about the business here in Italy. We enjoy ourselves. We can work. And we can play. And we don't have to keep our play strictly business. We don't have to be in a rush to finish either. We can take it slow."

His lilting Italian words in tandem with the stroking on my arm starts a subtle vibration in my lower tummy. Maybe it's not all about the finish to him, but suddenly I wish we'd at least get started. He purrs in my ear, calling me *bella regazza* again, just like he did on the beach.

Beautiful woman, that's what it means. Not "hot" or "sexy" like I'm used to with Tony.

I don't mind if he wants to call me beautiful, but I know he has other motives. I know that because I don't think I am beautiful. I'm not unhappy with how I look, and maybe I'm even pretty. But I don't think I'm beautiful because other men never bother to tell me that I am. Other guys, like Tony and even Day-Trader Dave, they just get down to business once it's been established that's where things are headed.

Whether it's true or not, it feels really nice to hear it.

I put my hand on Gianni's knee to let him know that I'm with him. He nods but refills our grappa glasses, deliberately clinks his against mine and drinks his slowly. In the soft glow of candlelight, his Adams' apple bobs as he swallows, the dimness can't conceal the single, strong vein that runs down the side of his neck.

I lean into him, pressing my body against his side. He's firm and warm and he dips his head and meets my mouth with his lips.

He kisses me. And it is so damn good. Soft, tinged with the liquor, lips and tongue and it's risky and new but it's not the least bit wrong.

He moves his hand off my shoulder, places it on my exposed thigh. Kissing me gently, his fingertips trace patterns upward on my leg. Thrumming inside,

I kiss him more deeply as his hand snakes up. I uncross my legs to give him easier access.

Gianni moves. Instead of kissing my mouth, he drops feather kisses on my cheek, his fingers rubbing the inside of my upper thigh. The *breva* kicks up again, and I bite my lip to control a shudder as his breath tingles in my ear. Instinctively, I slide my hand up his leg, his muscles tensing beneath my touch. Not lingering, I take hold of him and he sighs in my ear again, a heavy breath, hot and moist.

The waiter comes to check on us, I freeze, but Gianni doesn't. He nuzzles my ear again before turning to him and answering, "Bring us the dessert list," while his fingers dance dangerously higher, now brushing against the smooth fabric of my panties.

I blush and tuck my head down. I'm not sure the waiter is oblivious. He bows, but loiters to refill our wine. As he does, Gianni slides his fingers directly across the crotch of my underwear, firmly.

I reel. I don't know if it's from the sensation so much as shame. Shame that it does feel good, shame that I don't cross my legs or push him away. But he picks up my wineglass and feeds me a sip, a rather large gulp. As I'm swallowing, he kisses my neck and works his hand smoothly up my stomach, then back down, this time beneath my panties.

I squirm and take hold of him again as the waiter retreats. He sets down the wineglass and moves my hand off of him. Saying, "*Ralenta, regazza. Ralenta.*" *Slow down.* Slow down? That's what this guy with his hand down my underwear in a public restaurant is telling me...slow down.

But before I can protest or take hold of him again, he slides his hand, his strong, sure fingers, back down. Inside my panties, parting my slit, two bold fingers slip down the length of me, then roughly, heavily back up, and again partway down, settling this time on my sweet spot, pressing against the nub of my rapidly sensitizing clit.

My breath catches, my shoulders tense, and my insides quicken. The rush from the grappa taking hold in my brain, warming my body as surely as he's tuning me up, turning me on.

I'm wet already, slick as he slides up and down, again coming to rest and pressing against my pleasure button. This time, shortening the length of his stroke, moving those two fingers only an inch. Sliding up, waiting, kissing my neck, and then gliding down, sucking on my earlobe. It's so nasty, so risky, I know I should pull away, or push him away, especially before the waiter comes back. But I'm pulsing and as I allow him to slide a few more times, I'm wired on it.

Shallow breath and rapid pulse, champagne blood rushes through my limbs, concentrating and knotting at the delicious tension he's creating between my legs, begging for satisfaction. The waiter comes back with the dessert tray. And oh sweet mercy help me, I still can't pull away. Even as the waiter looks me in the face. I meet his eyes, he's explaining the desserts, pointing to samples on the tray, and Gianni keeps working his fingers rhythmically over my engorged clit. I tell myself the waiter can't possibly know what's going on as long as I keep it cool. Yes, Gianni's nuzzling my neck, but the waiter can't see his hands under the table, beneath the tablecloth, especially in this flickering light. I can do this, I can hold it together.

But as he keeps reciting the menu, Gianni picks up the pace, moving quick and firm, taking me higher, higher. God, this is awful, I'm close to getting off, I should stop this but I can't, it's within reach, it's just too good. I stay still, dropping my eyes to hide the telltale twitches. And when the waiter finishes his descriptions, just as I'm on the edge, Gianni stops his movements. I can't stop myself, I just can't help it, my back arches and pelvis pushes forward, seeking satisfaction, pressing myself, subtly grinding against his hand.

He moves his fingers away, pulling up slightly, rubbing small circles against the base of my stomach as he orders us a chocolate torte to share. It's horrible, even worse than the tantalizing indiscretion was, my nerves are screaming for release, my whole body in a knot and head swimming. The waiter takes his leave and instead of putting his hand back between my legs and finishing me off, Gianni removes it completely. Languidly, he brings his fingers to his mouth and licks them with a satisfied smile, telling me I'm sweeter than any dessert.

Now I can't decide if I want to fuck him or claw his eyes out. I slowly come back down as he feeds me the cake. And by the time we start walking back to his villa, the agonizing tension has subsided, but I still can't imagine wanting him more. I'm melting to him as he holds a strong arm around my waist. We walk in the cool night along the charming cobblestones, until we get to his villa, where he leads me the up the spiral staircase and through the mutedly lit hallway.

At the doorway to my room, he takes me in his arms and kisses me deeply, passionately, making me reel. And then, just like at the restaurant, he pulls away from me, bidding me goodnight, leaving me longing for more.

Confused, inside my room, as I get changed, a different frustration seizes me. As daring and delicious as that was at the restaurant, it was also a blatant manipulation. After he lectured me about romance instead of sex, he proceeded to play my body like a fiddle, turning it precisely into sex.

And then he took it away.

He asked me why I came to Italy, why I agreed to dinner with him.

I came to escape the silly games and the constant, hopeless potential of more than just sex. And when I let my guard down, he suckered me.

Climbing into bed, my body still buzzing at a low frequency, I could cry.

It all felt so easy and clean with the signing of some papers, and now, it's murky and dangerous again. Somehow, I've fallen right back into playing games for a man's affections. And I didn't even want his affections! I didn't ask for this. He opened up to me, and then he ended up turning me on only to show me off. Just like what Tony always loved to do.

I try to shove Tony out of my mind, but I can't. Angry, I refuse to give in to the pesky pull between my legs, because I know I'd end up fantasizing about him and I don't even want to give him that much power any more.

So I lay there, waiting for the itch to recede, festering about Tony and once again wondering what Gianni's real motives were for hiring me.

CHAPTER TWENTY

In the morning, after a few hours of fitful sleep, with daylight breaking and streaming through the open doors leading to the balcony and a soft breva billowing the silk curtains, I'm of a different mind.

With the morning light, it all seems clear. Even though by now I've learned that I have a hot-blooded temperament, that still doesn't stop it from galloping away from me. Last night, in the throes of my sexual frustration, I got overly agitated about the situation, much in the same way I'd always raise my own hopes with Tony and then allow them to be dashed when he didn't fulfill them. Gianni was playing a game, yes. But there isn't any malice in his game, and it's up to me what to make of it.

The problem with me is, my body reacts like a man's, but my mind is like a woman's. If he can follow through on what he started last night, he's offering me the best of both worlds. But first, I have to let him know that I'm up for fun, and maybe even romance. But I'm not to be toyed with. And the best way to do that is to play his game, and beat him at it.

Outside, on the balcony, I stretch and absorb the panoramic view of the lake with its snow-covered, alpine mountains bowing down to meet the tropical lakeside, two so seemingly different climates meeting and mingling and creating beauty. It's more majestic than I could possibly imagine. I have to strangle a wistful thought that I wish Tony could see this with me.

Directly below, a voice calls out to me. Gianni greeting me a good morning as he waves up to me and beckons me to join him. Downstairs, the staff is back on duty, and even though I'm not particularly hungry, the savory smells wafting from the kitchen tempt me.

We have a wonderful breakfast on the patio, and as the day warms up, we go for a ride on the lake in his boat. Later, as we come back in, we take a dip just outside his villa. I can't help but watch and admire him as he skims through the water, his lean body cutting efficiently through the gentle waves, the gleaming sunshine and wetness accentuating his physique. Even if he was a pauper, this guy would have women fawning for him.

I have to admit, I'm deeply attracted to him. I thought he was handsome immediately, and I took to his personality quickly. Last night was a pure physical reaction to the things he was doing to me. But now, today, I want him. There's no doubt about it. I'm still, unfortunately, in love with Tony, but I desire Gianni.

I honestly don't want to leave, but it is Sunday, and there's still too much work to wade through for me to relax enough to take a day off from it. So as the sun moves west in the sky, I tell him we should probably head back to Milan soon.

Hip deep in the lake, he wades next to me, wraps his arms around my waist and asks, "So soon? We haven't even had lunch yet."

"We haven't done a lot of things yet," I tell him.

With that, he leans in and kisses me. Strong, sure, and oh so succulent. As well as he worked my body last night, he's even better today, sucking and nipping and all-out making out with me in the surreal lake. I reel with it it's so good. Then the thought occurs to me of who I'm kissing. Gianni Loren. Ladies' man, man's man, man of the world and king of an empire. And I'm kissing him! He's kissing me! And it's fantastic!

Just as I'm dizzy with it, he pulls back, asking, "Shall we go inside?"

Much as I want him, I remember last night. So I tell him. "I want you so bad, Gianni."

He smiles and sighs.

"Last night, though, that was cruel what you did."

He smiles again, and I can see that he's smug. It's that fatuous self-love, a certain and yet breezy air of entitlement that prods me along. Telling him, "I understand what you're saying about us, and what you meant, about us taking our time. And I agree. But last night, if you're serious about having a romance with me and not just fucking me or fucking with me, that was a mean game."

"Lisa," he says. "It wasn't my intention to..."

"No," I shake my head. Still holding onto his shoulders, I lean back slightly and look him in the eye. "I didn't like it. You treated me like a toy. An object that you can control. It makes me wonder if you really want me, or if you're just collecting a new prize. I can't have a romance with someone if I don't think he wants me. Understand?"

"Lisa. I want you."

I back away. "How do I really know that?" "

"Come here," he says, pulling me tight against him. "Can't you feel that? Does that feel like I don't want you?"

I can feel him, bulging against his swim trunks, even beneath the water.

"Mmm," I nod, eyeing him warily. This would be so much easier to pull off if I didn't want him so badly. "Let's go upstairs," I tell him.

We pull towels around ourselves and then go in. Inside the villa, we wind our way up the staircase. Holding my hand, he leads the way, and instead of going to my bedroom, he leads me into what I assume is his, the master bedroom. It's even bigger than the one I was in, and just as luxuriously appointed. But before I can even get an eyeful, Gianni closes the door behind us and again takes me in his arms, kissing me demandingly.

"No, Gianni," I say. "Slow down." I move toward the bed and motion for him to sit. Taking a seat on his lap, I give him a deep kiss. Pulling back, I ask, "Do you want me?"

"Are you joking?"

"I mean it," I say. "Are you just horny? Or do you want me?"

"Lisa," he sighs, running his hands along my back, trying to soothe me. "I want you."

"I'm not a toy, Gianni."

"I know," he says, finally, the cockiness draining.

I stare at him, and he doesn't flinch. In these lights, his green eyes seem nearly translucent. I believe him. Almost.

"You aren't a toy," Gianni says again.

"I understand. Last night, I gave in to you. I trusted you. Do you know how difficult that is for me? You understand, don't you, about how Tony doesn't really want me? I know you think that sometimes Angelina doesn't really want you. You think she likes the idea of you. Last night, you told me we could do business and mix in pleasure. Now, I just want to make sure it's really me you want the pleasure with. Last night, I waited for you. Now, will you wait for me?"

He doesn't speak. He doesn't nod, he doesn't even blink.

I stand up. Screwing up my courage, I unfold the towel, neatly tucked under my arms, and hold it open, letting him look at me. It's not easy, because I know he's used to the perfect physique of his exotic lover, and I know I don't match those expectations. But his eyes move from my face to my body, slowly moving up and down, and though he doesn't say anything, I'm pretty sure he likes what he sees. I don't have the willowy, model's body that Angelina has. But maybe that's part of what he likes about me. If he meant what he said about me being beautiful, then he ought to enjoy this. I lower my arms, and drop the towel at my feet. Instead of moving back to him, I turn around, bending over at the waist to retrieve the towel, giving him a full view of my bottom.

I almost can't believe I'm doing this. Well, not undressing in front of him.

But what I'm going to do. I'm not shy, but I'm not a tease either. Usually. But last night, he teased me. If he was playing me, he'll learn a lesson. And if he wasn't playing me, this will definitely get him coming back for more.

Looking over my shoulder, I can see that Gianni's enraptured by my ass. It's even plumper than usual, those months working late instead of going to the gym still showing, but he doesn't seem to mind. I toss the towel even further aside and go back over and straddle his lap, settling myself on his knees. Brushing my cheek against his, I whisper to him. "Take off my top, Gianni."

Gianni gulps. He places his hands on my stomach, sliding under the damp material of my suit. I'm watching him as he brings his hands up to my front, cupping my tits.

"Take it off," I tell him.

Breath coming shallow, he slides his hands higher, pulling the material, freeing me as he pulls it over my head, up along my arms. He tosses it on the floor. As soon as it's gone, he goes back to cradling my tits in the palms of his hands. Pulse racing, my nipples hardening under his touch, he leans in to kiss my neck.

I evade his kiss and rise up off his lap. Standing in front of him, I allow him to take a long look at my body. I can tell he likes what he sees, and that gives me the courage to go on. His face is flushed, his hands on me had been strong but gentle. I bite my lip to keep my resolve.

I ask him again, "Will you wait to have me? The way I waited for you?"

He swallows again, nodding. "If that's what you desire, I will wait."

I crawl onto the bed next to him, then further up, settling my back against a stack of pillows.

"Gianni," I say. "Get up. Take your clothes off."

I watch as he hurriedly drops the towel and strips off his suit. His skin is smooth and golden, his legs are lean and strong. His upper arms and chest are just as defined and cut as his sinewy forearms. His stomach is tight and flat, the skin getting paler in his midsection where it's not exposed to the sunshine. His erection is standing at attention. When he's finished, he moves to climb on the bed on top of me.

"No," I say. "Stay there."

Looking at him, I want him to touch me. I want his hands all over me, and his body pressed close to mine. I want to kiss him, I want to lick him, I want to run my hands along his muscles and feel them, all of them.

Looking at him, letting my eyes roam where my hands want to go, I reach up and touch myself, imagining it's his hands running all over my body. First my neck, then my stomach, then I smooth my hands across my breasts, stopping to massage my nipples, pretending it's his mouth on them. Looking to his face, I see his eyes glued on my every movement, the rhythm of his breathing increasing, a hot flush coming to his face.

Taking a deep breath, scared and shy, but knowing it'll really set him off, I close my eyes and dip a hand under my suit bottom. I part myself with a few fingers and find the hot nub where my tension is centered, where it's been nagging me since last night. Already slick, I expertly work my clit, opening my eyes to check his reaction.

When I look up at him, he takes hold of himself and makes a move toward me.

Breathy, low, I just say, "No. Stay there. If you touch me," I warn him, "I'll stop."

He obeys. Stunned, seemingly riveted by my body, he stares at the deliberate movements of my hand beneath my suit.

I turn my head and bury my face in the pillow, hiding my shame. I meant to turn him on, figured I'd put on a show. But in the process, watching him undress, seeing his body and how it responded, I got genuinely excited. I don't know if I can follow through if this is real, but I'm throbbing beneath my hand and don't know if I can stop either.

Looking at him, it seems like Gianni's throbbing too. My suspicions are confirmed as he touches himself. Rubbing. He licks his palm and takes hold of himself again, slowly pulling on his cock.

I watch out of the corner of my eye, see the speed of his hand increase. "If you don't stop," I warn him, "I will." I pull my hand away from my slit and hook my thumbs around the edges of my suit, pull it down over my hips, rising to slide it over my butt, then sit up to kick it down my legs.

I toss it aside and lean back, one hand going to my breast, massaging, the other back between my legs. Above me, Gianni keeps stoking himself. "I mean it," I warn him. "Stop it."

Raspy, "Lisa," he says, pleading. "Please…"

"You can hold yourself," I cut him off. "But nothing else. If you try to touch me, this is over. If you try to get yourself off, this is over. Just watch."

As I start working my hand again, he moves, closer to the bed. I glare at him and reluctantly stop what I'm doing. He halts, gripping himself tightly, his cock clearly pulsing in agony.

I hold his gaze and go back to work on myself again. I meant to prolong it, to tease him with slow touches, to put on a show. But now I can't fake it, because it's real. Last night was enough waiting for me. My cunt is aching for release, and watching his frustration only makes mine increase. I go to work, gliding my fingers over my hot spot, each stroke demanding another. Pressing harder, rubbing more quickly, I begin to undulate my hips, grinding against my own movements.

Gianni seems ready burst, strung tight as a piano wire. Clutching himself, the veins in his neck standing out, muscles in his arm and neck cording with tension. I look to his erection, his fist curled around the shaft, so freaking tempting. I give up massaging my breasts and use that hand on myself too. Reaching down, sliding a few fingers inside, I buck as I close my eyes and imagine it's Gianni entering me.

Suddenly, I'm going at myself with both hands, working furiously. My hips grinding, a few fingers inside, my other hand slick and sliding, pleasing myself. Peeking out, needing another eyeful of him to fuel my desire, I see that he dares to pump himself. He's watching my body, not my face, so he's not aware that I'm watching, monitoring him. He goes lightly at first, but the more I buck, the faster my hands work, the more he picks up the pace.

Edgy, watching Gianni jerking himself with growing fervor, I moan and he looks to my face. I close my eyes, drive my fingers deeper, press and rub, and let out a long, low moan as I start to come. It's a hard one, rushing through my veins, shaking my body, my one hand still working away, dragging it out. Even with him watching, I don't stop. I coax the aftershocks, shivering, writhing with them. When I've had enough, I lay panting, exhausted. But opening my eyes, I see Gianni above me, starting to really go at himself. I force myself to sit up. Pushing the hair off my face, I say one word: "Stop."

Gianni grits his teeth and grunts. His hand slows, but doesn't relent.

"Gianni," I say. "If you don't stop touching yourself, you'll *never* touch me."

"Lisa," he groans, holding his cock tightly. "Please."

When I don't answer him, he glides his hand again. It must be killing him to stop at this point. He asks, "May I come on your breasts?"

"No," I tell him. "You can't come at all. You didn't let me come last night. Now you said you'd wait."

"Lisa," he groans it again.

I don't answer him. It must be sheer willpower on his part, because Gianni inhales sharply, lets it out slowly, and releases himself.

"Did you like what you just saw?" I ask him.

He swipes a hand across his brow and gives a terse nod, teeth still grinding together.

"Gianni," I say and wait for him to look me in the face. When he does, I tell him, "If you did hire me just to fuck me, I'm worth much more than a couple million bucks."

He nods.

"Now get dressed," I tell him. "We have to go back to Milan."

Naked, I sit on the bed and watch him as he pulls on a pair of boxers. I can tell he's furious with me. I can tell he's embarrassed. But mostly, he's frustrated. Silently, he pulls on slacks, and when I'm satisfied that he's suffered enough, I pick up my towel and suit and go back to my own room where I get dressed.

I assume that as I wander down the hall, he'll pull down his pants and finish himself off. Probably cursing at me as he does. But once I'm dressed and packed, I find him waiting in the foyer for me, still tight jawed, and I realize that maybe he did obey my wishes.

He's quiet on the drive, and just as I think I've blown it by pushing him too far with my stupid pride, he clears his throat, and then softly says, "I did not hire you to sleep with you. I don't know how to make that clear."

Smiling, watching the city of Milan rise in front of us, I say, "I believe you."

"Last night," he says. "It wasn't my intention to toy with you. I thought...I thought you were enjoying it."

It's embarrassing to admit it, but I do anyhow. "I was enjoying it."

"I just didn't want to go too quickly. I didn't realize..."

"How frustrating it was?"

"Yes," he says. He looks at me, and it's smoldering. "I thought it would heighten your desire."

"Gianni. It did." I lick my lips. "Did it for you? Today?"

"I'm not used to not having everything I want exactly when I want it," he says.

"I'm not a thing," I say.

"I know," he says. "You called my bluff about the romance, and I'm glad."

"You mean, you aren't interested in romancing me now?"

"No," he laughs. "I will romance you. But now I see also that you will be good at romancing me. For us, it goes both ways, Lisa." He takes hold of my hand and says, "The waiting, the not rushing, it's a little painful. But it is good."

Mutual Holdings

As the limo pulls up in front of the hotel, I say, "Why don't you walk me up to the room, Gianni. I think we've waited long enough."

He doesn't have to answer. The spark in his eyes says it all.

CHAPTER TWENTY-ONE

As we near the hotel, I can see the throng of photographers outside the building. As the limo draws closer, they press together and surround it.

"I apologize deeply," he says to me.

"What is going on?" I ask.

Sighing, he says, "I assume the picture they snapped yesterday has been released."

"So?"

Looking at me as though I'm stupid, he says, "So you are a new curiosity for them. They are all trying to get pictures of you now."

"You're joking, right?"

"Lisa, I'm not joking."

"But I'm just an accountant!" I yell.

"If you like, we can keep going and try to exit somewhere else."

"Will that work?" I ask him.

"I don't know," he says. "They have a way of finding me. They know my stops. We can just quickly push through them if you like. The doorman is here to help. They can't come inside the hotel."

"Go," I say.

"Yes?"

"Yes, just, go!"

And with that, he leans across me and unlatches the door. It swings out and one man has his body pushed in front of the photographers, and he holds out a hand for me. I take it, but even before I exit, the bright flashes start popping in my face. Strangers are jostling me, and as I blink and try to focus, they're shouting at me, asking my name. Asking me how I know Gianni. Asking me who I am.

"I'm just an accountant!" I say loudly, feeling them crush and surround me.

"Who are you?" another one asks, getting in my face.

"I'm an accountant," I say.

I swear I can detect a subtle riff, a diffusion of energy as the noise level drops, and I hear it being passed along, "She's an accountant." "Oh, it's just business."

But just as they're quieting, a random voice says loudly, "She left with him yesterday! They went to his villa on Lake Como!"

And with that, the snapping of pictures ensues as the crowd strangles around me again.

Suddenly, there's an arm around my waist, and Gianni is leaning close to me, pushing me forward, quickly moving through the crowd, and they actually part for him. In front of us, the doorman struggles to pry open the doors against their hovering bodies, but he gets it wide enough just as Gianni's whisking me to it, and then, quickly, through it. Once I'm inside, he pops his head back out through the doors and confirms what I'd been trying to tell them. He simply says, "She's my accountant. Mancuso, Mancuso & Russo of New York."

I can't help but smirk at that. Tony would probably kiss him on the mouth for that free publicity.

Gianni's speaking to the doorman, and as I turn around to enter the lobby, Mark is hovering right in front of me. "You little minx," he purrs in my ear.

"What?" I ask. "How? What are you doing here?" I ask him.

"I've been waiting for you all afternoon," he says. "I wanted to hear how it went with Mr. Fabulous."

"How did you know I was with him, Mark?"

"Oh, Lisa," he says. "The whole city knows."

"What?"

He hands me a newspaper, folded over to the society page, and there, under the headline *Mystery Woman* is a picture of me from yesterday as I was climbing into the limo with Gianni.

"The whole country knows," he says.

"Oh crap."

"God, Lisa! I think the whole world knows! This picture is everywhere!"

"Do, do you think Tony's seen it?"

"Honey, if he gets a newspaper, he's seen this."

From over my shoulder, Gianni says, "Oh my," as he looks at the paper. "Angelina."

"She's here," Mark says to him in a low, confiding tone.

Gianni seems distressed. "She's here? Now!"

Mark nods and tilts his head toward the terrace bar off to the side of the lobby.

"Oh Madonna," Gianni sighs.

"So what'd you do all night?" Mark asks directly in my ear. "Did you let him go over your figures?"

"Oh my God," I sigh.

"Oh my God!" Mark says and his head swivels and he watches a young man walk across the lobby toward the bar. "Who is THAT?" he asks.

Focusing on the guy, dressed in a sharp burgundy shirt, I can't believe what I'm seeing. "OH MY GOD!" I shout it. The boy turns his head, and I'm now positive. His eyes light up as he sees me, and he turns and comes toward me.

He gives me a warm hug, and I introduce him to Gianni and then Mark, saying, "This is my cousin, Ricky."

"Hello," Gianni nods.

"Hel-*lo*," Mark says, holding Rick's eye, and his hand, for quite a long time. Rick, he doesn't seem to mind.

To me now, Rick says, "Come to the bar, I have a surprise for you."

"This should be fun," I say, hesitantly.

Looking at Gianni now, he goes, "You're Gianni Loren? Your girlfriend is in there waiting for you."

"This should be a nightmare," Gianni says.

"This is too much," Mark says.

"Yeah," I agree. "That's exactly what I meant."

Placing his hand on my shoulder, Gianni looks at me and whispers in my ear, "Lisa. I leave this up to you how I handle Angelina. Were we on business? Or pleasure?"

I feel like I'm being suffocated. Panicked, worried as much for him as I am for myself, I say, "I'm just an accountant!"

"Oh-kay," he says and straightens up. Then, "No problem. But I'm going to need some expensive diamond jewelry. Fast."

CHAPTER TWENTY-TWO

Rick and Mark flank me as we enter the bar, my heart in my throat, worried that Angelina is going to attack me. I reassure myself that if she accuses me of fucking her boyfriend, I can deny it on technicalities.

But instead of a vicious assault, I'm greeted with warm, enthusiastic hugs. "Lisa!" they all shout, leaping from their seats and surrounding me.

"Lucy!" I hug her so tightly and am so shocked and pleased I nearly cry. She looks wonderful in a clingy aqua top with her milk-chocolate brown hair sleek in a ponytail. Then my other cousin is in front of me. "Marina!" I shout, disbelieving.

She doesn't release her wineglass, but throws one arm around my neck as she kisses my cheek, her dark, wavy hair loose and flowing down her naked, already tan shoulders. "Look at you," she says. "The talk of the town waltzing in here. Where's this man of yours?"

Gianni stepped off to make an emergency pickup at the hotel's jewelry shop, but I tell her, "It's just business. He's a client."

"So you're charging now?" Marina teases. "What? Tony couldn't afford it so you're hooking over here?"

"Leave her alone, Marina," Eva says, easing up behind her to greet me with a kiss, her blue eyes shifting from Marina to me and curling up as she smiles.

"I'm just teasing her," Marina says and takes a long gulp of wine. "Take a Midol, Eva."

Eva swivels her attention back on Marina. Confronting, "You haven't seen her in three years and you start off by calling her a hooker?"

"I'm so happy to see you both," I tell them, as I notice Lucy take a small step back, her eyes darting between the two of them.

"I can tease her and call her a hooker because we all know, and she knows, that she's the straightest woman here!" Marina insists as she casually flips a lock of her hair over her shoulder. Her impossibly dark eyes flitting briefly to Lucy as she says, "Except her."

"What's that supposed to mean?" Eva snaps, leaning closer to her. "She's the straightest one here. Are you implying something?" As usual, Eva's dressed in black, but it's a slinky, silky slip dress she's got on. Nevertheless, she still looks intimidating enough that I'd back down. But Marina doesn't.

"I didn't realize it needed to be implied," Marina shoots back, straightening her shoulders.

"Girls," Lucy says. "Please..."

"No," Eva says, "I want to know what she means by that!"

But before Marina can answer, it happens. Their outburst caught Angelina's attention, and she bolts over, furiously pointing her finger in my face. Simply accusing, "*Puttana de merde*!"

Literal translation: Fucking whore.

Result: Both Marina and Eva swivel to her, the friction they were generating between each other suddenly snaps on her. Eva squinting her kohl-lined eyes and going, "Excuse me!"

Marina moving in front of me, saying to Angelina, "Who the fuck are you?"

Luckily, before the smolder can spark, Gianni arrives, taking hold of Angelina by the waist and saying, "Darling. You recall meeting Ms. Russo in New York?"

She stares at me, breathing hard. He prods again, saying, "She is my newest accountant?"

Again, Angelina just breathes. Fumes.

Gianni, he holds out a box in front of her. Smooth, he says, "This weekend, after looking over some of my accounts, she assured me I could afford to buy you this."

Angelina's eyes flicker to the box, and then back up to me. Back down to the box. Gianni flips it open. Still gazing into the box, Angelina says in Italian, "Welcome to Italy, Ms. Russo. I hope the paparazzi don't interfere with your time too much." Then, looking at Gianni, she simply says, "Andiamo," and turns crisply and heads out, Gianni close on her heels.

Watching the scene, Eva is just speechless. But Marina cracks, "Well. I guess it's settled. She's definitely the biggest hooker here."

"What was that?" Eva asks.

"That," I say. "Is Gianni Loren and his girlfriend."

"Does he always buy her complicity so obviously?" Lucy asks.

"Yeah," I admit. "I think so. Every time we've met she's picked up some diamonds from him."

"I know who she is," Lucy says. "She's a model. I've seen a La Perla ad of hers back home. She's always so haughty and money-hungry?"

I say, "Keeping her calm requires more ice than Joe's crab shack on all-you-can-eat oyster night."

Eva smirks. "You mean if he wants access to her la pearl-a, he has to bring diamonds?"

"So," Marina quips, "you're saying that he has to bring ice if he plans on shucking?"

Mark, he cracks up. Saying, "You ladies are fantastic. Who are you?"

"I'm so sorry!" I say, remembering my manners as I introduce Mark. "This is my colleague," I tell them.

"Technically," he says, "I'm her employee."

"He's also my friend," I tell them, so that they know he's cool, and because

I'm proud of having made friends with him. "This is my cousin Lucy. She lives in Las Vegas where she's a hotshot chef. And this is Marina. She lives in Vegas, too. And she's a ..."

"Writer," Marina says as she shakes Mark's hand.

"And this," I tell him, "is my other cousin, Eva."

Squinting, Mark says, "You look so familiar. Have we met?"

"I don't think so," Eva says.

"And this is Rick. You've already met, but he's Eva's brother."

Lucy takes charge, leading us to a table where we can all take a seat. Asking, "Do they serve food in here?"

"Yes," I answer. "Want something?"

"Maybe. Soon," she says. "It was a long flight."

"You're not kidding it was long," Marina says. "I need something to drink." She drains her wineglass and flags down a waiter. Asking us, "Grappa, everyone?" before placing the order.

"What are you guys doing here?" I finally ask.

Eva points at Rick. Says, "His graduation present."

"Right! Congratulations, Rick!"

"*Grazie*," he says. "Your gift was very generous, Lisa." As Mark also congratulates him, Rick smiles at him longer than necessary.

"What about you guys?" I ask Lucy and Marina.

Lucy shrugs, saying, "Danny's been busy at work."

"Shooting the movie already?" I ask. When she nods, I tell Mark, "Her boyfriend is an actor, and he's filming his first big movie. In fact, believe it or not, Marina wrote it."

"Get out of here," Mark says.

"I wrote the book," Marina explains. "Not the screenplay." As the waiter brings the drinks, she reaches up on his tray and helps herself, taking a nice gulp of hers as she says, "Which is why they won't even let me on the set."

"Oh get over it," Eva says. "They won't let you on the set because it's being filmed in a casino you've been banned from."

"She's allowed on the set!" Marina says, pointing to Lucy. "She won't take me!"

"I won't go!" Lucy says. "Thanks to you my boyfriend is spending days on end half-naked in an elevator simulating sex with his co-star! I don't want to see that!"

"I can't believe you lived that," Eva says to Marina.

"It's fiction," Marina insists.

"Oh really?" I ask. "How is Miguel?"

Marina sighs. "Good. He's really good. He thanks you for all the Mets stuff you sent."

"So why are you here?" I ask her again.

Arching a brow, she says, "The movie option I got? It wasn't that much. I figured I'd come over here and check out some European casinos."

Eva says to Mark, "Because she's been banned from most casinos in the States."

Lucy goes, "If you'd held out for a movie deal from Tarantino you'd have made out better."

"I know," Marina says, gazing at her empty glass and tossing a thick lock of her dark brown hair over her bare shoulder. Eva pushes her full glass in front of Marina and calls over the waiter and orders a full bottle.

"I still don't get it," I say. "How, how did you guys know I was here?"

All eyes fall on Eva, so I look to her too. She simply says, "I talked to someone and they mentioned you were here. Said you might be a little homesick."

"Oh Madone," I sigh. "Did my mom call you?"

"Lisa, no," she smiles. "I saw Tony. He told me."

"What?"

"I had some tax stuff that I needed looked at so I dropped by your office. He told me what was going on." Adding, "But I don't think he knew about all this other stuff."

"Oooh, yeah!" Marina says. "Tell us all about Gianni Loren!"

"Honestly," I tell them. "There's nothing to tell. We were just on business this weekend."

"Liar," Marina says. "I can smell the sex on you from here."

"You can not possibly smell it from there!" I gasp.

"No, I can't," she says. "But now I know it's there!"

"I knew it!" Mark says.

"But I thought you were still in love Tony?" Lucy asks.

"I am," I say. "Sort of. He's not in love with me, Lucy. I came here to get over him."

"And the best way to get over one man is to get under another!" Marina says. Both Mark and Rick toast her on that one, but Eva sits quietly.

I ask Eva, "Tony told you I seemed homesick?"

"Yeah." Reaching in her bag, she pulls out a small package and hands it to me. Saying, "He asked me to give you this."

Opening it, I find my favorite skirt, the one my cousins sitting here now gave to me over five years ago. I get a little choked up thinking about how he must have found it in the hotel room and then bothered to save it for me. "Oh shit," I say. "Maybe he does love me."

Eva just stares at me.

Lucy says, "Of course he loves you, Lisa. Everything he does for you?"

"That's what I told her!" Mark says.

"Then what am I doing here screwing around with Gianni Loren?" I ask. "What have I done?"

"I told you that you needed to tell him how you feel," Eva says.

"I did!" I tell her.

"You did?"

"Yes!"

"Well. What'd he say?"

"He didn't say anything," I tell her. "I told him that I'm still in love with him, and he basically pushed me on a plane to Italy."

"Oh," Marina says.

"Ew," Lucy says.

"Uh," Eva says.

"That's, that's not right? Is it?" I ask them.

Eva scratches her neck. Saying, "I think, maybe, that Tony's just not quite ready yet to settle down. So you freak him out."

"Is that how your guys were?" I ask them. "Miguel, Vincent, Danny? Did they evade you once you told them you were in love with them?"

None of them answer me. It's not just Marina who takes a long pull on her drink, all of them sip and avoid my eyes, letting me know that I'm alone with this experience.

Finally, Eva says, "But it just doesn't make sense. So Tony's a hard-headed commitment-phobe. But look at the life he has. He's a construction worker, Lisa. And he became an accountant and built that firm. I think he did it for you."

"Either that or he just wanted to get rich with my help," I tell them.

"He is a greedy thing," Marina says. "But still..."

"Sometimes," Lucy says, smoothing out her already sleek ponytail. "You have to take a leap of faith based on just a kiss and a promise."

"Yeah," I nod. "But Tony's promise to me is over ten years old. And he doesn't even kiss me anymore."

"Wait a minute," Lucy says, wide-eyed. "He doesn't kiss you?"

"No," I say. "He kissed me twice in the past year. And once was only because Gianni Loren was watching us."

"I don't know what to say to that," Eva says.

Marina says, "The first time Miguel fucked me, it was with some guy who made him jealous watching us."

Lucy just glares at her.

"And another thing," I tell them, trying to convince myself. "The last time we had sex? He really went at it...hard! It wasn't very loving."

"Oh well," Marina says. "Last week, Miguel fucked me so hard that I've still got a bruise on my back from it."

Eva spits her drink with that as Mark and Rick crack up laughing.

"I'm just saying," Marina says. "Some good hard fucking isn't a bad thing."

Bitterly, glaring at Marina, Lucy says, "Unless it's your boyfriend in an elevator with an Academy award winning actress!"

"Okay," Eva says. "Really, you need to get over that, Lucy. It's not her fault."

"She wrote it!"

"Not in the screenplay!" Marina insists.

Waving over the waiter, Lucy asks in Italian, "Can I get a menu? We're going to need some food here. Quickly. Just bring some appetizers."

Rick speaks up then. "Tony's just scared, Lisa. Domesticity is frightening. I think he'll come around."

"Yeah." I nod. "Or he's just getting jealous now because he doesn't have me in the palm of his hand."

"Speaking of palm of your hand," Marina says and leans forward. "You have to tell us. Is all of Gianni Loren's money just making up for his, um, personal shortcomings?"

Everyone, and I mean everyone, including Mark and Rick, leans in as she asks that. Though I'd like to entertain them, I have to admit, "There is nothing short about Gianni Loren. Nothing on his person, and especially not his *comings*. Okay?"

Slowly, with a mixture of whistles and catcalls, everyone leans back in their seat as the waiter delivers some food. As silence falls, Lucy digs in, still obviously mulling the shortcomings comment as she picks up a sausage stuffed pepper and gustily pops it whole in her mouth. Marina, of course, reaches for the bottle of grappa and refills her glass.

Eva just stares at me, her blue eyes piercing until I say, "But just to be clear, we've only fooled around. We've fooled around a lot. But we haven't...you know."

"Mm," Marina says. "So you've frozen his assets, huh?"

"Something like that." I grin at her.

Eva keeps looking at me though, and I finally say, "Besides. Tony's fucking someone else."

Lucy stops chewing and exchanges glances with Rick. Eva shifts in her seat. I say, "What? I'm supposed to sit by in chastity while he screws anyone he wants?"

Marina, she goes, "Once, Miguel fucked a cheap blonde hooker. I caught him. I took him back though."

"And thank you for that, too!" Lucy hisses. "Do you know who's playing that hooker in the movie? It's that girl, you know the one, that one who broke up what's his name's marriage!"

"Relax," Eva says. "I thought she was screwing what's his name now."

"She was," Lucy nearly shouts. "But she's not now! Now she's single again!"

"Oh shit," Mark says. "And she's going to be filming a sex scene with your boyfriend?"

Lucy picks up another pepper and stuffs it in her mouth.

"Lucy," Eva says. "Danny loves you. It'll be alright. Just be extra nice and loving to him when you get home."

"Pfft," Marina says. "Be nice. This coming from the girl whose jaw unhinges."

I'm worried it's going to start another go-round. They always did have a volatile spark between them. But Eva just shakes her head and says, "You always were funny, you bitch."

Marina winks at her as she raises her glass, saying, "*Ti amo*, Eva." Meaning, I love you.

"I love all you guys," I tell them. "I can't believe you stopped here to see me."

With that, the loves fly around the table until Mark says, "I'd like to get to love you all!"

And Rick, the baby, the quiet, normally reserved Rick says to him, "Play your cards right and you'll have the chance to love me really soon."

This time, Marina spits her drink.

"Well, for what it's worth," Eva says, "I think Tony's going to come around, too."

Feeling bullied, I get a bit rankled. "Yeah, well, it's exhausting waiting for him to come around and love me. I feel like I'm never getting anywhere and it's stupid to keep trying. I feel like Sisyphus."

"Oooh," Marina says. "You better see a doctor, get that taken care of. They've got a shot, it'll clear it up like that!" She snaps her fingers.

Lucy, exasperated, says, "You illiterate ass. She said Sisyphus, not syphilis."

"I knew what she said," Marina says. "I was making a joke. Lightening the mood."

"It was a good one," Eva nods with approval.

"Damn right," Marina says. "Call me illiterate. Don't push me, Lucy. I didn't write the screenplay but I can call them up and suggest new scenes."

"Oh shit," Lucy says, reaching for another pepper.

"The poor girl is lovesick," Marina says, looking at me. "We've all been there. We know how it sucks. We have to stay upbeat here."

"Thank you," I tell her.

She goes, "Of course, none of us got to wallow in our misery with a gorgeous billionaire." She, Lucy, and Eva all toast and drink to that.

Leaning back, Eva looks at me and says, "Alright, enough with your pathetic and yet incredibly fascinating love life, Lisa. I have something very important to address with you."

"Oh!" I say. "You had some tax problems. You need my help?"

"No," she says, shaking her head. "It's not that. Tony handled it for me."

"Tony did it for you?" I ask, disbelieving.

"Yeah. Why? Is he a moron? Should I be worried it's wrong?"

"No," I say. "I just... Nothing. What'd you want?"

Looking around the table, she says, "We've been in Milan for less than four hours, and look at us. We've already gone shopping."

I can tell it's true. They all look stunning. So stunning, they could actually put Angelina to shame. Eva's wearing a sexy black slip dress with high heeled sandals. Rick's got an incredible burgundy button-down shirt on with tailored black pants. Lucy's wearing a silky, fitted skirt in vibrant, summery water hues to match the clingy aqua shirt. And Marina has on a sexy halter in shimmering silver. They look ready for a nightclub in Milan.

Eva goes, "You've been here two weeks now. What in the fuck are you wearing, girl?"

I smooth my hand across the plain brown pants of one of my standard suits as I look at my white cotton button-down shirt. I go, "I'm an accountant!"

Mutual Holdings

CHAPTER TWENTY-THREE

On Wednesday, deep in the afternoon, I get a disturbing phone call. It's Tony calling from New York. "Saw you in the paper, babe," he says. "Seems like you're enjoying ...the country. And they seem to be enjoying you. Mystery woman."

I sigh. "I'm just an accountant," I say.

There's a long pause. Then he says, "I miss...working with you. We haven't worked apart for this long in over five years."

"Uh huh." Wishing, praying he'd just say the words. He misses working with me. But I want him to miss *me*. It's close, but it's not quite the same thing, colleagues and lovers. Is he really so commitment-phobic he can't even say he misses me? Or is he giving me all he can to try to appease me?

"I'm very busy," I say.

"You can relax a bit," he says. "You're on retainer, remember?"

With that, I hang up on him.

Mark peers across his desk at me, giving me a sympathetic look. But when I glare at him, he tucks his head back down and shuffles some ledger papers.

Over lunch, he treated me to the oh-so-romantic details about his previous evening with my cousin Rick.

I sit there, festering for nearly an hour when I get a phone call from Gianni, asking me to come up to the office. Although I glare at Mark as I stand to leave, he doesn't back down. Instead, he grins smugly.

Gianni's office encompasses nearly half of the top floor of the building.

Once off the elevator, there's his secretary, and then to the left is a large boardroom, and to the right is his expansive office. His secretary waves me to go inside immediately.

Inside, I find him pacing the room, his hands stuffed into the pockets of his light grey suit, looking dapper in a soft yellow shirt with a bold orange tie.

"Gianni, what's wrong?"

Halting, holding his hands out, he says, "I don't think I can take it much more!" The desperate edge in his voice is unmistakable. I've never seen him so uncollected.

"What?"

"She's driving me insane!"

"Oh," I say. "Angelina."

"Why do I love her?" he asks, but it's rhetorical, not directed at me, and I'm thankful for that.

"Is she still angry about last weekend?"

"No. But she won't sign the pre-nup. That's what she's disturbed about. She left town again. She booked a shoot in Africa. Can you believe that? Africa!" He spits the word as though it's absurd. "She's taken that actor with her. She says if I love her I'd give her everything! I say if she loves me she wouldn't want anything but me! Who's right, Lisa?"

I just look at him but don't dare answer. But he demands again, and I finally say, "I guess you're both right."

"I know!" He throws his hands up in the air in disgust. Saying, "I'd give her everything if I knew she didn't want it!"

I just nod as he turns and paces the other way. But suddenly, he stops and turns back to me. Asking, "You signed those papers. Last weekend. Did it offend you?"

"Me?" I ask, stalling. Then, I decide to be honest. "No, I wasn't offended. I was glad to show you I was interested in you, not a lawsuit. It felt...liberating."

"You see!" he shouts.

"But I'm not Angelina," I tell him. "You two have a history, Gianni."

"We have a history alright," he fumes. "We have a history of her extorting everything she can from me!"

It's not the same, but I have the history of Tony withholding everything he can from me, so I can sort of understand where he's coming from.

"*Porcoddio*," Gianni exclaims. I think it's the first time I've heard him swear, and it takes me by surprise. Looking heavenward, he implores the ceiling, "Africa! With the actor! You know who I mean? What's his name! The one who left his wife for that actress!"

"I thought he was dating that actress now," I say.

"She dumped him," he says. "He's dating Angelina! He's going to Africa with her!" He takes hold of my arms and looks me in the eye, and I can see he's hanging by a thread. "What do I do?" he asks.

Maybe it's hearing about Mark's casual and easy fling with Rick. Maybe it's my cousins' words still echoing in my ears. Maybe it's the frustrating call from Tony. Maybe it's unfinished business from last weekend.

Or maybe, just maybe, it's that even though he's slightly unhinged, or even because he's unhinged, he's superlatively sexy.

But I answer him by swooping in and kissing him, full on the mouth.

It's not consoling, and it's not sympathetic. Greedy and hungry, it's a deep, lustful kiss. And he kisses me back. It's as though all his agitated frenzy gets poured out into kissing me. Hands on me, groping me roughly, his tongue thrusting, his breathing already intense.

It makes me crazy.

It's consuming, all out making out with me, me lapping it up and giving it back. A part of me reacts to the shock of the newness, getting turned on. Another part, disbelieving, immensely aroused as I realize I'm kissing Gianni Loren. Gianni Loren is panting and tongue-fucking me! He dates models and actresses and I'm just supposed to be crunching numbers for him but he's devouring me and letting me lick, suck, nibble him. It's intoxicating.

He presses against me, and I can feel him against my hipbone. He's not just letting me lick, suck, and nibble, he's aroused by it. He's loving it!

We're like teenagers in heat with it. In the office, no less!

It's not true love, but it's close enough. It's true lust.

I slide one hand of mine lower, rub him roughly through his pants. He stops kissing me, looks me in the face, his lips puffy and pink. Says one word, demanding, sharp: "*Ora*!"

Meaning: Now!

"Yes," I answer him.

Almost crazily, he pulls me to his desk, carelessly shoving pens and a stapler and papers aside with one fluid swoosh of his arm. I hop onto it, spreading my legs around his body as he leans into me, urging me down, kissing me roughly. I lay back, head whirling, body already fevered and rushing. My blazer is open and he yanks at the fabric of my shirt, pulling it out of my skirt, pushing it up over my stomach, above my breasts. He looks down at me, gazing at my torso and the exaggerated rise and fall of my chest, a serious expression on his flushed face.

My bra goes next. With both hands he takes hold of the underneath and shoves that up, tangling it with my shirt just below my neck. Still he doesn't touch me, he just looks. His flawless green eyes, watching as I breathe, my nipples already hard and distended. Unexpected, he doesn't touch me. Instead, he quickly untucks his own shirt and raises it up, exposing his taut stomach, his muscled chest. Holding it up, he crushes down on top of me, skin on skin, sliding himself against me, chest to chest as he claims my mouth again.

His intercom buzzes. His secretary saying, "Mr. Loren? Mr. Spillway is here for you."

He pulls himself off my mouth, says one word. "No."

"He says it's important, Mr. Loren."

Panting against my cheek, fanning my hair out across the desk with his heated breath, he waits a second. Sharply, "I said no!"

"Yes sir, Mr. Loren," she says. "I'll tell him you'll contact him later."

"Do not disturb me," he says.

That's when it hits me again. One of the most powerful men in the world is leaning over me, panting for me. Telling others to wait because of me. God help me, it turns me on.

Then, he's back on my mouth, his tongue thrusting, then waiting for me to respond. That, and the feel of his smooth skin against me gets me even hotter. Antsy, angsty tension collecting between my legs. I reach for him again, grabbing at him through his pants. He lurches with it, gasps into my mouth.

"*Protezione*," he sighs. I nod as he reluctantly climbs off me, moves to the other side of the desk and fumbles for a minute in a drawer until he finds a condom. I use the opportunity to sit up and tug off my underwear, quickly sliding them down my legs and hiking up my skirt and taking my place back on his desk. Gianni Loren's desk. The desk he's going to fuck me on!

Oh, God.

He comes back to me, but instead of urging me to lay back, he hands me the condom packet as he fumbles with his belt. Telling me, "Quickly. Hurry," as he stares at my exposed tits, my bra and shirt still tangled absurdly, hurriedly around my neck.

I get it ripped open and take the condom out while he unzips. He's so hard that the head of his cock is peeking out the top of his shorts. I push them down, bunching them up as he springs free. He's as hard as he was when he was watching me masturbate for him, and judging from the feel between my legs, I'm already as wet. I take hold of him, and together, we slide the condom on him. As soon as it's unrolled, he places a hand on my shoulder and pushes and I lean back for him. He takes hold of himself, but instead of immediately thrusting in, he bows and kisses my breast. Hot, demanding, he goes to the nipple and sucks – hard.

It's an electric mainline, shooting silvery pulses of desire straight to my crotch.

Lifting up, breathless, he lines himself up but stops to look at me. I guess it's one last checkpoint for him, making sure he can proceed.

"I want you, Gianni," I tell him. "Now."

Swift, sure, and deep, he thrusts in, forcing the last of my breath out of me. He lingers a moment, but then stands up. Instead of easing out and sliding in again, he takes hold of my hips, pulling me to the edge of the desk. I lift my legs and he hooks his arms under my knees, getting leverage, spreading me wide.

And then, he starts fucking.

Deep, just barely controlled, pistoning deeply and swiftly into me as I clench around him. Hard enough to shake me, him watching my face, my body as we meet and meet again. His usually easy and playful expression is erased, his face drawn into concentrated lines of passion.

It's incredible, a powerful mix of pleasure and pride; pleasure that he's giving me, pride that he's so rapt and eager to be doing it. Gianni Loren, he's loving fucking me!

"Lisa," he growls my name, watching my face. "I want to see you come."

I just moan, trying to concentrate on the rhythm, trying to lose myself in the sensations so I can do that for him, so I can take the ultimate release for myself from him.

His face pulls to a snarl as he picks up the pace, thrusting now as though he's seemingly possessed. Maybe edgy already.

"Tell me," he says. "Show me. Show me how to make you come."

Once again, desire eclipsing embarrassment, I'm hot and he feels amazing, thrusting and filling me, sweet friction and motion. But I know it won't be enough, not if he's getting caught up and ready. Pushing aside any last vestiges of modesty, I reach down and show him what to do. Him thrusting into me, I slide my fingers across my engorged clit and press. Sliding, pressing as the speed of his hips increases, I don't even fool around. Him watching intently, I start rubbing furiously.

He releases one of my legs and pushes my hand away, interrupting the ecstatic feeling for only a moment before his fingers take my place. Thrusting with his hips, he matches the pace I'd shown him as he massages my clit, stroking it quickly, pressing with surety, his fingers easily sliding with the excess wetness.

Pumping into me, rubbing me out, he looks rapt and enslaved to the moment. At this angle, I'm fully exposed for him, my sex on full display, up and open, accepting and reveling in his demanding ministrations, able to watch himself slide in out as I juice and clench for him. But then he looks away from my throbbing pussy that he's expertly manipulating, gazes briefly at my tits, rocking and shaking with his demanding strokes. He lands on my face, staring me in the eye.

I can't take it. Somehow, rubbing myself for him and watching the mechanics as we fuck is bad enough, but having him look me in the face as I eagerly take unbridled pleasure in the debauchery is too much to bear. I close my eyes and turn my head even as the heat starts to sizzle.

"No!" he barks, but still doesn't break his movements, bringing me close. "Look at me, Lisa."

"I, I, I can't," I pant.

"I want to watch you," he says. "Look at me." He rubs even harder, pressing deeper and going quickly, utterly relentless, setting me right on the verge. "You're beautiful," he says, and I open my eyes, trusting him, giving him what he wants, truly exposing myself to him.

We lock eyes, and I come hard. Shaking, contracting around him, holding my breath, letting him watch my most vulnerable moments.

Just as I thought he couldn't, he somehow kicks into overdrive, fucking now almost like a reflex, and then with one bone-rattling thrust, still looking me in the face, he comes fiercely deep inside me. He lists forward, catches himself on his hands at my sides as he strokes a few more times, elongating his own pleasure as he starts to breathe again.

"*Bella*," he sighs. Finally, closing his eyes, he lowers himself completely on top of me and seals it with a soft, wet, lingering kiss.

Some quiet time passes as we bask in it. Then, in my ear, he says, "*Que bella sboratta.* " The literal translation meaning, "What a great ejaculation."

The Italians, for as much as they talk about enjoying the moment and it not being all about the finish, their vernacular is heavily slanted to phrases that celebrate the big finish.

But, I'm inclined to agree with what he just said.

"My God," he says as he slowly climbs off me, taking hold of himself. Italian intimacy, he cups a hand around my sex, too, kisses my tit again. "You made me come so hard, Lisa."

"Me too," I tell him as he staggers to his feet, gingerly pulling off the condom.

"But the fucking, too," he says as he disposes of the condom in the trash-can. "It was incredible, that fucking."

"I know," I say, amused by the dissipation of his foul mood and the return of his normal, enthusiastic manner.

"It was?" he asks. "You're sure? It was good for you?"

I barely have enough strength to laugh, but I do, lightly. I tell him, "You couldn't tell? It was great, Gianni."

Taking a seat on the desk next to me, he says, "It's really a good thing I'm paying you for accounting and not fucking."

"What?" I say, mildly shocked.

"Two million," he says. "You'd be grossly underpaid."

I laugh again. Tell him, "Oh yeah? Wait till you see my accounting."

CHAPTER TWENTY-FOUR

After dressing and arranging my hair, I exit Gianni's office on still shaky legs. To my dismay, Mr. Spillway is lingering out there. I resist the urge to fidget and smooth my clothes again, reminding myself that I'd properly zipped and tucked and double checked everything before exiting, even as he stares at me with blatant disdain.

He can't know anything, I remind myself, trying to stay composed.

"Finished with your meeting?" he asks. "I take it you were banging out some numbers?"

I glance over at Gianni's secretary, but she's demurely typing on her keyboard with an earpiece in.

Spillway again, saying, "I knew it. You'd still better watch yourself, young lady. It's not unusual for him to get confused and go off half-cocked in pursuit of women."

Pissed, but also loaded with guilt for knowing that what I just did was purely unprofessional, I can't help but lash out as the American Jersey girl in me bubbles out in self-defense. Saying, "Trust me, Gianni was fully cocked just now."

With that, I punch the elevator button.

Back downstairs, I'm barely in the office when Mark looks up at me. With one glance, his eyes go wide and he says, "You little minx!"

"How can you tell!" I demand, smoothing my clothes again.

"You have to tell me," he says. "Did you do it on his desk?"

I just smile.

Wistfully, he goes, "Oh shit. I can't wait to see Rick tonight."

That night, at dinner, with all my cousins gathered around, my co-worker Mark stands and toasts me. Saying, "She nailed down the account of the most flamboyant billionaire in the world. And now she's nailed him."

Lucy and Marina raise their glasses. Marina drains hers after clinking against mine. Across the table, Eva raises her glass. She nods. In Italian, she says, "May he give you happiness."

Marina, she goes, "Fuck that. She can get her own happiness. May he give her multiple orgasms!"

And Lucy, she goes, "Screw orgasms. She can have those on her own, too. May he give her something lasting and eternal."

"Right," Marina says. "Lasting and eternal. May he give her jewelry!"

Mark and Rick laugh as they lean into each other. But there's a shift in the energy at the table, and I can tell the other women are having personal thoughts about their own loves instead of pondering my future. Eva sips slowly from her glass. Marina waves her glass, motioning to the waiter. Says just two words: "More grappa!"

And Lucy, she quietly ducks her head and winds her fork through her pasta, then eagerly gulps down a large bite.

* * *

The next day, my cousins scatter. Rick and Eva move on to Rome. Marina heads out for Monte Carlo. And Lucy flies home. At work, Gianni summons me to his office after lunch. Looking every bit the sly, sophisticated man of the world he is, he says to me, "I think we should go away for the weekend."

I smile, pleased that he still wants to spend time with me even after we've fucked without restraint. "I'll be looking forward to it."

"Oh. I meant now," he says.

"But, it's only Thursday," I tell him.

"But already I am desiring you," he answers, as though that's the end of it.

"No," I tell him. "My client wouldn't be appreciative if I blew off his account."

"I guaranty that your client will understand."

I puff some air through my lips. "My client might understand. But I wouldn't feel right about it."

"Let's make this quick," he says. "Tell me now, will you eventually back down if I persuade you? Or are you quite firm in your decision?"

"If you'd like to go somewhere this weekend," I tell him. "I'll be available Friday afternoon."

"As a date, you drive me mad," he says. "But as an accountant, I respect you even more, Ms. Russo. Have your things packed and ready Friday afternoon."

And sure enough, when Friday afternoon rolls around, instead of summoning me to his office, he comes down and meets me in mine. In the elevator, he says, "Are you prepared for the cameras? I believe they are outside, prying already."

I nod.

He goes, "If you like, you are free to tell them that you are more than my accountant."

When the door opens and the cameras press into my face, snapping pictures, asking me where we're going and what my business with Gianni is, I don't answer them at all. And later that night, at his villa on the lake, there is nothing business-like about our relationship.

Mutual Holdings

CHAPTER TWENTY-FIVE

The next morning, Gianni takes us out on the lake for a cruise on his boat. For growing up on the seaside as I did, I never really learned to fish, and he's all too happy to anchor and take the time to teach me.

For something as supposedly passive as fishing, I get a huge thrill when I feel the first nibble and Gianni gives me instructions on how to bring it in. It's only a small perch, but he's careful as he takes hold of it and slides his hand down its back to release it from the hook before tossing it back. My next catch, I panic for the fish as it's gasping and gyrating out of the water, hanging by my line. Gianni hangs back and laughs as I try to catch it, flopping on the deck. I move too quickly, and though it's another small one, when I take hold of it, the fins of its back spike into my palm. Startled, I drop it, but quickly catch hold of it again, this time properly, as Gianni steps in and again helps me release it from the hook.

When I finally pull up a decent sized trout, I'm still skittish, but able to handle the entire procedure on my own. As I lean overboard and release it back in the water with a satisfying plunk, it hovers for a moment, and then shimmies and swims happily away.

Gianni, he goes, "You can do anything, can't you?"

I raise a brow and say, "That's the American in me that appalls you so much."

"No," he says. "That's the American in you that I admire so much. I only dislike that it overwhelms the passionate Italian in you."

"You don't think I've been passionate with you?" I ask, incredulous.

He laughs. "I have no complaints, Lisa. Your passion is nearly overwhelming me! But I had to pry it out of you. And I wouldn't have even known it was there if I didn't look so hard. You hide it too well."

"*Grazie*," I tell him.

"That wasn't a compliment, my dear."

"It was to me," I tell him. "I met you as a business associate. That's all you should have seen."

"Why? Why would you try to deny an entire half of yourself? I don't."

I laugh. "But you're a man, Gianni. It's different for men. You can have your exploits splashed all over the papers and it only makes you seem more... potent. But if a woman has any exploits at all, that's all she becomes in other people's eyes. They see only the sex, not the other abilities."

"That's because women like you who are powerful at both try to deny it," he says. "Don't you see that? The more you claim and embrace about yourself, the more powerful you become. But until you start doing that, you keep that divide in place in people's minds by reinforcing the stereotype that it's one or the other."

"So you're saying if you'd seen me kissing Tony before you hired me that you'd have still respected my abilities?"

It's his turn to laugh, and I swear I see a blush creep to his face. But he admits it, saying simply, "No. I probably wouldn't have."

"You see," I say smugly.

"But I won't make that same mistake again with any other women," he says. "Because of you."

"Yeah, well, that's nice," I say as I cast another line back out into the lake. "But I'm still trying to get my own foothold in the business world and prove myself. I can't afford to take risks like that yet."

"You underestimate yourself," he says. "But this proving yourself thing, that, I can understand."

Shocked, I tease him. "So says Fortune 500's man of the year. How could you underestimate yourself?"

"You are impressed with what I've done," he says it as a statement, not a question. "I'll tell you a secret. Making a lot of money isn't so hard."

"Pfft."

"It's true," he says. "Once you have begun, it gets much easier. And you shouldn't be so impressed with me, Lisa. I didn't start from nothing. Not like you and Tony. My father left me a small fortune."

"Yeah," I say. "And you ran it into an empire."

"Do you know why?" he asks.

I just look at him, because it had never really occurred to me to even wonder why.

He goes, "Because I was trying to prove myself. Not just to others, but to me." He lightly taps his hand against his heart as he says that. "I love what I do, don't get me wrong. I love to build things and watch them grow. But I did it to make myself seem worthwhile."

I'm a little shocked. But then I ask, "Did it work?"

He shrugs. Says, "Partly." Then a cagey smile. "I won't lie. It felt good."

"I knew it," I say.

"But it doesn't feel half as rewarding as being in love," he says. I turn and gaze out at the impossibly deep blue of the water, pondering that. He says, "Don't fret, my dear. You are well on your way."

"In love?" I ask him. "With you?"

"Ah," he says. "Maybe! If we are so lucky. But I meant the money. They say the first million is the hardest. Now, you have that."

I look up at him and have to squint from the brightness of the sun. I tell him, "Yeah. Well. I'm still trying to earn that million bucks."

"I have no doubt you will," he says.

After a prolonged silence, it's his line that gets the next bite.

Mutual Holdings

CHAPTER TWENTY-SIX

That night, we're in his sinfully soft and plush bed. We've gone slow so far this evening. Earlier in the day, anchored out on the middle of the lake where the two disparate beauties of the mountains and lake merge together into one seamless landscape with the flourishing, beautifying touches made by man surrounding us, we had rushed and frenzied sex under the beating sun with the waves rocking us back and forth. Now, instead of animal heat, we took our time undressing; kissing and caressing each other. Gianni still wants me, evidenced by his formidable, sheathed hard-on. But instead of seeking instant gratification for his cock, he's currently feeding his mouth by licking my knee, tickling the underside of my foot as he enjoys my body. I'm turned on. He doesn't have the overwhelming physique that I'm accustomed to with Tony, but he's gorgeous in his own right.

Taking a page from him, instead of rushing for completion of the act, I decide to linger and enjoy it. As he sinks on top of me, seemingly preparing to enter me soon, I kiss him deeply. A part of me, I know, is making up for things I can't enjoy with Tony. Kissing, stroking; all the sensual delights that turn sex into more than fucking. But yet another part is already lost in the physical pleasures, reveling in the sensations of the moment.

Even as I kiss Gianni, I press against his chest, pushing him off me. But instead of moving him away, I move with him, rising up and turning, positioning myself on my side as I get him on his back. He doesn't mind. In fact, I think I can see a glint of appreciation as I run my hand along the smooth skin of his chest, down the sleek form of his torso.

Climbing on top of him, I take my time and take my fill. Sucking at his neck, tracing wandering patterns with my tongue across his shoulders, all the way down to his stomach. Lower, along the tender muscles where his tan line ends, revealing the pale, delicate flesh that leads to his groin. He's being patient with me, and as a reward I dip lower and take him in my mouth. Above, he sighs approvingly. I'm not a fan of the taste of condoms, but he doesn't seem to mind having it on, so I suck anyhow. I go to work on him and he responds, showing me approval by stroking my hair. Ever the gentleman, even as he seems to be getting edgy, he doesn't grab my head. In fact, as his hips start thrusting more quickly, he suddenly tugs on my shoulders and pulls me off.

I don't mind. It got me itchy to watch his tension rise. So when he says, "Lisa. Fuck me," I'm happy to oblige.

Straddling him, I reach down and line him up. But instead of taking him, I first lean forward and kiss him deeply, taking a mouthful. Thrusting my tongue against his, I lower myself onto him slowly. Easing down until he's buried deep even as our breath mixes and he accepts my hungry tongue.

It's like that, satisfying all my physical cravings, that I start to rock. His hands move to my hips and start guiding me, increasing my pace immediately. But still kissing him, I reach back and take hold of his wrists, pull his arms off of me as I slow down. I place his hands above his head and hold them tight. He's plenty strong enough he could shake me off if he wanted to, but I stop and look down at him, and I can tell he doesn't mind. "The hurried American," I whisper in his ear. "She wants to go slow."

In answer, he raises his hips slightly, getting himself deep as he says, "*Mostrami.*" Meaning: Show me.

So I do.

Rocking and riding him slowly, kissing him with my breasts pressed against his chest and keeping his hands above his head, him stretched out beneath me, placidly accepting and handling it is immensely, deeply satisfying.

I make it last as long as I can, but when it starts getting intense I have no choice but to release his hands and rise up for more leverage to start grinding harder. He's watching me and I like it, because he shows me he appreciates what he sees. Instead of guiding my hips, he uses his hands to smooth his palms across my thighs, up along my stomach. Finally holding and massaging my breasts.

It's so good, a sheer physical rapture so close. Grinding and rocking, watching him and his labored breathing, I think he's close. "Gianni," I sigh. "Can you come soon?"

Ever the gentleman, he says, "After you."

"I'm close," I tell him.

"*Andiamo*," he encourages, licking his lips, wiggling his hips, pushing up against me even as I thrust onto him.

A whispery shiver goes up my spine, setting me on edge.

"Lisa," he calls my name.

"Gianni," I answer him, biting my lip and then holding my breath, waiting for it to overtake me as I rock and force it; watching him struggle to hang on pushing me to the brink.

"Lisa," he calls as the feeling inside me zings me so hard I'm going to tumble over the edge any second. I rock and take him deeply, feel the tingles starting to expand. He sighs, "*Ti amo*."

Ti amo.

Literal translation: I love you.

My interpretation: Disaster.

But I can't help it.

"Oh fuck!" I nearly sob, my heart bottoming out as I stop thrusting and grinding. But it's too late, and once again, my body can't be tamed and I suffer the reverberating shocks of an orgasm as it overtakes me.

I squeeze my eyes shut and turn my head, clenching my jaw even as I involuntarily shudder with the liquid heat coursing through my veins and my cunt continues to devour the thrusts of Gianni's cock, lighting me up like a pinball machine. Even as I twitch and come with undeserved, unwanted shocks of ecstasy, I force the rest of my body to obey. Rising up with forced and jerky movements, I climb off him, grabbing between my legs and squeezing my own sex, not to intensify the orgasm, but just as a reflex, hoping to quash the burning pleasure.

It's also too far along for him. Even as I pull off him, his breathing is shallow, and though he's now exposed and abandoned, he falls victim to an unassisted orgasm as his hips thrust the air and his cock shudders, squirting into the feeble protection of the condom. Immediately he grabs his deserted erection, fisting and stroking himself to ultimate completion without the help of my body to finish him off.

When he's barely finished, he nearly yells at me, in Italian, raspy, but loud: "Are you crazy?"

The despair is seeping through me now, finally my body comes down enough and I flop helplessly next to him. Him demanding, "What the hell was that for?"

I could say something smugly clever, something about how it's not all about the finish. But I don't. Barely holding back tears, I demand of him, "Why'd you say that?"

"What? What the hell did I say?"

"You know what you said!"

"WHAT?"

"How could you say that! Tell me you didn't mean it!"

"I don't even know what the fuck I said!"

"How could you not know?"

"I was on the verge of a great orgasm, Lisa! I babble plenty of things when I'm like that. And you wrecked it."

"You got off anyhow," I say.

"Unfortunately! And it was much weaker!"

"How could you say that?" I demand.

"WHAT? WHAT DID I SAY?"

"You said the one thing you shouldn't have said!"

"I don't even know what I said!" he insists.

"I don't see how you could become so rich if you're so stupid you can't even remember two minutes ago!"

"WHAT DID I SAY?"

"You know what you said!"

"Oh my God," he groans. Then he roars, "MOST WOMEN WOULD KILL TO HEAR THAT FROM ME!"

"I knew you knew!"

"*TI AMO*!" he shouts it again. It rings off the walls, probably floats out over the balcony and seeps into the lake, waking the trout with its absurdity.

"WHY?" It's my turn to demand.

"BECAUSE I DO! I LOVE YOU! I LOVE YOU!"

"Oh my God," I say and bury my face in the pillow, and now the tears do fall. I can't stand it. "STOP IT!"

He places a hand on my shoulder and I try to shake it off, but can't. Him asking, "Why don't you like it?"

I nearly sob. Saying, "Because I see how miserable you are with Angelina not loving you enough. Because I know how badly it hurts the way I love Tony and the way he doesn't love me back. Because I can't stand the thought of being that source of pain for you!"

Gianni, the idiot, he starts laughing. "Get up," he says. "Look at me."

"No," I say.

"Lisa, get up and look at me."

I blink open my eyes, still wet with more hot tears threatening to fall. He laughs at me. Says, "You really are an American. You all try to hoard it instead of accepting it. I love you because you don't want to hurt me. I just like you so much that I love you, that's all I meant."

"Gah," I just scoff, finally getting the tears under control.

"Frankly, Lisa," he says. "I think you love me, too."

That nearly gets me to crying again. That gets him to laughing some more. Him saying, "You love me."

"I want to love you, Gianni," I sniffle as I sit up, wiping my face. "Maybe I will. But I'm just...I'm sorry, I'm still..."

As my words trail off, he says, "You're still in love with Tony." When I nod, he says, "I am still deeply in love with Angelina."

"But you said..."

"And I meant what I said. I do love you. In a different way, I love you."

"You mean, like, like a friend?"

"Yes," he nods once.

"Oh," I say and blink.

He goes, "Like a friend that I also enjoy having sex with." Scowling now, "Most of the time I enjoy it."

I can't help but laugh. It was kind of rotten, what I did.

"Don't you like me, Lisa?" he asks. "I thought you did. Very much."

"Oh my God," I say. "Gianni. I adore you."

"You like to fuck me," he says. "And you like to fish with me."

"Yes," I answer.

"Then if you adore me and you like me, how can you not love me?"

"I thought you meant something else, I guess."

"Like I said, you are so American, Lisa. But now you're in Italy, and you're with me, an Italian. If you love me, you can tell me. In our culture, we enjoy sharing love," he says. "The other kind of love," he sighs, "the something else that you mean, maybe for us, it will come to be. Maybe it won't. But what we already have is love, isn't it?"

I feel absurd now. I look at him, and a rush as hard and liberating as an orgasm hits as I realize what he's saying. One of my fears is that no one likes me. And here's a guy, a great guy, and he likes me so much he loves me. And I freaked out over it. I am a fucked up American. I can't help but tell him. Quietly, I go, "*Gianni. Ti amo.*"

"*Benissimo*!" he shouts, throwing his hands in the air. "*Ti amo*, Lisa," he says easily.

"*Ti amo*!" I say, loudly.

He gives me a warm hug, pulling me close, saying, "There is always hope for you." Then, after a beat, he pulls back and looks at me seriously. He goes, "I want you to promise me something. As a friend who loves me. Oh-kay?"

"What?" I ask.

"Promise me that you will never fuck up another ejaculation like that for me again."

* * *

Later that night, lying there with Gianni, a sense of peace comes over me. It's not often in this life that we're lucky enough to be with someone who's in perfect synch with us, feeling the exact same things we are.

If only we were feeling those most intense things for each other.

But right now, what we have is good enough. He may be a little bit coy sometimes, because that's just his nature: Wary and protected, he's probably not always immediately sure of who likes Gianni, or who likes the billionaire. But he certainly wasn't coy or closed to me tonight. He's also more giving and generous than nearly anyone I've ever met.

That's when it comes to me, almost in a flash. He may be generous to a fault, but there's no way he'd have invested the money that he has in me professionally simply to make it personal. That'd be anathema to what he's looking for; it'd be starting up another relationship like the one he has with Angelina. He hired me to do a job. He hired me to assess his net worth. It sounds simple, like a bottom line job. But from what I glean, his wariness and diligence has paid off over the years.

And now I see he's not just cunning about personal affairs. He was protected and coy about the underlying reasons about hiring me.

Resting there, on the verge of sleep, the puzzle pieces slide into place as the memories replay. And it's with that sense of calm that finally, I'm able to get my hard-wired, accountant-trained, detail-oriented brain to relax and see the big picture.

CHAPTER TWENTY-SEVEN

Sunday night, after returning back to Milan, I ring up Mark to meet me for cocktails downstairs.

"How's Rick?" I ask him after he orders his drink.

With a melancholy tone, he says, "Still in Rome."

"Gonna meet him again next weekend?"

He shrugs, saying, "He'll be in Venice by then."

"Oooh! I've always wanted to go there."

"I don't know," he says. "I think I might just stay here."

"Why? I thought you and Rick hit off?"

"He's a little young," Mark says.

"Oh. You need someone a little more mature, huh?"

"Me? No," he says and looks up at me. "I like him. I just think maybe *I'm* too old for him."

"Mark. You're twenty-seven."

"Exactly," he says. "Gay years are like dog years. It makes me feel like a sugar-daddy."

I laugh. Saying, "Except he's got all the cash."

"How's that translate in Italian," he asks. "Sugar daddy, I mean."

"Uh," I stumble. "I'm not really sure what the slang expression is for it here. Literally it'*s daddy dello zucchero*, but I'm sure they have an expression for it."

"Anyhow. When I'm with him," he says, "I'm the experienced one. The wise one."

"So?"

"I've never been that before! I've always been the young boy-toy!"

"With Tony, I was always the grown-up. He was the fun one."

"I'm not sure I'm ready for that," Mark says. "Besides, I think he probably wants to hang out with more people his own age, that's all."

"Did he say that?"

"No. In fact, he asked me to meet him in Venice."

"Well, then, if you want to go, you should go."

"Yeah, but, Lisa. What if he's just being polite?"

I laugh at that. "Mark. My cousin is a lot of things. But being polite for the sake of it is not one of those things."

"Are you sure?" he asks.

"Want me call him and see what he says?"

His eyes light up with that. "Can you pull it off without being obvious?"

"Of course."

"Oh!" he says it so suddenly it startles me. "Speaking of probing phone calls. I got one this weekend."

"From who?"

He purses his lips before answering, "My boss."

I try to act nonchalant, taking a small sip of my grappa. "Tony checking up on you, huh?"

"No, it was pretty clear he was checking up on you."

"Come again?"

"Is that an expression you used very often this weekend with Gianni?"

"Mark!" I can't hide the blush seeping across my face, and I know Mark is going to know it's not from the grappa.

"Mmmhmm," he says with a nod. "I knew it. And that's what Tony wanted to know."

"Wait a minute," I say. "Tony asked you if I'm fucking Gianni?"

"He tried to dance around it," he says. "He asked me how it was going. Said he saw last weekend's picture in the paper. Then, he asked me what you were doing this weekend."

"What'd you tell him?"

"I told him you were gone away with Gianni."

"You didn't!"

"Yes I did," he says. "He's jealous, too. Very jealous!"

"He said that? That he's jealous?"

"He didn't come out and say it no. But I know."

"Are you sure?"

"Lisa. There are two things I know about in this world. I can depreciate an asset and I can read men."

"Mmhmm," I say. "Then how come you're having trouble reading Rick?"

"Because he's still partly a boy!"

"Yeah, well. If Tony can't even admit that he's jealous, then he's still a boy, too."

"He'll come around," he says. "It's so obvious that he's in love with you. He's just a typical commitment-phobic male. But he's already pining away for you."

"I'm not so sure about that, Mark."

"Trust me. Once he sees the big picture, that he really could lose you, he'll wake up. In the meantime, you get to fuck the rich right out of Gianni!"

I laugh at that. But then I say, "Speaking of fucking the rich right out of Gianni, I think I finally see the big picture about us being here, Mark."

"What do you mean?" he asks.

I take a nice gulp of grappa, lean in close, and then say, "I have a hunch. I think we've been going about this job all wrong. We're auditors. I think we need to put the overview aside and start chasing some details."

"What do you mean?" he asks.

"Remember those transactions we put aside to investigate later? Well. It's later."

* * *

By Tuesday, Mark and I have gone back three years and discovered the multitude of payments to various independent companies. By consolidating records and searching based on names and types, we've found them coming from every one of Gianni's major operations.

I don't want to draw suspicion, but I'm too driven by this to let it rest and in the event that I'm wrong, I don't want to waste too many weeks on a paranoid goose-chase. Mark and I are working late at the hotel. While I've been tracing transactions, I've leapt him ahead to investigation of the companies. He's munching on a cold slice of pizza when he says, "This doesn't make sense."

"What?"

"C'mere. See this? This one right here, it's a subsidiary."

"Of what?" I ask, leaning down over his shoulder to look at his screen.

"Midaco Enterprises."

It takes me a minute because we've breezed through hundreds of company names the past few weeks. But this one sticks out because I recall the kerfuffle it caused when I'd asked about it. That's when I know for sure. Euphoric, I throw my arms around his shoulders, squeeze and smooch him on the cheek. "It makes perfect sense, Mark!"

He goes, "I'm sorry, *Ms. Russo*. But I still don't get what this means."

"This means, Mark, that's I'm still not sure who it is, but I am sure that someone is literally fucking the rich right out of Gianni Loren."

"Do, do you mean...You think this is fraud?"

"YES!" I shout it, shaking his shoulders. "*Frode corporativa*!"

"*Frode corporativa*!" he repeats. Then, "Holy shit!"

"*Merda santa*," I correct him. "Actually, I think this situation calls for *porcoddio*!"

"*Porcoddio*," he gasps. "This is unbelievable!"

"I know!"

"And we found it!"

"I know!"

Rising, he looks at me wide-eyed, stunned but excited. "We're so good!"

"I know!"

"What, what do we do now?" he asks. Then, "Wait. Wait. Are you sure? Why would Gianni do this? Why would he hire us and risk us discovering it?"

"Because he didn't do this," I say. "I think he hired us so that we would find it!"

Hand covering his mouth, he gasps, his eyes getting even wider as I can see him figuring it out. "He suspected someone of embezzlement!"

"Yes!"

"But he didn't want to tip his hand!"

"YES!"

He can't contain himself now. "This is scandalous!"

"Yes, I know!"

"We, we have to trace everything and prove it all out and figure out who this is!"

"I KNOW!"

"How? I mean, how, how do we do that?"

"I don't know," I admit. "I think we're going to need some help though."

It's past midnight here, so I know our offices are closed back in New York. But I'm so excited I can barely wait. And with Mark breathing and getting more worked up about this as we look things over and discuss it, we get whipped into a veritable frenzy of a geeky, accountant-high. I want Tony started on this first thing in the morning, and there's no way that I want to make the call from Gianni's office, because much like him, I want to play this cool until I have everything nailed down.

So I put in a call to Tony's work line with the intent of leaving him a message, asking him to begin a clandestine investigation on Midaco Enterprises. I put it on speakerphone so that Mark can say hello, too. As expected, when

Tony doesn't answer, it flips over to his voicemail, but as I start leaving a terse message, the phone picks up.

Breathy-sounding, a female voice says, "Ms. Russo?"

"Jill?"

"Uh. Uh-huh."

"I thought I dialed Tony's extension?"

"Mm-hmm," she says, her voice clipped and strained. "I'm just working late. I needed something... in here." It's not just the sound of her voice that's odd, I can hear a rustling sound in the background.

"I just wanted to leave a message," I say.

"Oooh, okay," she says, but it's nearly a groan. I glance at Mark, but his face is ashen, and I know I'm not the only one who's thinking what I'm thinking.

I should hang up, but instead I stay on the line, listening intently. Saying, "I need an investigation done on another company."

"Okay," she says. But then, as she does, unmistakable, there's a sound. A human noise. Not speaking words, but definitely masculine, a muffled but audible guttural grunt. As I glance at Mark, whose eyes go wide as he covers his mouth, Jill makes a hushed shushing sound.

I've heard enough. To think I was appalled when Tony was eating me out and she barged into the office. Now she has the audacity to talk to me on the phone while he fucks her? I say, "I'll call with details tomorrow." Hurriedly, I click the disconnect button before I hear any more.

Looking at Mark, I can see it written all over his face that I was definitely hearing what I think I was hearing. I ask, "Is that the sound adult males typically make when they're pining, Mark?"

And he goes, "Lisa. Isn't that the sound you've been making with Gianni while you pine for Tony?"

I have to admit, he's got a point.

CHAPTER TWENTY-EIGHT

Wednesday morning, I decide to leap ahead and take a sharpshooter approach to the investigation of Midaco Enterprises. Mark, he says he's not only up to the task, he seems anxious to do it.

I arm him with his artillery – a single invoice.

He takes a deep breath, and I send him off to the elevators. I didn't want to color his perceptions in case I'm wrong, but I did warn him that it might be a bit unpleasant. I don't want Mark to get yelled at. But I'm willing to bet that Spillway is going to get very aggressive with him.

It's the cab driver incident that made me formulate the theory in the first place. When Gianni had that minor fender-bender in New York, he was clearly in the wrong and in a very vulnerable position. Spillway didn't miss a beat in intimidating the cab driver though, presumably so that he'd back off. Then, when we first arrived here in Milan, Spillway got irrationally acrimonious with me – when I'd inquired about a Midaco billing.

I know Gianni suspects. He may be generous and even eccentric, but he's also a top-notch businessman. He shielded his true motives from Spillway with the Mets ruse, probably because Spillway is so legally entangled in his organization that he can't extricate him lightly.

Suspicion is one thing. Proof is another.

When Mark returns, he's flushed and breathless. His hand shakes as he places the invoice back on my desk. Leaning close, he tells me, "He chewed me out. Really bad."

I can't help but smile. I still have to prove it, but now I'm fairly certain that Midaco Enterprises is in some way going to lead back to Michael Spillway.

Still close in my ear, Mark says, "I can do you one better, though."

I glance at him, questioning.

He goes, "Before I asked about the invoice, I figured I'd try to ingratiate myself. You know, make some small talk to gauge his mood."

"And?"

"And he was in a very good mood."

"So he only attacked you after you asked about the invoice?"

"Not only that. We chatted a few minutes. I was looking around his office, admiring some of the things. He has a picture of his family on his desk, and I complimented him."

I just stare at him, not understanding where he's going with this.

He says, "His son is named David, and his wife is named Colleen."

I exhale slowly. Say it softly. "Michael, David, Colleen. Mi-Da-Co."

"What do you think of that?" Mark asks.

And I say, "Not so clever for a lawyer."

* * *

On Thursday, after Gianni returns from lunch, I buzz his secretary and ask for a meeting with him.

When I enter his office, he's leaned back in his chair, gazing out the window. He asks breezily, "I was thinking maybe this weekend we could take a trip to Rome?"

"Not now," I say, holding tight to two files. One is stuffed with a printout of the past year's dubious payments, and the other is background information about Midaco Enterprises and a number of its subsidiaries. "I know why you hired us, Gianni."

"Oh?" is all he asks. But he does turn from the window to look at me.

"I may be good in bed," I say. "But I'm not worth two million bucks."

"Debatable," he says with a laugh.

"No one is that good. That's why you asked for a pre-nup from Angelina." His brows raise, but before he can say anything I say, "And you certainly don't need someone to tell you how rich you are, Gianni."

His lips purse, and he's on the verge of saying something, but he refrains, still playing it close to the vest. He knows I know. And he knows I know that he knows. But it's how he likes to play the game – cagey. I don't blame him. A little anticipation does make it better. Or, hopefully, in this case, it'll also ease the sting.

I prod again, saying, "I found what you wanted me to find."

Smiling, he nods. Asking simply, "How much?"

I toss the one folder on his desk. "This year alone, over seventy million. It goes back ten years, maybe more. Mark is still running the numbers, but it looks like over five hundred million dollars."

His smile wanes. He swallows, and I can see the shock hitting him. He suspected, but I don't think he ever imagined it was so much. No one would cry for Gianni Loren. He's more affluent than most people can ever even dream about. But that still doesn't make stealing from him right.

I can see he's struggling with it. Not looking at me, he asks, "Who is it?"

"Spillway. But he had to have help."

Now he looks up at me, curious, questioning.

"Your other accountants, Gianni." I hold out the other folder for him. He takes it, but doesn't even open it. I say, "Spillway was smooth about it. He set up shell corporations and had consultant fees paid to them, and they all funneled back into one larger corporation. I could see how your accountants would miss the connection between these companies. But I don't see how they couldn't have questioned the fees paid."

"But," he says, looking confused. "They are reputable businesses, these firms I used."

"Yeah," I shrug. "So was Arthur Andersen. It happens. People can be bought. They're greedy."

"And you?" he asks.

"Uh," I'm not sure how to answer that about myself. Or, maybe I'm afraid to. How else can I explain being in love with Tony and yet lapping up the affection I'm getting from Gianni?

But then he clarifies, saying, "Do you think I'm greedy? For wanting to get it back?"

"No," I tell him, looking him in the eye. "I think you want what you've earned. And there's nothing wrong with that."

"Why?" he asks. "I was very generous with him. I don't understand."

"Because you're so generous, Gianni. Because you give so much, some people feel like they're entitled to even more from you."

He lowers his eyes. "Like Angelina?"

I answer as honestly and as kindly as I can. Saying, "I don't know."

He sighs. "What do I do now?"

That I do know the answer to. "You get your money back from Spillway, that's what."

CHAPTER TWENTY-NINE

As I'm getting ready to exit the elevator on Spillway's floor, he's waiting to board. He says, "Going down?"

No, but you're about to, I think. But I've learned a thing or two about not tipping my hand from Gianni, and I don't want to take away his coup de grace when he shocks Spillway with the information that he's been discovered. He had toyed with the idea of confronting him on a personal level before involving authorities, but I warned him of the practical downside – it could allow Spillway enough time to empty out all the accounts and effectively disappear. So instead we made the calls and got his accounts frozen, and everything will be handled through the courts with a full investigation by the *Commissione Nazionale per la Società e la Borsa*, better known as CONSOB, which is the equivalent of the American SEC. Normally, starting investigations and actions like that would take weeks, if not months. And I'm sure this will take a long time to sort out. But it was easy to get the ball rolling. It's amazing what you can get done in an hour when you toss around the name "Gianni Loren" with authority.

"Actually," I tell Spillway. "I was in a meeting with Gianni and he needs your help."

He rolls his eyes but pushes the up button as he climbs on with me.

When we get to the entrance of Gianni's office, I glance at his secretary, who nods to allow us entrance. Then, she picks up the phone to alert building security and the financial securities investigators along with police who are waiting nearby in the boardroom.

In the office, Gianni's sitting on the corner of his desk. Though his gloomy mood has passed, he's not yet back to his formidably carefree self. He looks at Michael, and I'm expecting a storm of accusations and insults. But I guess that's more the Jersey streak in me than the Italian. Or maybe Gianni's just still genuinely hurt. Or, maybe he just has more class than even I ever gave him credit for. He just holds out his hands and says, "I just need you to answer one question for me, Michael."

A long, heavy pause. And then Spillway bites. "What's the question, Gianni?"

"Why have you stolen from me?"

Immediately, Spillway denies, saying, "I don't know what you're talking about."

But Gianni must be done with the games, because he simply rises and hands Spillway copies of the files I'd given him earlier. He says, "I paid you well. Why?"

Spillway glares at him. "This is ridiculous," he says. "This woman has brainwashed you, Gianni! You don't understand..."

"I understand everything! And I want to know why! My father trusted you. I trusted you. You are a wealthy man because of us."

"No," Spillway spits. "You're wealthy because of me! I helped your father build this business and then he turned around and handed it over to you. A spoiled, insolent little brat. I'd worked for everything here and you had it handed to you! I was just taking my small slice of what I richly deserved."

"Whether you deserve it or not," Gianni says, "I earned it. And now, I'm taking back what you took from me."

"I'm not giving you anything," Spillway says.

With that, Gianni nods at me. I say, "If you're not willing to freely return what you've embezzled, then I'm quite sure the courts will order you to do so. You're a lawyer, I'm sure you know all about what's going to happen."

"I knew you were trouble from the start," he hisses at me.

"You shouldn't have tangled with me, Michael. You know why?"

He just glares at me silently, so I say, "You're a lawyer, but I'm an accountant. You may be good with the rhetoric and the words, but I'm good with facts. You should never screw with an accountant. Because whatever you try to bury, we'll dig up."

"You little bitch," he says.

"*Abasta*!" Gianni shouts at him. "You can exit this office on your own. The police are waiting outside."

As he turns to go, I can't resist one more dig. I hold my hand out, pointing my index and pinkie finger at him as I say, "Who got the horns, Spillway?"

As he leaves, he's taken into custody. There will be more, plenty more, including possibly years of lengthy investigations and litigations. And it's quite possible that Gianni may never even recover a single penny. But given the little information Mark and I were able to dig up about Spillway and Midaco, I think there's a good shot he'll recover a fairly large portion. And if nothing else, we've now stopped the bleeding.

But I know this is about much more than just the money.

When the commotion has died down, I close the office door and stand next to Gianni, again gazing out the window of his office onto the streets of Milan below. Placing a hand on his shoulder, I say, "I'm sorry."

He taps my hand, telling me, "You have nothing to apologize for, dear Lisa."

"I just mean, I'm sorry this happened. I feel bad for you."

He chuckles lightly, but it doesn't seem ironic. He goes, "Don't ever feel bad for me, Lisa. I'm so lucky it should hurt."

"You're lucky because someone stole over five hundred million dollars from you?"

"Yes," he says, enthusiastically. "I'm lucky because I could afford to have someone steal that much from me!'

I can't help but laugh and agree with that.

"And I'm even luckier," he says, "because someone cares that it happened. You know, you probably could have confronted him, taken a cut, and kept quiet."

"I know," I say.

"Why didn't you?"

"Because you paid me a lot of money to help you. No matter what Spillway says, he's wrong for what he did."

"Suddenly two million for your services seems like quite a bargain, doesn't it?" Smiling, he goes, "You certainly did smash those numbers, didn't you?"

"Ahh, you could've paid me next to nothing and I'd have still helped you out."

"I believe that," he says. "But why?"

I put it as simply as I can. It's my job. It's not my nature to fuck someone over like that. But also, because of one simple fact. I say, "Because I like you, Gianni."

He smiles and bumps his hip against mine. Saying, "I like you too, Lisa. And I have an offer for you."

CHAPTER THIRTY

Back downstairs, poor Mark is still running numbers and figures and compiling all the data. He lights up when I enter, and I make his day even brighter by saying, "Mark, knock it off for the day. In fact, knock off for the weekend. Get headed out so you can meet Rick in *Venezia*."

"But there's so much..."

"It'll still be here Monday," I tell him. "I think we've earned a nice little break. In fact, it'll be here on Wednesday, take until then, at least."

"Seriously?" he asks.

"I'm as serious as corporate fraud, Mark."

He smiles and says, "I have to tell you something."

"I have to tell you something too," I say.

"Mine is really important," he says.

"Mine too!"

"Ladies first," Mark defers.

"Do you like Milan?" I ask him.

"A hell of a lot better than New York," he says. "Why?"

"Because Gianni has asked us to stay here, permanently."

"*Porcoddio*!" he shouts. His hand goes over his mouth, his eyes wide.

"You like that?" I ask him.

"*Lo amo*!" he says, meaning, I love it.

"Good," I tell him. "Now get the hell out of here and enjoy your long weekend. Then, after we get this stuff wrapped up, you're taking a nice long vacation. *Capisce*?"

"*Capiso*," he says. "But wait. Wait, wait. You haven't heard my news yet."

"Oh, I'm sorry."

"Uh, that's *mi dispiace*," Mark corrects me.

"Oh, stepping up the Italian already, are we?" I tease him.

Taking a deep breath, Mark says, "Are you going away with Gianni this weekend?"

I flutter my lashes. "Yes."

But Mark isn't smiling. "Ok. But I think you should know this first."

"You're freaking me out a little bit here. What is it?"

"I had to call the office. I lost a file and I wanted to see if Tony could send it back to me. But Tony wasn't there."

"Oh," I say, "that's no problem, we have duplicates. We can get another copy of whatever you need from the system here."

"I know. It's not that. I talked to Jill."

"Oh."

"Tony's not fucking Jill."

"How, how do you know that?" I ask him.

"Because Jill is fucking Louis."

"*Porcoddio*," I gasp. It's my turn to cover my mouth in shock. "Are, are you sure?"

"Oh, I'm positive," he says.

"That was Louis we heard with Jill the other night?"

"Yes!"

"Louis the maintenance guy?" I ask, to make sure.

"Yes, Lisa. Yes!"

"Oh my God. Good for Jill. Louis is adorable!"

"I know!" Mark nearly shouts. "I'd nail him!"

I start laughing. Asking, "And they do it on Tony's desk?"

"That's why she's worried. She's afraid you're going to rat her out to Tony."

"But, wait," I say, my mirth draining. "Then that means..."

"Exactly," Mark says. "Tony hasn't been fucking her at all."

"Holy shit," I say.

"*Merda santa*," Mark corrects me.

* * *

Gianni offers me Rome for the weekend. But he still seems reticent, I dare say he even looks tired. I know there will be ample paparazzi in Rome. It's early in the evening, so I tell him I'm content to just stay here in Milan, that he's free to go relax.

He frowns at me. "*Bella donna*. Being with you does relax me. And so does my villa. Is that acceptable?"

"I love it there," I tell him.

"You have done much for me today, but may I impose for one more thing?"

"Sure," I tell him.

He takes a deep breath. "Lisa. You are a smart woman. You are ambitious and driven. And you are beautiful and kind-hearted. But you are not perfect. You still have a terrible singing voice."

I smile at that. But then he drops a bomb on me. Saying, "And you dress for shit."

My jaw goes slack. "I, I do not," I say.

"Really," he says, shaking his head. "You do."

"Is it that bad?"

"It's a little bad," he smirks. "I've never seen so much brown and white in my life."

"But," I say. "I'm an accountant."

"Still," he says. "Come. We are in the fashion capital. Dolce, Armani,

Prada, Versace! Please. Let's go pick you up a nice dress for dinner?"

I admit it, I'm a little steamed. Mostly because, I suspect he's right.

I go a little Angelina on him. Saying, "Fine. But you're buying it."

Putting his hand on the small of my back, he gently pushes me forward and leads me to the elevator. He goes, "You make two million dollars for this job and you still can't buy a dress?"

"I just saved you five hundred million dollars today," I say.

"No," he corrects. "You discovered that I've lost over five hundred million dollars. You should take pity on me!"

I laugh. "I thought you didn't deserve pity?"

"You got me," he says as he punches the button. "Come now. I'll buy you two."

With all the choices, it could take us all night. But honestly, I'm a bit tired now too. So we stop at Dolce & Gabbana and the first one that strikes my fancy is the one I pick up. It's silky and sexy; a vibrant, lusty red. It's not the least bit business-like. Revealing and clingy, as I try it on, I'm not uncomfortable about it. Suddenly, it doesn't matter if anyone else sees me as simply a sex object instead of an accountant.

I know what I am. I'm both. And those two facets of me, body and brain, don't have to negate each other. Instead, they work together to balance me out. I've done my work for the day, now it's time to enjoy my play tonight.

But despite my previous teasing, I pay for the dress. Not because it'd be inappropriate to accept a gift from Gianni, but simply because it feels like I've earned a splurge on myself. I do, however, let him pay for the shoes to match.

Instead of taking the limo, Gianni drives us in his candy-apple red Ferrari, and I swear it's the one that we got fixed in New York. "No," he tells me as he pulls out onto the highway. "It's a twin. I kept that one in the States."

"Really? It's just sitting there, in a garage?"

"*Si*. Down in Miami. You like the car?" he asks as he shifts gears and takes it even faster. My heart pitter-patters with the increasing speed, a flood of adrenaline coursing through me as he smoothly steers and cuts us through the countryside.

It's an amazing feeling, yet I smirk as I recall an even more amazing feeling involving a car like this. "Enzo," I sigh aloud with the memory. Then, "I like it very much," I admit.

"There's only one thing better than driving this Ferrari," he tells me. With a knowing smirk, he goes, "Driving the Ferrari, and then having sex on it."

"I know."

"You and Tony, yes?"

I just smile.

He does too, and I know he's entertaining memories of Angelina. After a beat, he goes, "It's a bit awkward, yes? Getting a good position?"

"We managed," I say.

"Us too," he laughs.

The drive in the car goes quickly, and we're at the villa before sundown.

That evening, he takes me to dinner at the same restaurant where he first got so bold and got me turned on to him. This time, though he behaves, the *breva* is even balmier and the silky fabric whispering across my skin is a sensual delight. But the dynamic between us has already changed, a nearly tangible difference in the soft environment.

The edge, for us, has already dulled.

We're easier with each other, but the contentment we've found doesn't quite equal fulfillment.

After dinner, as we sit sipping grappa, he takes my hand and says, "Why can't love be this easy?"

I say, "So that we always appreciate how lucky we are when we have it."

We walk back to his home slowly, languidly, hand in hand.

CHAPTER THIRTY-ONE

We're out on the balcony of Gianni's bedroom, enjoying the last shreds of sensual darkness before the sun rises to officially start another day. It's quiet out, but it's not a heavy or bereft silence. It's peaceful.

I slip my arm around his waist, and I gaze up at his handsome face. I almost can't believe what I'm about to do. He respects my mind. He lusts my body. And I truly believe that he loves my heart. And I love his.

But it's just not quite in the right way.

He's handsome. He's rich. And most importantly, he's good to me.

Out of all the potential fish in the sea, he's one of the very best. In fact, he's Moby Dick.

But I'm going to toss him back because there's another fish that still permeates my soul. And Gianni, he's already been hooked by another fisherman.

Maybe it is my choice to love Tony. Maybe it's not my fate, but my conscious choice. So I'm going to willingly go back to New York and work with him and keep trying to push that boulder of love up the mountain while Gianni struggles to tame Angelina. Who knows – maybe in two years, or five years, or someday down the road Gianni and I will revisit our brief romance and realize that we made a mistake by not trying longer, trying harder, really working on this together. Maybe then it will work.

But for right now, I can't give up on the love that already gives me fulfillment, and I don't think Gianni can either. The thought of spending weeks, months, a year away from Tony is more torturous than the thought of spending the time with him in vain.

Camus reasoned that Sisyphus must be happy because pushing the boulder was his purpose. It gave him meaning. I love my work, and it gives me meaning. But having only work in my life would make it a relentless grind. We need some relief, we need some joy. And Tony gives me that happiness.

I love him. He's etched indelibly into my psyche and carved into my soul. Sometimes, I'm not sure if it's love of the man or love of the memories, but then I realize that they're inseparable, my memories of him and the current man. They're twined together and corded around my heart.

I may be a programmed, American workaholic. But I've also got that passionate Italian blood running through my veins. I can finally accept my sexuality on my own terms, and now I have to accept what drives that passionate blood. I long for Tony. Because deep down, I'm also a Jersey girl at heart.

Sisyphus, he was condemned to his fate of pushing that boulder because he tried to cheat the gods out of his death. He loved life so much that when his time came to die, he found a loophole and lived another lifetime. For revenge, the gods cast him to his lonely mountain to pursue a futile task. I'm only going to get one lifetime. Tony is still the one who makes my pulse race. He makes this life of mine wonderful enough that if I have to shoulder the burden of him not reciprocating, I have to accept that.

Leaning close, I kiss Gianni's naked shoulder softly, because even though it's physically exciting, I no longer desire to kiss his face, his mouth. I say, "*Ti amo.*"

He puts his arm around my shoulder, kisses the crown of my head and answers, "*Ti amo.*"

"I'm going back to New York," I tell him.

"I know."

"Are we fools?" I ask him.

He holds me tighter, and gazing out upon the dark lake, he says, "Truly, Lisa. I believe we are."

I sigh. "You could give me the world."

He shrugs, but I can tell that although it's an earnestly humble gesture on his part, there's still the underlying confidence where he knows he could serve it up at the asking.

"The problem," I tell him, "is that I don't want you to give it to me. I want to earn it myself."

"And I have already promised my share of it to another," he says.

"I wish it had worked between us."

He smiles at me. Says, "We want too much. Nearly anyone else would take what we have together and be satisfied. It is this hot, Italian blood in our veins, coursing through our hearts. It makes us lusty and greedy."

I laugh. "I thought those were the good things about us, Gianni."

"Oh, it is! We are wretched, sinful creatures. Dante could write and write about us. Lusty, proud, greedy. But we also love. I suppose that's our punishment, that our love is so true."

I swallow thickly. Looking heavenward, I silently pray for him. A prayer that Angelina releases him from his misery and loves him back, the way he deserves. The way I can't.

Reaching out, he strokes my face, lingering. In the darkness, his green eyes are heavy-lidded, and soft. I take hold of his wrist and place a kiss in the palm of his hand. I tell him, "I'm going to miss you so much."

"Then don't miss me," he says.

"But, Gianni. You're in love with someone else. I'm in..."

"Not like that," he says, stroking his hand through my hair. "*Capelli rossi*," he sighs, commenting on my red hair. "The sign of a true Milanese beauty. Lisa, maybe in another life somewhere, we'll be a magnificent couple. But in this one, we're friends. And that doesn't have to end. You'll leave soon. But we'll say *Ciao*, not *Arrivederci*. Always, we will talk, yes?"

"I'd like that, Gianni. Very much."

"Good," he says, surprisingly in English. His posture going rigid, his voice takes on his business tone as he says, still in English, "Because you're also my accountant now. After everything that's happened, how the fuck am I supposed to trust anyone else?"

"I appreciate that, Gianni. And I'm more than happy to stay on. All you have to do is say those magic words."

He goes, "Billable hours."

Both of us laughing, I say, "I think Mark will be happy to stay on permanently here in Italy."

"And you?" he asks. "You'll make frequent trips. Yes?"

"Yes," I tell him.

"Mark," he says. "He's quite good?"

"He's excellent," I tell him. "I wouldn't have found the problem without him."

"So he is an expert at smashing numbers, too!" He says it brightly. Just as I'm about ready to correct him on the phrase, I decide against it. He goes, "I like Mark. He is trustworthy. Yes?"

"Very," I tell him.

"Am I correct in my thinking that he's also gay?"

"Yes," I say, hesitantly, worried that he'd ask that.

But Gianni says, with a smug smirk, "Then I must have him also sign the papers you did. The sexual harassment releases. Just in case I miss you too much and can't resist him."

I crack up.

From below, there's a violent splashing in the water at the lakeshore. Above the line of the mountains, the sky is starting to lighten, a pale-grayish blue creeping up through the previously impenetrable inky dark. Squinting,

I can make out a small boat just off the edge of shore, and I see movement, but can't discern the figures.

"What is that?" I ask.

"If it's the paparazzi, I'm going to sue their ass for trespassing," he says. Louder now, he leans over the railing, switching back to Italian, "You hear that? I'm going to sue your ass if you have a camera!"

In English, from below, "You're a fraud, Loren!"

I know that voice. I know it as well as I know my own. "Tony?" I shout.

"Lisa?"

"What are you doing?"

"He's a fraud, Lisa!" he yells. "He's been embezzling from his companies!"

"Oh dear lord," I sigh.

"You hear that, Loren? I've caught you! You're going down, pal!"

"Tony, stop it," I say. I can tell exactly where he's standing by following his voice, but I can only make out his silhouette.

Gianni, he's laughing. Quietly, he turns to me, asking, "You're quite certain that this is the man you prefer to me?"

"Like you said. I'm a fool."

In the distance, the pale blue increases on the horizon, now obscuring the remaining stars hovering above.

Tony shouting up, "If you're going to stay here with him, you should know what's going on, Lisa. I'm giving back his stupid retainer and going public with this information!"

Gianni, he says to me, "I thought Angelina was a handful. Dear God."

"I'm so sorry," I tell him.

"No problem," he tells me. "But he seems quite agitated. I think you'll need some jewelry to help calm him. I have a nice watch you could give him."

"No, I think I can handle it."

"He's a thief!" Tony shouts up to us.

Gianni nudges my shoulder with his. "I think that he is maybe jealous of me. Maybe he hates me."

I just sigh.

Tony hollers, "He's a scumbag, Lisa! Did you know he's still screwing that model, too?"

Gianni goes, "I think maybe this jealousy is a good thing for you."

"I better go talk to him," I say.

Gianni says to me, "Go take care of your man." Leaning over the railing again, Gianni hollers down, "You've got me, Tony!" Egging on his fury with, "I've amassed a fortune by stealing. From myself."

I hurry down the staircase, wanting to quiet Tony down not only so he stops making a fool of himself, but also before he wakes up everyone else in the house. Outside, there isn't even a hint of chill in the air, but the glow of oncoming daybreak brings about a slight mist across the lake. With the sky expanding above, the shadows playing across Tony's face dissipate.

He's soaking wet, and glancing at the small motorboat, I figure he must have had trouble hopping out of it. "What are you doing?" I ask him.

He stares at me for a second. The second stretches into a minute. Then, looking back up to the balcony, he runs a hand through his hair and points to Gianni, but tells me, "I've been going through those files you sent to our office, Lisa. This guy, he's been methodically embezzling for years now."

"It's not Gianni," I tell him. "It was his lawyer, Spillway."

Tony looks confused. Glancing back and forth between me and Gianni, finally he goes, "What?"

"We found it already. Mark and I. He wouldn't say it, but I knew Gianni hired us for a reason. He suspected Spillway of ripping him off. I found it. Mark and I got all the proof we need and Spillway and a bunch of Gianni's other accountants have already been fired and the accounts frozen while an official investigation starts."

"Oh," he says. Then, "Shit." Looking up to the balcony, he waves, says, "Sorry."

"I appreciate you looking to protect me from myself, Tony," Gianni hollers down. It's light enough now that I can see an amused look on his face.

"Uh, nice place you got here."

With that, Gianni goes back into his bedroom.

"What are you doing here?" I ask Tony.

"I, I thought you should know," he says lamely.

"You couldn't call me? You had to hunt me down?"

"I couldn't get you in Milan. Mark told me where you were. It's no big deal, I just flew over. And then, rented a car. And then, uh," he says, looking to the tiny boat, lilting on the waves. "Then I had to get this. To get here."

"Why?"

"I just, I thought you should know. Before you got too entangled with him."

"Uh-huh."

Straightening his back, he goes, "Our company. I couldn't let something like this go and then have it discovered by someone else."

"Well, it's not what you thought. Gianni's not a villain, Tony."

"Yeah," he nods. "So... he's what? He's a good guy, I guess?"

"He's pretty much the perfect man," I tell him.

Looking at the ground, he asks, "So I suppose you'll be staying with him, then?"

I could make it easy for him. I could tell him the truth right now, that I'm still hopelessly in love with him. That I've already decided to come back to New York. I can see the truth now, I guess I always did see it. Gianni was offering to share his empire with me. But from the start, Tony's been trying to build an empire for me. A man who's trying to protect his professional reputation might fly on a redeye to Milan. But only a man in love will rent a boat to get to Bellagio at the break of dawn.

But it hasn't been easy for me. I've been carrying the weight of this relationship for a long time. And sometimes, like right now, I just need to hear the words.

Shots of brilliant pink are streaking the underside of a few wispy clouds nestled into the now powder-blue sky above the mountains as a few golden rays burst upward with promise.

"Is there any reason why I shouldn't stay here?" I ask him.

Tony runs a hand through his hair again, and then wipes his hands across his face. I can see his chest expand as he takes a deep breath. Looking me in the eye, he lowers himself to his knees. Gently, he reaches out, takes hold of my hand.

My heart pounds so hard it feels like it's going to thump out of my chest. In this light, his dark eyes seem bottomless.

"Lisa," he sighs. "I love you. I've always been in love with you."

That translates into the sweetest music my ears have ever heard.

Weak-kneed, pulse-pounding, it's more euphoric than sex. It's more euphoric than making a million dollars. And it's as weightless as light itself.

"I'm not a billionaire," Tony says. "Sometimes, I'm a jackass. Okay, most of the time I'm a jackass. But that's why I need you. You balance me out. And I promise, if you still love me, if you give me another chance, I'll love you every day for the rest of my life."

This guy, my guy, Tony? He's never broken a promise to me yet.

The first slice of sunshine peeks above the lowest dip in the Alps behind him.

"I still love you, Tony."

He exhales roughly, a smile pulling at the corners of his mouth.

"And I'm coming back to New York with you."

He leans his forehead against my stomach, wrapping his arms around me. "I thought I lost you," he says.

I twine my fingers around a ringlet of his thick, dark hair. "Get up," I say quietly. "Kiss me like you mean it."

He rises, takes me in his arms, literally lifts me off my feet and lays the sweetest kiss on me I've ever felt in my whole life. I wrap my legs around his waist, hold tight to his neck, and kiss him back.

The soft pink, misty light of dawn illuminates the quiet blue of the lake, a diffuse glow rising up to the snow-topped mountains, with creamy villas chiseled into the slopes. Before long, the sun will intensify and warm the day, but the mild *breva* will keep it in harmony. Then, it will be beautiful. But right now, for a few lingering moments, it's perfection.

Pulling back just slightly, but still holding me tight, Tony takes a look around. He goes, "Chissakes, Lisa. You must be in love with me. You're giving up this?"

"Mmmhmm," I sigh. "And you really must be in love with me. You waded through all that paperwork for me."

"It was awful," he admits with a laugh. "But worth it."

"You could've just called, you know. Told me you loved me. That would've done it."

Squeezing me tight, he says, "I know that now. I just...I was really jealous of him, Lisa. And I didn't see how you couldn't fall for him."

"It's just money, Tony," I tell him, and that's when he sets me back down on the ground.

He says, "It's not just the money. It's a lot of money, Lees. And he's good looking, and I guess maybe he's sorta cool. And the first time we met him, I could tell he wanted you."

"Yeah, well. But I want you."

"Sometimes, I think you're the jackass," he says.

"Tony!"

"Hey, I'm just saying, I wouldn't blame you. If he came on to me I'd have a hard time turning him down."

"You're an idiot," I tell him.

"Yes," he nods. "But I love you. And that's the smartest thing I could do."

"Baby," I say. "You were ready to throw away two million dollars for me?"

"You're worth a lot more than that, Lisa."

"Well, that reminds me of something," I tell him. "I said I'd come back to New York with you. But after all this work here? I think it's time I got a raise."

His hand goes over his heart with mock hurt as he goes, "Oh! Already! We're back to the dirty talk."

"Tony," I say in a warning voice.

"Listen babe," he says. "I'll give you everything I've got. But I think we just lost our biggest client, so I don't know how much there is to give."

I take hold of his hand and look him in the eye, but I can't keep the smile from my face as I tell him. "We're keeping the Loren account."

He eyes me, his one brow cocked. "Yeah, but wait till you tell him you're not staying with him."

"I already told him," I admit.

"Wait a minute," Tony says and drops my hand. Motioning back up to the now empty balcony, he says, "You broke this guy's heart and he's still letting you keep the business?"

"It's a done deal," I tell him.

Gape mouthed, staring at me, he drops to his knees again. Placing his hand over his heart, he says two simple words: "Hail, Caesar!"

"Get up, you fool!" I start pulling him to his feet, but I never could handle Tony, and he pulls me down with him, into the soft sand, kissing me greedily.

When he takes a breath, I lay the rest on him. "Mark helped me a lot," I tell him. "We have to make him partner."

"Yeah," he says. "Um, all that digging through the files I did?"

"Uh huh."

"Jill may have helped."

"I fucking knew it!" I nearly yell, but he shuts me up with another kiss. Deep and wet, I go docile.

Pulling back, he goes, "She just helped, I swear," he says. I keep eyeing him, and he goes, "And it was only paperwork! That's all she helped with. But I think she needs to be made partner, too."

"Good," I tell him. "Let her and Mark suffer through tax season next year."

He nods toward the house, asking, "Think your ex in there will feed us breakfast along with letting us keep the account?"

"I think so. But I thought you were jealous of him."

"I was," Tony says and looks me in the eye. "When he wanted you. When I knew you were with him, it nearly killed me."

"And now?"

"I still don't like it," he says. "But I feel sorry for him, too."

"You feel sorry for Gianni Loren?"

Tony nods. Says, "He's got all the money in the world, but I've got the most priceless treasure."

As I'm kissing him, everything else drips away. The strength of his body pressing against me is the most glorious feeling. Until he pulls back again. I can hear the sound of doors slamming inside. Then, from up on the balcony, loud, distinctly clear, a female's voice shouts, in Italian, "I signed the fucking pre-nup! You belong to me, now, Gianni Loren!"

"Angelina!" Gianni shouts, and I can hear the joy in his voice.

Her again now. Demanding, "Now get that accountant out of here!"

"Tony," I say. "I don't think we should stay for breakfast."

Gianni answers her. Saying, "Fine. But you should know that she just saved us over a half-billion dollars that people were stealing from my companies. That's what she's been working on."

"She can stay as long as she likes," Angelina says. "Cook her some breakfast."

"We can stay for breakfast," I tell Tony, skipping the verbatim translation.

"Baby, you are good," he tells me.

"One thing though!" Angelina says. "She can't continue to be photographed with us looking how she does. For Christ's sakes, Gianni, buy her some decent clothes!"

After a long, wet, satisfying smooch, with everything I've ever wanted having fallen into place, I ask Tony: "Is it true? Do I really dress so badly?"

And he says, "Oh babe. I love you. But your clothes are for shit."

The End

About the Author:

Susan DiPlacido lives in Pennsylvania, plays in Nevada, and loves to write. She is the author of two previous novels, *24/7* and *Trattoria*, and a winner of the Moondance Film Festival Spirit Award for her short story, "*I, Candy*". She can be found online at *www.susandiplacido.com*.